MW01232285

Bidding on Brooks

THE WINSLOW BROTHERS, BOOK #1
THE BLUEBERRY LANE SERIES

KATY REGNERY

SPENCER
HILL
PRESS

Bidding on Brooks
Copyright © 2015 by Katharine Gilliam Regnery

All rights reserved. No part of this book may be reproduced or transmitted in
any form or by any means, electronic or mechanical, including photocopying,
recording, or by any information storage and retrieval system, without the ex-
press written permission of the publisher, except in cases of a reviewer quoting
brief passages in a review.

This book is a work of fiction. Names, characters, places, and incidents are used
fictitiously. Any resemblance to actual persons, living or dead, business estab-
lishments, events, or locales is entirely coincidental. Use of any copyrighted,
trademarked, or brand names in this work of fiction does not imply endorsement of that brand.

Please visit www.katyregnery.com

First Edition: May 2015
Katy Regnery

Bidding on Brooks: a novel / by Katy Regnery—1st ed.
ISBN: 978-1-63392-079-8

Library of Congress Cataloging-in-Publication Data available upon request

Published in the United States by Spencer Hill Press
This is a Spencer Hill Contemporary Romance, Spencer Hill
Contemporary is an imprint of Spencer Hill Press.
For more information on our titles visit www.spencerhillpress.com

Distributed by Midpoint Trade Books
www.midpointtrade.com

Cover design by: Marianne Nowicki
Interior layout by: Scribe Inc.
The World of Blueberry Lane Map designed by: Paul Siegel

Printed in the United States of America

The Blueberry Lane Series

THE ENGLISH BROTHERS
Breaking Up with Barrett
Falling for Fitz
Anyone but Alex
Seduced by Stratton
Wild about Weston
Kiss Me Kate
Marrying Mr. English

THE WINSLOW BROTHERS
Bidding on Brooks
Proposing to Preston
Crazy about Cameron
Campaigning for Christopher

THE ROUSSEAUS
Jonquils for Jax
Coming August 2016

Marry Me Mad
Coming September 2016

J.C. and the Bijoux Jolis
Coming October 2016

THE STORY SISTERS
Four novels
Coming 2017

THE AMBLERS
Three novels
Coming 2018

Based on the best-selling series by Katy Regnery,

The World of...

The Rousseaus of Chateau Nouvelle
Jax, Mad, J.C.
Jonquils for Jax • Marry Me Mad
J.C and the Bijoux Jolis

The Story Sisters of Forrester
Priscilla, Alice, Elizabeth, Jane
Coming Summer 2017

The Winslow Brothers of Westerly
Brooks, Preston, Cameron, Christopher
Bidding on Brooks • Proposing to Preston
Crazy About Cameron • Campaigning for Christopher

The Amblers of Greens Farms
Bree, Dash, Sloane
Coming Summer 2018

The English Brothers of Haverford Park
Barrett, Fitz, Alex, Stratton, Weston, Kate
Breaking up with Barrett • Falling for Fitz
Anyone but Alex • Seduced by Stratton
Wild about Weston • Kiss Me Kate
Marrying Mr. English

Art ©2015 Paul Siegel • paulsiegelstudio.com

For Melissa Molloy, sailor extraordinaire, and her (totally hot) beau, Ciaran, for making sure my lines were straight and sails were full.

And with thanks to Dr. Jen for answering 1,001 heart-related questions.

CONTENTS

Chapter 1

"Please, Skye. Just listen. You're the perfect person for this. You've got to help me out."

Skye Sorenson rolled her eyes at Brooks Winslow, adjusting the brim of her baseball cap as she swept past him and headed down the dock for her next job.

"I mean it, Skye. I'm up a tree . . . and we're friends. Can't you give me a hand?"

Dreamy Delight needed a new float switch and bilge pump, which would be difficult to manage with Brooks Winslow standing on the dock, looking casually gorgeous as he yammered at her about some charity event he wanted her to attend.

Gazing at her hands, she noted they were still covered with engine grease from the oil change she'd just handled on the outboard motor of a J-24 sailboat. Not wanting to get black fingerprints on the white fiberglass of the motorboat she was about to service, she took a bandana out of the back pocket of her overalls, then turned to face Brooks as she wiped her fingers.

"Are you going to follow me around all afternoon if I don't listen?"

"Umm . . . pretty much."

She sighed with feigned annoyance. "Fine. You have my attention. Tell it to me again."

Brooks looked relieved and gave her a small grin that *damn it*—made Skye's stomach flutter.

"Knew you wouldn't let me down."

"Haven't said yes to anything yet," she said, shoving the bandana back into her pocket and crossing her arms over her chest.

"My sister, Jessica, is back in Philly this summer to get married. To keep busy, she's organized some big benefit for the Institute of Contemporary Art. She and her girl-friends thought it would be fun to volunteer their single brothers to be auctioned off."

"Auctioned off?"

"Yeah . . . a bachelor auction."

"Some sister," said Skye, unable to keep the teasing from her voice.

"It's for charity," he said defensively, running a hand through his waves of jet-black hair.

"Okay. So you got roped into it." She thought back to an old movie she'd seen once where women were auctioned off as dates. At each of their feet had been a pretty lunch basket, and the man who was the highest bidder won a homemade lunch with the girl of his choice. "What do you have to do? Have lunch with someone?"

"Oh, no," he said with irritation, pursing his lips. "Nothing that painless. Jess wants to make money. *Big* money. She had to think bigger than lunch."

Skye stared up at him. "Dinner?"

"Nope."

"Two dinners?"

"Nuh-uh."

She gestured to the sleek Sportscruiser moored at the end of the dock that she was supposed to be working on. "I'm out of guesses, Brooks . . . and that pump isn't going to fix itself, so—"

"A sail. She's auctioning off a sail. With me."

"Well, I don't know why you're complaining. You love sailing. You love women. What's the problem?"

Skye tilted her head to the side, looking at Brooks' way-too-handsome face with a cheeky grin.

Long ago Skye had accepted the fact that Brooks would never see her as anything but a great mechanic, a proficient sailor, and a longtime friend. She was—honestly and truly—satisfied with that status quo between them. He was rich and powerful, an ex-Olympian and world-renowned sailor from Philadelphia, while Skye lived a much quieter life, working as a "handyman" at her dad's marina in Maryland. What they had in common was a deep love of boats and mutual respect for one another's nautical skills, and that was just enough to keep their friendship intact.

The first time Skye had ever seen Brooks Winslow was the day he came down to her father's marina to claim the fifteen-foot Primrose wood-hulled sailboat gifted to him from his parents for his fifteenth birthday. He swaggered into Sorenson Marina, flashing his perfect smile at her, and her ten-year-old heart had grown wings as she'd discreetly followed him down the dock. She was instantly infatuated with Brooks, of course, but much more, Skye harbored a deep devotion to his Primrose, the most beautiful little double-ended Daycruiser she'd ever seen. Her stomach had been in knots as she walked behind him from a discreet distance, hopeful that he would handle the little sailboat with the grace and care she deserved. But Skye's worries turned out to be unfounded. He'd treated that pretty boat with respect and skill, and Skye had breathed deeply with relief, whispering, "I'm gonna marry you someday," as he sailed away.

Twenty years later, Skye knew two things for certain:

One, that Brooks was one of the most talented, natural, organic sailors she'd ever met in her life. Heck, he'd made it all the way to the Olympics and come home with a medal to prove what Skye had always known—that any boat was safe in his hands. She respected him more than most of the sailors she knew.

And two, the chances of her ever marrying him were next to none in the approximate area of zero. He was gorgeous and rich and talented and fascinating . . . and completely out of her league.

"Not a one-day sail," Brooks continued in a terse voice, jettisoning her memories as he prompted her back to their conversation. "Not even two. Jessica signed me up for a cruise. From Baltimore to Charleston."

Skye felt her eyes widen as she stared at him. "That's a week. Minimum."

"Yeah."

"Crew?"

Brooks grabbed the back of his neck with his hand, rubbing. "Nope. It's supposed to be . . . romantic."

A romantic cruise. For a week. Alone. With Brooks.

Lucky girl, she thought, ignoring the ridiculous spike of jealousy that jabbed a little at her heart and made her feel instantly guilty.

She couldn't help her attraction to him, but the fact that it was totally unreturned made it manageable in a way that didn't hurt. For heaven's sake, it wasn't like she had *feelings* for Brooks beyond friendship. She just liked looking at him. Her eighty-year-old granny's heart would flutter at the sight of Brooks' thick, dark hair, flashing sea-green eyes, square jaw, muscular body, and perennially tan hands that handled a boat with the same finesse that he probably handled his women. Noticing Brooks' good looks didn't make Skye unique or special, and it didn't mean she wanted more from him than friendship either (she tried to convince herself). It just made her human.

"Romantic," she murmured. Turning away, she looked out at the harbor where sailboats bobbed up and down in afternoon sun.

"Yeah."

"But you won't know who she is," said Skye, "until she wins you."

"Bingo," he said.

"And then you'll be trapped at sea for a week."

"Precisely."

"She could be *anyone*."

"Yep."

"Does your sister really hate you?"

Brooks scoffed. "No. But she really loves modern art."

"Okay. Yeah. It's a pretty sucky situation. But how can I help?"

He grinned. "You can bid on me."

Brooks had been friends with Skye Sorenson forever, which meant a lot to him because Brooks had a hard time making lasting friendships with women. Such friendships always seemed to turn into romantic entanglements, and the camaraderie was ultimately sacrificed when he walked away from the friendship and the woman. But not so with Skye because he didn't see her in any romantic light whatsoever and had it on good authority that her interests lay elsewhere—with her boyfriend, Patrick. In fact, Brooks thought of Skye almost on par with his sister, Jessica, and respected her skills on the water as much as any man he knew.

She and her father, Jack, ran a first-class marina on the Chesapeake Bay, and they were the only people on earth he trusted with the care and maintenance of his several sailboats: a Primrose he'd had since he was a teenager, a Passport Yacht, and—soon—an antique cutter. Totally obsessed with boats from a young age just like him, he'd known Skye was a kindred spirit early in their friendship. Their mutual respect had ensured a level playing field when it came to boats and sailing. If he was forced to skipper a weeklong jaunt down to Charleston, Skye would be the perfect person to accompany him.

Having sailed with her many times before, he knew her to be an excellent crew: she'd pull her weight on deck, and if they ran into any problems—mechanical or weather-related—there was no woman he knew who would be better equipped to assist him. They'd both enjoy the challenge of trying to achieve maximum speed on the antique sailboat, and Skye would be an equal partner, rather than a spoiled debutante who wanted to be waited on while she worked on her tan. In short, he'd simply enjoy himself a lot more if Skye agreed to go with him.

She stared back at him like he had a screw loose, and he forced himself not to smile. No stranger to Skye's frank assessments of messed-up situations, especially as they pertained to anything sailing-related, he expected a quick rejection.

After searching his face for several long seconds, she finally looked away, putting her hands on her hips. "Bid on you? With what? The millions I have lying around? I don't have that kind of money, Brooks."

It surprised him that she didn't say no. Hope surged.

"No. But I do."

"You're going to *give me* the money to bid on you?" She looked up at him from under the brim of her cap. "Why don't you just donate it to your sister's charity and back out of the auction?"

He took a deep breath. "Winning the sail with me is the *headlining* auction item. Jess thinks it'll be a big draw."

Skye rolled her eyes. "Like 'The Bachelor' at sea, huh?"

"Something like that . . ." He winced, hating to share the next bit of information, but knowing it wouldn't be fair to keep it from her either. "With the cameras to prove it."

"*Cameras*?"

"Jess has arranged for a photographer from *Celeb!* magazine to meet the boat at Virginia Beach, Hatteras in the Outer Banks, Myrtle Beach in South Carolina, and Charleston. They're going to do an article in their online magazine." Realizing what this could mean to her within the context of "The Bachelor" analogy, he rushed to reassure her. "Not that we'd have to touch or kiss or anything for the camera. No way. Absolutely not."

"Absolutely not," she echoed softly, quickly dropping his eyes. She paused for a moment, picking at the black cuticles of her oil-stained fingers before looking at him. "I don't think I'm the right person for the job. I haven't been sailing a lot lately. Sorry, Brooks."

She turned on her heel and started walking back down the dock. Brooks watched her go—her ass completely hidden by rumpled, unshapely overalls—before refusing defeat and running after her, because the thing was? Skye was the *only* person for the job.

What did she mean, she hadn't been sailing a lot lately? That couldn't be true. She loved sailing. And besides, she was a crackerjack sailor, a low-maintenance companion, and perhaps—most convenient of all—she was taken, and since Brooks was wholly disinterested in anything remotely romantic with her, that made her the perfect choice.

"Wait, Skye! Wait. Come on. Hear me out."

Skye turned, her expression incredulous. "Hear *what* out? Why in the hell would I want to put on a dress and go to an auction . . . bid on you . . . and then have to sail with you to Charleston, stopping along the way to . . . to *wave* for pictures? Even friendship has its limits. Call me when you need racing crew or a maintenance check on the Prim."

Her mention of one of his boats made him consider playing his trump card early, but he decided to try another tactic first. Cajoling.

"You don't have to wear a dress to the auction. I don't care if you wear this," he said, wrinkling his nose as he gestured to her stained overalls. "And c'mon! You love seaboard cruises. I know it and you know it. And so what if you have to smile and wave for the camera a couple of times? Big deal. It's for a good cause, Skye."

"I'm up to my eyeballs in work here," she said. "Don't you know a million girls you could ask?"

"I'm not interested in the romantic aspect of this. I just need a good sailor who will pose for a few pictures. And listen, I'll pay you. I'll pay you to crew. Going rate."

Her voice had an edge when she answered. "I don't need a second job, Brooks. Find someone else."

She turned on the heel of her beat-up Top-Siders and kept walking. Left without any other options, Brooks called after her, "And here I thought you'd be interested in crewing a custom-made, fully-restored, 1929 sixty-two-foot cutter."

He watched with hope and amusement as Skye stopped in her tracks. Brooks knew exactly how tantalizing was the morsel he dangled before her.

"Did I mention steel frame, teak topside, and pitch pine bottom planking?" he asked, taking a step toward her.

Her shoulders moved subtly, like she had suddenly gotten the shivers, and he took another step closer.

"You could have the whole aft cabin to yourself, Skye. Two berths. Built in. With the original head en suite."

Was he honestly wooing his friend to sail with him by selling her on the antique boat's original bathroom? Why, yes. Yes, he was. He had resorted to the equivalent of sailboat seduction, because the thought of being trapped on a sailboat for a week with some privileged, stuck-up miss who had no respect for the art of sailing was unbearable.

"And one other thing," he said, pushing one of two thick, blonde braids off her shoulder and practically whispering in her ear. "Well, two, actually. Original pitch pine mast *aaaand* Douglas fir boom . . . still . . . intact."

At that, she whipped around, her eyes wide as she licked her lips and pursed them together. "Damn it, Brooks."

He grinned at her. "Did I mention it's for charity? Plus, you'd be doing a favor for a friend, which means I'd owe you one."

"When would we lift anchor?" she asked, narrowing her eyes as she pulled her bottom lip between her teeth in thought.

Brooks' eyes flicked to her lips, then lifted quickly. "Auction is this Saturday night. Cruise starts on Sunday the weekend after."

"Two-week round trip?"

"One week," said Brooks, forcing himself not to chuckle at the sudden change in her demeanor. "Flight home's on me. I'm planning to stick around Charleston for a while and get the cutter outfitted with new fixtures."

"And you'll pay me?" she reconfirmed. "Going rate for crew?"

"Absolutely."

Skye paused, Patrick's face flitting through her mind. Her boyfriend, Patrick Flaherty, was presently circumnavigating the globe on a maxi-catamaran and was on month four of the two-year journey. Skye planned to meet him in Mexico in August as one of three planned visits they'd agreed upon before he left.

Pat knew Brooks, of course. They were members of the same yacht club, about the same age, both exceptionally good looking, and had competed against one another in local regattas many times. And though Skye had sensed a rivalry between them, especially on Pat's side, he wouldn't take issue with her helping Brooks out on such a short cruise, would he?

No, of course not. That would be ridiculous because she was Pat's girlfriend, and regardless of how shamefully handsome Brooks was, he and Skye were just friends. For heaven's sake, he'd just made it abundantly clear that he had no interest in romantic entanglements and didn't even want to touch her for the sake of pictures.

All she and Brooks had in common was boats. And rationally, thinking of everything she could learn from a world-renowned sailor like Brooks, she'd be foolish to pass up the chance to watch him skipper up close for a week. Anyway, when Pat heard about the 1929 cutter? He'd more than understand why she couldn't turn down Brooks' offer. Antique boats were the cheese to her mouse, and Pat knew it.

As though he knew what she was thinking, Brooks asked casually, "Hear anything from Pat lately?"

"I'm talking to him tonight," she answered, ignoring a niggling feeling of guilt. "He's in Panama."

"Wow. He made it in four months. Not bad."

Skye sniffed. "Speed was one of his priorities."

"He crossing over land or via canal?"

"Canal . . . but he couldn't guarantee four knots, so he's being tugged tomorrow."

Brooks grinned at this bit of information, and Skye frowned. The idea of Pat's little thirty-foot boat being dragged along the famous canal by a tugboat somehow felt ridiculous, which made her feel defensive on Pat's behalf.

"Pat's a good sailor," she said.

"No arguments here," he said. "You don't think he'll mind, do you?"

"Mind?"

"You and me doing a weeklong while he's away?"

"Don't be silly!" she exclaimed too quickly as her cheeks flushed. "We're just friends."

"Exactly. I don't even see you as a girl, really. Just an awesome sailor."

Skye blinked at him, taken aback by his words and how offhandedly he'd shared them. Skye didn't dress and act like a typical woman, but that didn't change the fact that she *was* one. And though this information really shouldn't have surprised her, and even further, she ought to have been pleased that he admired her for her nautical skills more than anything else, it pinched that he didn't "see her as a girl."

"Will they *let* another *man* bid on you?" she sniped back, turning around and stalking down the dock to *Dreamy Delight*.

"Oh, come on," he said, his voice immediately taking on a sheepish tone as he realized he'd insulted her. She heard his footsteps behind her but didn't stop until she felt his hand on her shoulder. "Hey! Skye, come on. I just meant that we're not like that—we're just friends, which actually means quite a lot to me."

"Why's that?" she asked without looking back at him, her ego still bruised.

"Because I don't have that many female friends . . . and I definitely meant it when I said that you're one of the best sailors I know. It's true. You are."

Skye turned around, surprised by his confession about not having many female friends because she'd never thought of Brooks Winslow as lacking much in his life. It made her soften toward him, even as she suddenly felt self-conscious about her dirty overalls, braided hair, and baseball cap.

"I get it. I'm flattered that you'd want me to go with you."

"So you'll do it? You'll bid on me?"

The hopeful expression in his deep-green eyes was her undoing, and she offered him a grudging smile.

"How much can I spend?"

"As much as it takes," he said, grinning back at her.

"And one other thing," she said, still smarting from the "I don't even see you as a girl" comment and unable to resist an opportunity to prove to the world that a boat mechanic, the daughter of a marina owner, could manage a boat as pretty as the one Brooks was describing. Plus, it might be her one chance—her one opportunity—to ever call the shots on a boat like that. She may as well go for broke. "I get to skipper."

Brooks' smile faded a little. It was one thing for her to crew his boat, but the skipper of any maritime vessel called all of the shots. Maybe he wouldn't want to give up that privilege. *How badly does he need me?* she wondered. Would he trust her to be in charge of such a sumptuous boat?

As his eyes narrowed, Skye worried for a moment that she'd overplayed her hand and was about to say "Just kidding" before he suddenly answered.

"Every other day you can skipper. We'll switch off."

She grinned broadly and nodded, sticking out her hand, which he clasped in his.

"You just won yourself an auction."

Chapter 2

Although Westerly, the Winslow family estate in Haverford, Pennsylvania, technically still belonged to Brooks' mother, he was the only Winslow in full-time residence this summer. As the eldest of five Winslow siblings, Brooks would inherit the sprawling estate one day, but the Winslows practiced an open-door policy when it came to any family member staying at the estate whenever they wanted, for as long as they wanted, which meant that Brooks' siblings were constantly coming and going from the nine-bedroom, fourteen-thousand-square-foot mansion.

As he pulled into the circular driveway in front of the house, the front door opened and his little sister and youngest sibling, Jessica, bounded down the stairs. She and her fiancé, Alex English, were back in Philadelphia for the summer, and although Jessica wasn't living at Westerly—she was living with Alex in his downtown apartment—she was using Westerly as "Wedding Planning Central."

"Brooks!" she exclaimed as his BMW convertible rolled to a stop.

"Hey Jess!" he greeted her, stepping out of the car and pulling her close for a hug.

There was an eleven-year age difference between Brooks and Jessica, and after their father passed away many years ago, Brooks had stepped in as a surrogate father for her. In fact, he couldn't be prouder to be walking his little sister down the aisle in three short months.

"How's the wedding planning going?" he asked, putting his arm around her shoulders as they headed into the house.

"Divine! I finally got the caterer booked, and even though they refused—initially—to let Daisy English do the cake, I won them over."

"With your charm?"

"With my wallet." She shrugged, grinning at him.

Daisy was Alex's sister-in-law and owned the most popular bakery in Haverford, *Daisy's Delights*, but she was still making a name for herself with local caterers.

"It's not like you could have used someone else," said Brooks, knowing Jessica's great love for her new family, who were—conveniently—lifelong friends and next-door neighbors of the Winslows.

"Unthinkable. Plus, Daisy's cakes are really good."

With Jessica still beside him, Brooks checked his watch, heading back to the kitchen to see if Mrs. Pugh, his housekeeper, had left something out for a late lunch.

"So, um," said Jessica as they entered the kitchen and Brooks dropped his arm from her to open the refrigerator. "Are you still pissed at me?"

"Pissed?"

"About the auction?" Jessica hopped up on the kitchen counter, her face contrite when Brooks glanced in her direction.

"I'm still not thrilled," he said, thinking, *It's going to cost me a lot of money.*

"I know. I should have asked first . . . but I was sure you'd say no."

"Safe bet," he confirmed, taking out a ham and brie sandwich wrapped up carefully on a plate. *God Bless Mrs. Pugh.*

"By the way, I need an invite sent to the Sorenson Marina in Havre de Grace, Maryland."

"You're inviting a marina owner?" asked Jessica, furrowing her forehead.

"Yeah. They service my boats."

Jessica rolled her eyes. "I'm sure the marina people will be big spenders."

Brooks looked away from her to hide his smile. "You never know."

"Well, you can comfort yourself that it's for a good cause," persisted Jessica.

"Uh-huh. So you've said. Though I still don't understand why Preston, Cameron, and Christopher got off scot-free," said Brooks, referring to his three younger brothers who were all as unattached as Brooks, yet spared the humiliation of being auctioned off "for a good cause."

"Do you want an honest answer to that question?" asked Jess.

Brooks grabbed a can of Diet Coke and walked through a swinging door to the small, round breakfast table in the morning room with Jess at his heels.

"No. Lie to me."

"I'm serious," said Jess. "If you want to know, I'll tell you the truth."

He sat down and placed a white linen napkin on his lap from the place setting before him. *Hmm. Do I want the truth?* From Jessica's tone, it might be loaded. Not entirely a stranger to his little sister's attempts to "help" his love life now and then, he wondered if this was just another ploy to add to the pile . . . only one way to find out.

"Sure. Go for it."

She took a deep breath, then fixed him with her emerald-green eyes, her words coming out in a rush. "You're thirty-five and you're not married. You're not even dating anyone.

Aren't you lonesome? You travel around the world training teams and reporting on races. You don't have a real home. Don't you want a wife and children? Don't you want to settle down? I'm worried about you!"

Wasn't this always the way? he mused. People who were hit with the "true love stick" wanted everyone else around them to be whacked too.

"No need to worry," he said, taking a big bite of his sandwich.

"You're not thirty-five?"

"I am."

"Are you seeing someone?"

"I'm not."

"Aren't you lonesome?"

Brooks flicked his eyes to Jessica's face before digging into his sandwich again, realizing that he didn't have an easy answer for her.

Was he lonesome for companionship? No. He had plenty of friends—at the Penn Alumni Club, at the hunt club, and at his yacht club down in Maryland, not to mention it was a rare day that he didn't see Pres, Cam, or Chris.

Was he lonesome for female company? No, again. There were plenty of women who were happy to ease that particular loneliness . . . for a fee. He used a discreet service that he called when his "needs" arose.

Was he lonesome for a wife and children? Did he want to settle down?

He glanced up at his little sister's expectant face before looking away and taking another bite of his sandwich.

N—*Hmm.* He wanted to say "No" because saying "No" would be best. He even thought the simple word and envisioned it, but somehow his mind wouldn't *say* it, which made his heart clench painfully.

Too busy for a love life by having the responsibility of male head-of-family thrust on him when he was seventeen, he'd missed out on college girlfriends, careful to spend his college weekends at home with his grieving younger siblings. And by the time his mother, Jessica, and Christopher had relocated to London, he was graduating from college and utterly devoted to training, conditioning, and racing to be a part of the Olympic sailing team. In 2000, that dream had come to fruition, and Brooks medaled on behalf of the USA at the Summer Games in Australia, which had led to over a decade of promotional speaking, endorsement tours, and judging races and regattas for major television networks. Although Brooks was home for the summer in preparation for Jessica's wedding, he had an offer for a short-term consulting job in San Diego he was considering, and as soon as Jess was married, he'd set up TV, consulting, and judging gigs from October through Christmas.

A wife and children.

Brooks hid the wince he felt by taking another bite of his sandwich.

Truth be told? Deep, deep in his heart, he longed to fall in love, and he had always sort of dreamed—as one dreams of impossible things—of becoming a father. But he'd kept himself from actualizing that dream because if he was honest, the idea also scared him stiff. He was thirty-five, and his own father had passed away from a totally unexpected heart attack at forty years old, leaving a widow and five fatherless children. Brooks had had an up-close seat to his mother's grief and his siblings' deep loss and confusion. He'd done his best to be a good big brother and substitute father, attending Jessica's father-daughter events at school, and helping with Christopher and Cameron's Boy Scout meetings whenever possible. Having a taste of fatherhood at such an early age hadn't deterred Brooks from wanting his own children one day; it had just strengthened that desire in his heart.

But he couldn't lie. In a very real way, he was frightened that if he allowed himself to fall in love and have children, he'd only end up abandoning them if he met his father's tragic fate. And that wouldn't just be heartbreaking, it would be irresponsible.

So it didn't really matter what he wanted. What was best for him was to keep a wide circle of friends for companionship and seek out safe, anonymous encounters when he felt the need for a woman. But he kept his heart carefully guarded, off-limits, and impenetrable to love, so that he'd never find himself gasping on an early deathbed, leaving tearstained faces behind.

Unwilling and unable to answer the uncomfortable question for Jessica in any simple manner, he defaulted, as he often did, to the stern tone of an older brother out of patience for his little sister's shenanigans.

"I'm fine, Jess. I don't require—or appreciate—your interference."

She gave him a sour look, tilting her head to the side before resting her elbows on the table. "Well, I still haven't answered *your* question, but now I will. I entered you in the auction because I'm hoping that if you get trapped on a sailboat for a week with a nice woman, you'll let propinquity take over and fall in love."

Brooks blinked at Jessica, quickly looking away before she saw him smirk at her outlandish suggestion.

He couldn't help it . . . thinking about Skye's shapeless body in men's overalls, the filthy, omnipresent, grease-stained bandana sticking out of her back pocket, battered Top-Siders covered with dried sea salt, and a face largely hidden by the brim of a beat-up Orioles cap, he almost laughed. Like every other man on earth, Brooks had a favorite type: blonde, blue-eyed, and willowy, with an ass and breasts that a man could hold onto in bed and legs that went on forever. He wanted the type of girl who made other men turn around and gawk with envy when she walked into a gala, who knew how to be feminine and graceful and still take care of a man's needs without awakening his heart. He knew his type, and it *didn't* include a certain marina mechanic who was more comfortable with a socket wrench than a champagne glass.

"Yeah, well. Good luck with that," he said, grinning to himself that he'd somehow managed to foil Jessica's matchmaker intentions.

She huffed. "I'm not giving up on you, Brooks."

He took the last bite of sandwich and swallowed as he stared at his little sister. "You probably should . . . or at least trust me when I say that it's not going to happen this time."

Jessica rolled her eyes as she stood up, but she did that superannoying thing girls sometimes do: as she headed out of the room, she tossed over her shoulder in a knowing, singsong voice, "Never say never, Brooks. Never say never."

Whenever she could, Skye tried to catch the sunset over the marina. The way the oranges, golds, and purples colored the clouds, reflecting off the water and silhouetting the tall masts of sailboats was—hands down—the most beautiful thing in the world.

After Brooks left her, the bilge pump job had taken twice as long as she'd anticipated because it wasn't a pump problem, but a wiring problem that had led to hours of testing the electrical board on the boat. Happily, it was now completed, and she'd saved the owners a couple of hundred dollars by not having to replace the pump. She'd done a good job, and per usual, she took a great deal of pleasure from a job well done.

As she watched the sky turn from blue to Technicolor, Skye thought about how much she liked working with and for her father. She'd learned about boats and their maintenance from the best, and although she'd grown up without the benefit of a mother, she felt certain that her father's love and affection had more than compensated for her mother's absence.

Her mother hadn't loved the simple life of living by the water in Maryland and had left for Los Angeles to be a singer when Skye was a little girl. If she hadn't cheated on Skye's father before leaving, Skye would have probably forgiven her mother for leaving, but she still remembered her father's pain at learning of her mother's betrayal. Though her mother had tried to explain the very tawdry adult situation to eight-year-old Skye before her flight to LA, Skye had already sided with her father. Her relationship with her mother had suffered irreparable damage. Not to mention, her mother's lifestyle once in LA was R-rated, at best, which meant that aside from a couple of visits to Maryland over the past twenty years, Skye had barely grown up with a mother at all.

"D'ja fix that pump, Skye?" asked her father, ambling down the dock where she sat, making it bob up and down. The pleasing sound of water lapping against the sides soothed her like a beloved lullaby.

"Sure did. Nothing wrong with the pump, Pop. Just a wiring problem."

"Figures." He grinned, taking a seat beside her and looking out at the dramatic sky. "Nice one tonight."

"A beauty," she agreed, pulling off her cap and taking the rubber bands out of her tight braids. She ran her fingers through her soft, blonde hair until it flowed past her shoulders in waves. "Hey, Pop. I took on a crewing job. Week after next. Sunday to Sunday."

"With Brooks Winslow?" asked Jack Sorenson, giving his daughter a side glance.

"Yeah. How'd you know?"

"He asked me if I could spare you for a week before coming to find you."

She nodded, appreciating the fact that Brooks respected her work enough to check with her boss before offering a job.

"You haven't been out on the water much lately," her father noted.

She shrugged. She didn't feel like discussing the reason or the *someone* who'd stolen a little bit of her love for sailing. She was just relieved that Brooks Winslow was giving her an irresistible opportunity to get back out there.

"Just you or a full crew?" he asked.

"Just me. And what's that tone for?"

Her father took a deep breath. "You know I have the utmost respect for Brooks as a sailor, right? Man knows his way around a boat better'n most." Skye nodded, unsure of where this was going. "But you sure you want to crew for him solo?"

"Promised I would," she said and couldn't resist adding, "and he's letting me skip."

"Is that right?" asked Jack, eyebrows lifting as he nodded in approval. "Well, that's a lot of responsibility."

She still sensed reticence in her father's tone. "What's up, Pop? What's your objection?"

"Let's just say I don't like the sort of women Brooks occasionally brings down here."

Intrigued, Skye grinned at her father. "And what kind of woman would that be?"

"The kind that arrives in a taxi and leaves in a taxi."

"What do you have against taxis?"

"Always a blonde. Always in a skimpy dress and heels. Always meets him here. But never for a sail," he said, raising an eyebrow and looking at her meaningfully.

"Oh," said Skye, understanding perfectly. Her father was most comfortable with boating types, and Skye knew that the type of girl Brooks preferred was sophisticated, working in the city, taking taxis everywhere, dressing fancy, and not showing an interest in getting out on the water.

"To each their own. We can't all have the same interests."

"Just so long as *his* interest isn't *you*," her father said, giving her a pointed look.

Skye looked away from her father, anxious not to miss the last of the sunset and feeling a little protective of Brooks and his right to privacy where his personal life was concerned. He wasn't hurting anyone, was he? If he liked more cosmopolitan girls, it wasn't up to her or her father to pass judgment.

"I can't see how it's any of our business, Pop."

"But it doesn't make me want to dance a jig that my blonde-haired, blue-eyed daughter is crewing with him for a solo weeklong."

Skye faced her father and rolled her eyes, Brooks' words about not seeing her as a girl running through her brain and stinging all over again. "Blonde or not, he doesn't see me like that. I can guarantee it."

Her father hefted himself up from where he'd been sitting. "No way to guarantee that, Skye. Man can feel something out of nowhere and decide to make his move . . . and a boat's got tight quarters."

She looked up at her father and gave him a reassuring smile as she stood beside him, hugging herself against a cool breeze that blew back her hair and made goose bumps rise up on her arms. "I promise you, there's nothing to worry about. Brooks and I are just friends. I'm going to help him crew that gorgeous boat and fly home a week later. The only love affair on this cruise'll be me and the cutter," she said confidently.

"If you say so," said her father, grimacing. "Would help matters if your *boyfriend* wasn't gallivanting all over the world without you."

Her father adopted a tone when he said the word "boy-friend," which chafed at Skye a little. She knew her father wasn't Pat's biggest fan, but she wished he could try a little harder to see what an organic, sensible match she and Pat were.

"From the moment you met him, he was always upfront about circumnavigating," she reminded her father.

"Seems to me his original plan changed pretty abruptly," her father reminded her in turn.

Skye shrugged, determined not to let her father see that his words had hit a soft spot. She didn't want to give him another reason not to like Pat.

"I know. I know. It's none of my business." He turned and started back up the dock before pivoting to face her. "It's just . . . you didn't have a mama around. You know, to talk about things like this—boys and such. I raised you a lot like my Pop raised me, and sometimes I feel like you . . . well, like you missed out on things. Hope I didn't raise you wrong. But even more, I hope you use your head, Skye Rose, especially where Brooks Winslow is concerned."

She wished he wouldn't worry so much, but there didn't seem to be any way to reassure him that Brooks Winslow wouldn't make a move on her in a million years. She walked over to him, leaning up on her tiptoes to give his cheek a kiss. "You are the best father I could have asked for. And you raised me just right."

His white beard prickled her lips for an instant before she let him go, turning around just in time to note, with a little disappointment, that the sun was already gone.

Chapter 3

Two hours later, Skye had showered off the marina stink, had changed into comfortable, pink terry cloth boxers and a scoop-neck gray T-shirt, and was sitting in front of her TV eating a grilled cheese sandwich as she waited for Patrick to call her on Skype.

She and Pat had met years ago when they both sailed Lasers for the Northern Chesapeake Cruising Club. At the time, Patrick worked as an investment banker in Baltimore and was married to his now ex-wife, Dionne. When he and Dionne split three years ago, he was looking for a new crewmate, and a mutual friend had suggested Skye. Remembering one another at first sight—and the races in which they'd bested each other over the years—they'd clicked instantly.

Though their relationship hadn't moved quickly—it had taken two years for their first kiss, they still didn't live together, and neither had ever broached the topic of engagement or marriage—that didn't bother Skye because it felt so comfortable. Pat didn't seem to care that she dressed like a tomboy and almost always had motor grease under her fingernails, and she didn't mind that he spent more time praising the cut of his catamaran than coming up with romantic surprises for her.

She convinced herself she didn't need that stuff—she just needed someone who cared for her and shared her interests. They were compatible, spending every spring and summer weekend on the water, and winter weekends playing paddle, visiting with friends, and heading south to Florida and the Caribbean to get in some seasonal sails. Pat had a love of boats that surpassed Skye's. For the first few months of dating, she never grew weary of listening to him talk about his dream of circumnavigating the globe. She honed her skills, getting out on the water as much as possible to be sure she was lithe and quick, ready to anticipate Pat's every need and be the best possible teammate for him.

The twist? He'd always talked about them going *together*, so it was a surprise when Pat finally announced that he'd quit his job for the trip, but that he wanted to go solo.

Skye's face had fallen. "But I thought—"

"I know, Skye. I know we always talked about going together, but I just feel like this dream started before I met you. It was one of the reasons Dionne and I broke up, and I can't shake the feeling that this is just an adventure I'm meant to enjoy alone. I think it's my destiny."

"Your . . . destiny."

"Not to mention, I'm just taking the Cat. Another person is extra weight, you know? And you're a decent crew, Skye, but I want to make good time, and you're not really a racer. I want to do this my way."

Extra weight. Like her 120-pound body would be such a deterrent to his speed.

A decent crew. Not even a good *sailor.* A *decent* crew.

She *was* a racer. She'd been racing sailboats since she was a little girl, and Pat knew it, which led her to one conclusion: Pat didn't think she was a *good* racer, and Skye, who'd always felt proud of her sailing skills and assumed she could hold her own, was crestfallen. If he'd backhanded her across the face it couldn't have stung more. But unwilling to rock the proverbial boat, Skye had swallowed her hurt feelings and offered him a brave smile. "It sounds like you've made up your mind."

"I have."

"Well . . ." she said, embarrassed and upset, but trying her best not to succumb to tears or out-of-character, girly overemoting. "I hope you have a great time, Pat."

"Aw, Skye, you're the best. I knew you'd understand. And listen, after I go once? I'll know all the pitfalls and challenges. Someday when we go together, it'll be smooth as glass." He'd paused, grinning at her. "You know what, babe? You *are* a great mechanic. Maybe we could work on the Cat together before I go?"

Taking some comfort from his reassurance that they'd go together "someday," and pathetically grateful for his compliment about her boat-maintenance skills, she'd helped him tune up his catamaran to a place of safety and speed, and even shed a few rare tears as they waved good-bye on a chilly March morning . . . that also happened to be their eight-month anniversary.

Now here it was, toward the end of June, and they'd spoken four times on the phone (about once a month). When Pat got a signal at sea, he'd occasionally e-mail her too, but it just wasn't enough contact, and unsurprisingly, Skye had really started missing Pat over the past few weeks. Being apart was really starting to bother her. Further, she was having doubts about whether a monogamous—though fairly new—relationship was capable of weathering a two-year absence. It made her heart hurt because she truly cared for Pat and didn't want to lose him. As a solution, she wondered if it might be a good idea for them to push up her visit to Mexico. Instead of waiting two more months to see him in Mazatlán, maybe they could meet up in three or four weeks' time in Santa Cruz or Acapulco. As much as Skye didn't want to put pressure on their relationship, this week also marked a year together, the first anniversary of their first kiss, and perhaps their relationship did need to feel a bit more solid—with them both committed to a real future together—to weather the year and a half of separation up ahead. At any rate, she had butterflies in her stomach because she planned to discuss it all with him tonight.

When her phone started ringing, she jumped, quickly putting her sandwich back on her plate. Muting the TV, she sat cross-legged in front of her laptop screen and clicked to answer the call. Suddenly, Pat's face took up her entire screen, and she beamed at him until her cheeks hurt.

"Pat!"

"Skye! Hey, babe!"

He waved at her, and she waved back, unfamiliar tears pricking her eyes because she was so glad to see him.

"How are you? How's Panama City?"

"Bueno and bueno!" he said enthusiastically. "I got in two days ago, and I've been having a blast. What a great city!"

Her smile faded just a touch as she processed the fact that he'd been on land for three days and hadn't called until now. Then she chastened herself. Did he really want to call her all the way from Panama and risk that she wouldn't be home? Maybe the boat had had issues that needed to be dealt with, and surely he'd needed to restock, right? No, it was good that he'd stuck to their agreed-upon time to talk. It showed commitment, thoughtfulness, and consistency.

"How does it feel to be on land again?"

"Huh? Oh, yeah!" He turned to the side for a second, smiling at someone before looking back at her. "Hey babe, I'm with Inga and Helmut right now. They're circumnavigating too." He panned his phone to the side, and Skye was suddenly looking at two very blonde, very tan, very good-looking people who were waving back at her enthusiastically.

"Hi," she said politely, waving back. "Nice to meet you."

"You too," said Inga, with a broad, confident smile. "Patrick is a—how you say?—good sport."

"Oh," said Skye, nodding. "Yes, he is. Where are you from?"

"Sweden!"

Suddenly, Inga jostled in her chair and looked back flirtatiously at her boyfriend, grasping his cheeks and planting a passionate kiss on his lips. At a loss, Skye watched the make-out session until a chuckling Pat reappeared on the screen again.

"How about those two? Feisty, huh?"

"It looks like you're having fun," said Skye, trying to be happy for him, but feeling the distance stretch between them dramatically, in more ways than one.

"Babe, it's like this awesome club. Everywhere I go, I meet other sailors circumnavigating, or doing long stretches. The stories I could tell . . ." He shook his head, laughing again.

"I bet," she said, offering him a nervous grin. "Um, hey, I sort of wanted to talk to you about some—"

"Oh, yeah, man! That's the way!" Pat was looking at Helmut and Inga with a wide grin. He finally turned back to the screen to look at Skye. "Sorry. They're like, full-on making out in an Internet café. Crazy. What were you about to say?"

Starting to feel upset that he'd called her from such a public place instead of making a quiet call to her from his hotel room so they could really catch up, she didn't feel like talking about Mexico anymore. Not only concerned that he was too distracted to engage in a thoughtful discussion, Skye was private about her personal life, and she wasn't too keen about Inga and Helmut eavesdropping. Hopefully she'd catch Pat over e-mail at some point over the next couple of weeks and bring it up then.

Scrambling for something else to share, the next thing that popped out of her mouth was, "I'm crewing a restored 1929 cutter for Brooks Winslow next weekend."

Pat's head, which had been turned toward his friends, whipped forward, and his expression straightened. Suddenly, she had one hundred percent of his attention and couldn't help a fleeting feeling of satisfaction.

"Brooks, huh? Is that right? Where to?"

"Charleston."

"Huh. That's a week. Minimum."

"Mm-hm," she said, adding slyly, "and he's letting me skip."

"What? *You?*"

"Yeah. Every other day," she said, raising her chin in defiance of Pat's opinion of her skills.

"Well, that's . . . great, Skye," said Pat unenthusiastically. "Should be interesting."

"Have a little faith in me, Pat."

"Sure. There's a first time for everything. It'll be a great learning experience for you." He gave her a thin smile. "Who else is going with you two?"

"Um, no one," she said softly, wondering if it would make Pat a little jealous and hoping that it would. Part of her was hurt that he couldn't be happier for her, and she was still feeling upset that he'd chosen to make their once-monthly call a social affair with his new friends in such a public place.

Pat raised his eyebrows, looking annoyed. "Brooks does love his blondes."

"What does *that* mean?" she bit back.

"Nothing," he said, his voice flat. "I hope you have a great trip. Good luck skipping."

She was about to say, *"I don't need luck! I know what I'm doing!"* when Pat looked back at Inga and Helmut, holding up his hand. "No, no. Wait for me. I'll finish up here, and we can go together." He looked back at Skye, his eyes cooler now. "Last night on land for a while. I guess I'll go make the best of it."

Suddenly, she forgot about Brooks and his boat, and her heart clutched at the thought of not talking to Pat for four more weeks.

"Pat," she said, "how about I meet you in Acapulco instead? In two weeks?"

He massaged his scruffy, blond chin with his thumb and forefinger, staring at her with surprised, blue eyes. "Oh, I don't know, babe. You already have the ticket for Mazatlán."

"I'm sure I can trade it in." She looked down and swallowed, gathering her courage before looking back up at Pat. "I-I miss you."

"Aw, you're sweet, babe," he said, his expression softening a little. "How about I try to e-mail you after I get through the canal? We'll talk then and make a decision?"

Skye nodded, unsatisfied with leaving the conversation this way, but not eager to make waves. "Okay."

Pat tilted his head to the side, pursing his lips. "Don't be mad, Skye. That's selfish. I have to do this for me. You know it's my dream."

"I know, Pat. I just wish we could—"

"Oh, my God, you guys! Get a room!" he exclaimed to his friends, laughing. He turned back to Skye. "I gotta go. Um, talk soon, babe?"

"Sure." Skye tried, but she couldn't even force a smile. "Pat, wait! Happy—"

"You're the best," he said, looking away from the screen to laugh with his friends as his finger clicked to disconnect the call.

"Anniversary," she whispered to herself.

Skye stared disbelievingly at the blank screen for a beat before getting up and stomping to the kitchen. She took a beer out of the fridge, opening it by resting it on her kitchen counter and dropping the heel of her hand over the cap. Then she stomped back to the couch where she snapped the cover of her laptop closed. Disappointment welled up inside of her as she reviewed their conversation, or lack thereof.

The only thing he'd shown a little bit of interest in was her cruise with Brooks, and even then he'd been argumentative and curt. It clearly bothered him that she was crewing for Brooks. Why? He and Brooks weren't the best of friends, but she'd seen them hanging out on occasion, and they'd raced together more than once. That comment about Brooks loving his blondes? What was *that* all about? Why did everyone seem to assume Brooks asking her for a routine crewing job was just a ruse for seduction? It wasn't. He'd made that abundantly clear.

She shook her head, tilting back the bottle of Bass and taking a long sip. Was she being selfish for wanting to see Pat sooner than later? It didn't feel selfish. It felt like a last-ditch attempt to get their relationship on level ground before it unraveled from the time and distance away from each other. She stared out at the harbor view afforded by her condo and wondered if it was even possible to save her relationship with Pat at all . . . because despite the fact that he'd called her in the company of friends, been distracted, gotten jealous about Brooks, called her selfish, and missed a chance to wish her a "Happy Anniversary" . . . the thing that ended up bothering Skye the most was that when she told him she missed him, he hadn't told her he missed her, too.

Brooks had several personal rules about using Elite Escorts for his personal needs in addition to the nondisclosure agreement he'd had them sign before ever making a booking with them and the standard precautions he took to ensure safe sex. Mostly, these rules were to guarantee that any sort of relationship or emotional intimacy was avoided.

The first was that he never gave his real name to the girls and asked them to use a pseudonym, as well.

The second was that Elite was never to send him the same girl twice in a row.

And the third was that they never, ever met at Westerly.

Because Brooks spent so much time on the road, he didn't have a bachelor pad in the city like his younger brothers. This meant that he asked most of his "dates" to meet him at the Sorenson Marina. Not only was the marina an hour away from Philly, where he was less likely to run into people he knew socially, but the Passport 47 Yacht he moored there boasted all the comforts of home, including a queen-sized bed and a bedside table stocked with condoms.

Pulling into the parking lot around seven thirty Friday evening, he decided to track down Skye to reconfirm the plan for tomorrow night since it was thirty minutes until tonight's date, Holly M., would arrive by taxi to meet him.

The little marina shop where Jack Sorenson worked had closed at seven, but Brooks knew from personal experience that Skye was probably still tinkering with an outboard motor or changing a starboard lightbulb before heading home for the night. She often left the mundane projects for the end of the day.

Walking out on dock eleven, he found her squatting on the wooden boards, staring at a raised propeller, one hand full of tangled line and the other holding a fish-gutting knife. Unlike almost every other time that he'd seen her, this evening she had her cap off, and her white-blonde hair was escaping from a long, thick braid in wisps and strands, blowing lightly in the evening breeze. He was mesmerized by the light color of the soft strands in the dying sun, and his gaze slid without permission to the contrast offered by the graceful line of her neck. Her complexion was tan after a lifetime's worth of heavy-sun sailing, and the light-blonde tendrils of hair teased the warm-looking skin. Skimming his eyes still lower, his gaze paused at a tiny, brown beauty mark at the base of her neck. Without warning, he felt his heart quicken. His tongue darted out to lick his lips, and his body began to tighten just as she whipped her head around.

"Brooks!"

He was grateful for the slight sunburn he'd gotten while playing tennis yesterday because it covered his blush as he snapped his eyes up from her neck to her face.

"Hey, Skye."

"Don't sneak up on me," she said, turning back to her work. "It's creepy."

He cleared his throat, refusing to let his mind linger on the unexpected and unwelcome thoughts that had just been firing through his head, heating up his body.

"What are you up to?"

"Uh . . ." she muttered, gesturing to the obvious mess in her hands. "Fishing line got tangled all around this prop. Trying to get it out, but it's good and stuck in all this seaweed. Give me a hand?"

"Sure," he said, squatting down on the other side of the propeller and getting a better-than-usual look at her face with her omnipresent cap gone.

"Here," she said, handing him a balled-up wad of fishing line mixed with gobs of gooey seaweed. "Hold it tight so I can cut it out?"

He tugged on the ball of line to tighten it, pulling back strands as she snipped and staring at her face as she worked. Her features, which he hadn't checked out at close range in quite a while, were elegant—a lovely contrast to the playful dusting of freckles over her nose. Damn. Skye Sorenson was the rare combination of cute *and* pretty, a look that Brooks had always been attracted to.

"Stop staring at me," she said without looking up.

"How do you know I'm staring at you?"

She glanced up. "Well, aren't you?"

"Yeah." He stared at her eyes now, which were huge and dark blue.

"So, cut it out," she said softly, dropping his eyes. "It's making me nervous."

He sighed, raising his gaze over her shoulder to stare at the boats bobbing in a neat line behind her.

Yeah, Brooks, he thought. *Cut it out. This is Skye Sorenson, your tomboy friend who's doing you a big favor. Graceful necks and kissable beauty marks have no place in this equation . . . not to mention, Pat probably wouldn't appreciate you sizing up his girlfriend's cute-versus-pretty ratio.*

"You all set for tomorrow?" he asked crisply, intent on shifting his thoughts away from anything inappropriate and back to their business at hand.

"What's tomorrow?"

His eyes darted back to her. "Skye, come on! You promis—" It took him a second to realize her shoulders were shaking from laughing. "Not nice."

"Wow. You're really in knots over this auction . . . no pun intended." She flicked her twinkling eyes to his. "A promise is a promise. I'll be there. But tell me this . . . how are you going to slip me the money when I win?"

With his free hand, he reached into his breast pocket and pulled out a credit card. "I got you a credit card."

"You applied for a credit card in my name? How?"

"It wasn't hard."

"You had to steal my social security number to do that," she said, concentrating on her work as she spoke. "Not sure how I feel about that, Brooks."

"Not hard doesn't equal illegal. It's my account. I just had your name put on the card."

"I see," she said. Then, cutting the last of the line, she fell back on her bottom. "There! Phew!"

Brooks chuckled softly. Something he'd always liked about Skye was how hard she worked. He'd never seen a woman as good with her hands as Skye, as good at fixing things. Most of the women he knew socially were far more sophisticated and much higher maintenance. They wouldn't be caught dead in overalls with seaweed stuck between their manicured fingers.

Skye reached down for the credit card with a slimy hand and looked at it before sliding it into the breast pocket of her overalls. Then she grabbed her cap from the dock beside her and mashed it on her head. She pulled the slack line from his fingers and stuffed it all into a garbage bag. "What's my credit limit?"

"Five hundred thousand dollars."

Her face jerked up to look at his. Her pink lips parted in shock, and he silently cursed her hat because he didn't have a good view of those dark-blue eyes widening. "Are you crazy?"

Brooks shrugged. "I trust you."

"You do? I don't know if *I* trust me with that much money."

"Well, I figure you have to get something to wear too. I was kidding when I said you could wear your normal duds," he said dryly, gesturing to her overalls.

"Oh, really?" she asked sarcastically, looking at him, lips pursed in annoyance. "Because I'm a total moron, and I thought this would be appropriate for a gala."

"Did you already get something to wear?" he challenged.

She stared at him for an extra moment. "No."

"I rest my case. Spend whatever you want. Maybe go to Saks Fifth Avenue in Bala Cynwyd. That's where my sister goes." He paused. "Do you have somewhere to stay on Saturday night?"

"I'll drive home afterward. Sunday's a busy day here," she said, standing up, the garbage bag bumping against her leg. "Anything else?"

He grinned at her. She was always working, always moving. Did she ever take a break? When she did, what did she do? He didn't know a ton about her life outside of sailing, and suddenly, he wanted to know.

"Why?" he asked, looking up at her from where he still squatted on the dock. "You have somewhere you need to be?"

"It's almost sunset," she said.

"And?"

"I like to watch it from dock five."

"Every night?"

She nodded, leaning down to latch her toolbox and pick it up. While she was bent over, Brooks noticed the taxi pulling into the upper parking lot.

"So, I'll see you tomorrow?" she asked.

"Yeah," he said, glancing up again to see an elegantly dressed, blonde woman exiting the cab, but surprised that he didn't feel a hot jolt of anticipation for what was, hopefully, coming.

Skye followed his glance, turning to look at the cab, then rolling her eyes at him before walking away.

As Brooks made his way in the opposite direction, toward Holly M. in her sleek updo, sexy, black cocktail dress, and high heels, he couldn't help but look back at the solitary figure standing at the end of dock five, and just for a moment, he wished that he was standing there, too.

Chapter 4

Skye pulled into a parking space at the Saks Fifth Avenue in Bala Cynwyd, a suburb of Philadelphia, at four o'clock on Saturday afternoon. For lack of a better plan, she would find a fancy dress and shoes, buy them on Brooks' credit card, and then hang out in a nearby Starbucks before getting dressed in the coffee shop bathroom and heading to the auction. Then? She planned to sit in a chair, bid on Brooks, win him, pay for him, get back in her car, and go home, preferably stopping in the ladies' room on the way out of the Ritz-Carlton to change back into her jeans, T-shirt, and flip-flops.

Throwing her sunglasses back into their case, she grudgingly left the comfort of her car and headed into the department store, almost immediately feeling like a fish out of water. The salespeople mostly ignored her as she headed over to a store directory, but she couldn't help noticing that most of the women shopping looked much older and more polished than Skye.

"God, what am I doing here?" she muttered, trailing a stained, stubby fingernail along the glossy sign detailing the myriad departments spread all over the store.

"Can I help?"

She jerked her head up at the sound of a male voice, turning to her left to find a man beside her dressed in a shiny, gray suit with a light-pink shirt, darker-pink tie, and hair that looked like it was being held in place by a whole can of hair spray. *Is that eyeliner?*

She shook her head. "I don't think so."

"Sure?" He leaned closer to her. "Don't take this the wrong way, but you don't look like a frequent flier."

"Huh?"

"Have you ever visited Saks before?"

"No," she said, still trying to find the department called "Fancy Dresses."

"Well, I practically live here. Minimally, I can direct you to the right place."

She looked at him again and sighed. "Okay, thanks. I need a fancy dress for a gala."

He leaned back sharply, looking surprised. "*That*, I would not have guessed, honey. Follow me."

Turning quickly, he headed back through the rows of makeup and costume jewelry, and Skye clip-clopped behind him trying to keep up, her flip-flops making a racket along the elegant marble floors. Stopping in front of the elevators, he pressed the "Up" button.

"I'm Clay," he said, grinning at her and holding out his hand.

"Skye," she said, shaking it gratefully.

"The elements," he said, raising one carefully shaped eyebrow as he gestured for her to precede him onto the elevator. "Earth and sky. I knew I liked your energy."

Unaware that she had a likeable energy, Skye grinned back at him, laughing softly. "Hey, I know you're a guy . . . but do you think *you* could help me find something?"

"What's our budget?" he asked shrewdly, giving her a once-over and pursing his lips.

Skye shrugged. "Whatever it takes."

"My favorite words!" he said, his face animating. "Where are we headed? With whom? When? I need the deets, Skye."

"Gala in Philadelphia at the Ritz-Carlton. With Brooks Winslow. Tonight."

"Color me impressed," he said, fanning his face as he held the elevator door open for her. "Brooks Winslow who was in the Olympics?"

Skye nodded.

"Girl, he's hot! But for heaven's sake. Tonight? What do you have against a little planning?"

"We have almost four hours!" said Skye, trailing after him again. "How much time do I need to buy a dress? I mean, I thought I'd kill some time in a coffee shop somewhere nearby before getting dressed, and—"

"Honey." He stopped his brisk walk and turned to face her. "We are going to need *all four* of those four hours. No joke." He took a cell phone from his pocket, dialed two numbers, and pressed it to his ear. "I need patented leather slingbacks brought to Ladies Formal Wear." Glancing at her feet, he grimaced as he continued, "Make that closed-toe pumps. Eight and a half. But sexy. Patent leather clutch, too. And I need Monique and Darlene at the salon ready for an updo and mani in"—he shot a quick look at the gold watch on his wrist—"seventy minutes." Gesturing to her breasts, he covered the phone for a moment. "Thirty-four C? Or thirty-two?"

"Thirty-two C," mumbled Skye, dumbstruck by Clay's pace and efficiency.

"And a bustier. Comfortable. Thirty-two C. And medium Spanx . . . because *every* woman needs them. When? Now, now, now, darling."

He pressed the end button on his phone and turned to Skye with a beaming smile. "Ready for some fun?"

Brooks pulled his phone out of his tux breast pocket, check-ing the time again, and then flicked his eyes to the entry of the Grand Ballroom with a frown. As far as he could tell, Skye still hadn't shown up and it was eight forty. The auction was set to begin in about twenty minutes.

For most of the evening, he'd hunkered down with his brothers for protection, but once or twice, overeager bach-elorettes had cornered him to share their commitment to winning the cruise to Charleston.

Felicity Atwell, who'd once dated Brooks' good friend, Barrett English, had been especially enthusiastic, running a tapered finger along his cheek to caress his lips and share her plans with him.

"I don't care what it costs," she'd hummed into his ear, her uninvited tongue flicking out against his skin. "I'm winning you tonight. I've already cleared my calendar for next week and told my bank to authorize a quarter million. You and me, Brooks. I'm packing light, but I'll be sure to bring my hottest string bikini."

Preferring to be the aggressor in his dealings with women, Brooks backed away from Felicity, almost blurting out that a string bikini was one of the most inappropriate pieces of clothing to bring on a weeklong ocean voyage when he was distracted by Margaret Story, who sidled up beside him.

"Felicity," she asked, adjusting her black-rimmed glasses. "Why don't you go away and stop annoying people?"

Felicity looked momentarily affronted, then recovered quickly and gave Margaret a snarky look. "Flat-chested Mar-gie. Nice dress . . . for a funeral." Looking back at Brooks, Felic-ity ran a tongue over her glossy lips. "I'll see you later, lover."

As Felicity sauntered away, Brooks turned to his child-hood neighbor. "I owe you."

"Great. Let's settle up. Tell me where Cam is."

Cameron and Margaret lived in the same apartment building, and they were presently sharing the same contractor who was renovating Cam's master bathroom and Margaret's kitchen. From what Brooks could gather, they were developing quite a rivalry over Geraldo's services and attention.

"What's he done now?"

"He signed for a shipment of kitchen tiles. And now they're missing . . . which means Geraldo's at a standstill until they can be found."

"Let me guess . . . he's working on Cam's bathroom in the meantime."

"Brooks, you're a genius," said Margaret sarcastically. "Is he here?"

"He's around," demurred Brooks, catching sight of Cameron's broad smile as he slipped out the door behind Margaret.

"Tell him I'm looking for him, all right?"

"Oh, sure. Will do. Hey, Margaret . . ." he started. He had to figure out a backup plan just in case Skye wasn't coming, because he was fairly certain he wouldn't survive a week trapped with Felicity Atwell. Maybe Margaret could bid on him?

"Huh?" she asked, turning around.

But the thing is? Lately Brooks had been sensing an undercurrent in Cameron's voice when he mentioned his "contractor wars" with Margaret . . . like maybe he was enjoying it all a little too much. Like maybe it *mattered*. Like maybe *Margaret* mattered. And even though Brooks wouldn't be asking Margaret to help him out as anything but a favor from a friend, it wasn't worth it to rile Cam, or worse, to hurt him.

He shook his head. "Nothing. Forget it."

"I guess the auction's about to begin," she said sardonically. "Good luck."

"Yeah. Thanks."

Taking one last look at the entry to the ballroom, Brooks cursed softly and shook his head as he headed toward the stage where Jessica was rounding up the bachelors. *Even the best laid plans can go to hell*, he thought. And right now, hell looked like a week with whiny, desperate Felicity Atwell.

After Clay helped her find a champagne-colored, floor-length dress covered in matching crystals, he'd walked her over to the Salon & Spa where two ladies had worked on her hair and a third had given her a "terribly needed" manicure. When the technician had finished the manicure, she'd gone to work on Skye's face, asking her to "close her lids," "purse her lips," and "pout" as she applied makeup.

At some point, Clay had returned with champagne-colored, shiny shoes that weren't absurdly high, a small, champagne-colored purse that looked like a big wallet with a gold bow, and some undergarments. Finally, he'd returned one last time with gold and diamond hanging earrings (he'd whispered in her ear that they were called "chandeliers" and "good paste") and an assortment of five perfumes to try. When Skye exited the changing room at the salon and looked in the mirror, she didn't recognize herself—nor, she suspected, did Clay, who clapped his hands and swiped at his eyes.

"Honey, you are *gorgeous!*" he exclaimed, shaking his head and trying not to cry. "A legit work of art."

Skye had giggled, self-conscious, but pleased. Her hair was parted to the side, and they'd made a loose bun in the back with tendrils escaping that looked sweet and summery, not overdone, and her makeup was light and natural-looking. Staring into the mirror, Skye grinned at her reflection and had only one triumphant thought: *Let Brooks Winslow tell me he doesn't see me as a girl* now.

Charging the $4,200 afternoon on Brooks' credit card with a single swipe, Skye had waved good-bye to her new friends, tucking Clay's business card in her purse and promising to e-mail him all about the gala.

The one thing Skye hadn't counted on? Traffic. Lots of it.

So much, in fact, that the eight-mile ride from Saks to the Ritz—which should have only taken fifteen minutes—had already added up to twenty-five. Flicking her glance to the clock on her dashboard, she cringed. It was after eight o'clock, and if Skye didn't figure out a way to get there faster, she was going to miss the nine o'clock auction and break her promise to Brooks.

Opting for backroads and shortcuts, Skye pulled in front of the Ritz at eight fifty-five, exiting the car without the help of the valet and tossing her keys to him efficiently. Grateful that she had chosen the one-and-a-half-inch "kitten heels" in lieu of the three-inch high heels Clay had originally tried to convince her to purchase, Skye picked up her skirt and ran into the lobby, stopping at the concierge to ask about the ICA event.

Five minutes later, at nine o'clock on the dot, she walked up to the check-in desk. A well-dressed woman gave Skye a surprised look. "You are?"

"Skye Sorenson. I'm late, but I'm on the list. Has the auction started?"

The woman chuckled softly and gave her a knowing smile. "Hoping to win a rich bachelor?"

"Something like that," she said, clutching at her dress as she adjusted the punishing waistband of her uncomfortable Spanx.

"Well, they've only just started. Brooks Winslow is up for grabs!"

Skye's face froze, and she grabbed the auction paddle out of the woman's hand without another word, racing into the ballroom.

"Two hundred thousand dollars! Going once! Going twice!"

Flustered beyond belief and scrambling to find her voice, Skye held her paddle high in the air and yelled from the back of the room, "Two hundred and ten!"

From where he stood beside Jessica at the podium, Brooks could just make out the paddle waving in the back of the room accompanied by Skye's out-of-breath voice. His eyes fluttered closed in a brief moment of relief as he pictured her rushing to put a second coat of epoxy on a fiberglass patch before realizing she was running late, throwing on some cheap, wrinkled dress and rushing to the hotel. Well, he didn't care why she was late, even if her dress was made from bedsheets or if there was epoxy still smeared all over her face and hands. All he cared about was that Felicity Atwell's bid had just been beaten.

"Well, now," purred Jessica, glancing at her older brother with a beaming smile. "This is about to get interesting, friends. We have a last-minute bidder! Now, let me remind you, ladies, my brother is a world-class athlete . . . if you know what I mean. An Olympic medal winner. Do I hear two hundred and twenty?"

Brooks let his gaze pass over the audience, trying not to rest on Felicity, but groaning inwardly when she raised her paddle again.

"That's two hundred and twenty," said Jessica.

"Two-thirty," yelled Skye clearly from the back of the room, her hand and paddle visible over the elegantly dressed guests who stood behind the back row of chairs.

"Two hundred and thirty thousand dollars going once. Going twice—"

"Two hundred and forty thousand," said Felicity, shooting a dirty look to the back of the room before fixing her blue eyes on Brooks and forcing a brittle smile.

"She's like a dog with a bone," whispered Jessica, covering the mic.

"That's for sure," said Brooks, catching Alex English's amused look. He sat in the front row alternating between looking at Jessica with devotion and laughing at Brooks with glee. "And tell Alex if he wasn't with you, he'd be up here, too."

"Oh, he knows," said Jessica, winking at her fiancé, who raised his eyebrows suggestively in return.

Brooks rolled his eyes. He was no stranger to the heat between Jessica and Alex, but all things equal, he'd just as soon pretend she was still his virginal little sister, thank you very much.

"Two hundred and forty thousand dollars for the new wing of ICA! The generosity in this room humbles me," said Jessica into the microphone.

"Two-fifty!" yelled Skye, lifting her paddle again.

The crowd gasped.

"Lord, Brooks, a quarter million dollars to spend a week with you? Who's back there?" whispered Jessica, straining her neck, then into the microphone, "Two hundred and fifty thousand dollars! My goodness gracious! Can we ask the mystery bidder to please come forward?"

Brooks braced himself for the crowd's response to his tomboy friend presenting herself in some skirt and T-shirt combination with dirty fingernails and a straggly braid. And likely wearing eau de epoxy. *Oh well*, he thought, grinning to himself. Skye was saving him from Felicity and ensuring him a decent week of sailing, and frankly, that was all that mattered.

All that mattered until the crowd parted.

When it did, his jaw dropped, like the hinge had just been busted. The most beautiful woman he'd ever seen stepped between the tuxedoed shoulders of several male guests, striding confidently up the center aisle where eager bachelorettes checked her out with wide-eyed envy. Her blonde hair was pulled back in a soft bun, and her slim body sparkled with crystals on a dress that outlined the perfection of her figure, including the mouthwatering valley between her breasts that spilled precariously over the top of the elegant gown. From her ears dangled two twinkling earrings, and her face, tan and even with pink, pouty lips and sexy, wide eyes made the blood in his head sluice south to just below his waist.

He blinked. His mouth lolled open. He didn't care. He couldn't help it. Hell, he couldn't believe his eyes.

She stopped about halfway up the aisle and gave Brooks a shy grin, then turned her deep-blue eyes to Jessica. "Here I am."

Jessica chuckled softly, "Well, hello! And you are?"

"Skye Sorenson."

"Welcome, Skye."

"Thanks," she said, deftly twirling her paddle back and forth in her clean, manicured hands as every pair of eyes in the room—especially the male ones—stared at her.

Included among them? Brooks. And although he knew he probably looked like an ass for ogling her when they'd been friends for years, he simply couldn't look away. For a decade, since Skye had turned twenty and quit college to work for her father, she'd been bumming around the marina in beat-up overalls and that old Orioles cap. *This* is what she'd been hiding? This fresh, wholesome, delicate beauty? She rivaled any woman in the room, any woman in the world, and the flash of heat he'd felt from peeking at her neck yesterday evening turned into a full-fledged fire as he drank in her loveliness.

"Wow," he finally sighed, mirroring the sentiments of every other man in the room.

From where she stood, Skye beamed at him, her eyes sparkling with pleasure.

"Sorry I was late," she mouthed, cringing adorably and shrugging her bare shoulders apologetically.

Brooks smiled back. He couldn't answer. He couldn't do anything but stare at her with a blank, dumbfounded grin.

"Well, mystery bidder!" said Jessica, composing herself. "You've bid two hundred and fifty thousand dollars for the pleasure of my brother's company. I hope he's worth it."

A ripple of soft laughter spread through the crowd of guests, many of whom, Brooks noted, were still staring at Skye with curiosity, lust, or envy.

"Going once! Going twice! Sold! Mr. Brooks Winslow sold to Miss Skye Sorenson!" Jessica banged her gavel and bowed her head in thanks. "And I thank you for your generosity."

"You're welcome," muttered Brooks, noticing several men shifting their positions closer to Skye to congratulate her on her win. His fingers curled into a tight fist in response.

"We'll take a quick break now," said Jessica breathlessly, "and return in fifteen minutes to start the bidding on our next three bachelors!"

As the music started up, Jessica placed her hand on Brooks' arm. "Who is she?"

"An old friend," said Brooks.

"A . . . *friend*?"

"That's right."

"And I assume you put her up to this?"

"Does it matter?" he asked. "Your plan's not going to work. Sorry."

Jessica gave him an incredulous look and chuckled slyly. "From the way you're looking at her? I'd say my plan's working out beautifully, big brother."

"She's a friend, Jess. Nothing more."

"Mm-hm," murmured Jessica, giving him an annoying wink.

"She has a boyfriend," he said emphatically, cutting his eyes back to Skye and thinking that she wasn't *acting* much like a woman who had a boyfriend, grinning at all of the new admirers who surrounded her. "He's a mutual friend, who would probably appreciate it if I rescued her."

"'Rescue her,'" she said, using air quotes. "Is that what you call it when you're about to go pee on a woman's leg?"

His brain worked to come up with an adequate rejoinder, but before he could say anything else, his sass-mouthed little sister turned around on her ridiculously high high heels and sauntered off the stage.

Chapter 5

One moment, Brooks was standing on the stage glowering at her, the next he was pushing through the crowd to stand beside her.

"Give me a second with my date, eh, gentlemen?" he asked sharply, offering sour looks to the handsome men who were surrounding her.

Skye turned to him, trying to conceal the fact that her breath actually caught at the up-close sight of him in a tux. She would have bet a million dollars that nothing could beat the sight of Brooks in shorts and a T-shirt, tan and wind-blown as he guided a boat out of the harbor. It smarted to know she would have lost that bet.

"Hey Skye," he said, his eyes flicking quickly down her dress and then back up to her face. He licked his lips, locking his eyes with hers. "Didn't know if you were coming."

"Sorry I was late," she said out loud this time, aware that her heart was thundering as she recognized the look on his face. Brooks was looking at her the way she'd looked at the Prim so long ago—like he saw something stunningly beautiful, something he wanted—and it was unsettling, but she discovered with a surprise that came from her relative inexperience, not at all unpleasant.

For most of her life, Skye had been the "friend." With the exception of a high school boyfriend, a couple of college flings, and Pat, she hadn't been pursued very much by members of the opposite sex for anything but friendship. The sort of attention she enjoyed tonight was foreign to her, but she couldn't deny it was exciting.

He offered her his arm, and she looked at it for a moment before realizing he wanted her to take it.

"Do you dance?" he asked.

"Not well."

"I'll take my chances."

She placed her unusually clean hand on the arm of his tuxedo jacket and let him lead her to the dance floor. As he put his arm around her waist and laced his fingers through hers, her belly fluttered, and she wondered about this new electricity between them, and even more, she wondered if he felt it, too.

Judging from his darkened eyes that still fixed on hers with a piercing gaze, she figured there was a good chance he did.

"So, when I said to buy a dress, I didn't expect this. You look . . . breathtaking."

"Thank you," she said, her cheeks flushing and her belly fluttering again in a way she hadn't felt in ages, the realization of which made her feel guilty since Pat was her boyfriend. The thing was, she couldn't remember the last time she'd felt butterflies with Pat, which only served to make her feel worse.

"What?"

She looked up at Brooks. "Huh?"

"You're frowning."

"Oh," she said, giving him a cautious smile. "I was just thinking . . . I talked to Pat last night."

Brooks' eyes cooled a little. "How's Panama?"

"He's having a great time."

"The Cat holding up well?"

"Umm . . . yeah," she said, though she had no idea how Pat's catamaran was doing because she'd barely had a chance to talk to him. Suddenly, her guilt took flight, and she didn't want to talk about Pat anymore because she still felt hurt by their crappy conversation last night. "So, the cutter. When's it coming?"

"Should be at the marina by Tuesday. Will you check it out for me?"

She grinned. "A school of sharks couldn't keep me away."

"It's supposed to be sail-worthy, but I'll take her out for a test run on Wednesday. You're welcome to come along if you like. We can stretch her legs a little in the bay before heading out to sea on Sunday."

As tempting as his offer was, she had a lot of work to catch up on before their trip next weekend, plus she was a little confused by the feelings she was having for him tonight. A few days apart before their weeklong cruise would probably be a good idea. She'd deal with her feelings about the phone call with Pat and remind herself that Brooks was a friend and nothing more—Pat was her reality.

"Let me check my workload, huh?"

"Sure thing." His eyes rested on her face, dropping to her lips for a moment before cutting to her eyes again. "Can I ask you a question?"

"Sure."

"I had no idea you could look like this. Why don't you ever, you know, dress up?"

"You mean . . . so people would *see me as a girl*?"

Brooks flinched. "God, I'm a jackass. Did I actually say that to you?"

"Uh . . . yeah. It would be hard to forget."

"Let me make up for it," he said, raking his eyes slowly down her face, lingering on her lips, tracing the line of her throat to her breasts, which barely grazed the front of his shirt, but puckered into tight points from the heat of his perusal. Finally he snapped his dark eyes back to her face, his breathing slightly more shallow and his voice a little gravelly when he said, "I promise, from this day on, to *always* see you as a girl."

Her cheeks flushed, and her heart did crazy flips as her tongue darted out to moisten her lips. She wanted to look away from him, but found she couldn't, almost like she was seeing him for the first time. Though she'd never stopped noticing how gorgeous Brooks was, something about the way he looked at her now made him feel new to her, and it was both exciting and confusing.

"Mr. Winslow and Miss Sorenson, over here!"

They looked simultaneously toward the voice, and a bright flash suddenly blinded Skye, making her stumble as Brooks tightened his arm around her to keep her from falling.

"Terrific shot. One more?"

"Hey," said Brooks dropping her hand and shielding her eyes as they stopped dancing. "That's enough."

The photographer grinned at her in a way that bordered on smarmy and made Skye instantly uncomfortable.

"That was one dramatic auction."

"I guess it was," said Brooks in an unfriendly voice. "You are?"

"Guy Hunter. From *Celeb!*?" He grinned, holding out his hand, which Brooks shook quickly. "I'll be meeting you two at Virginia Beach, Hatteras, Myrtle Beach, and Charleston. I'm here to document *the love*."

"The love?" murmured Skye, grateful that Brooks had pulled her possessively against his side.

"You two lovebirds on an ocean voyage. So . . ." said Guy, leaning closer to Skye, "you must have pretty deep pockets, huh, Miss Sorenson? Or can I call you Skye?"

Ignoring Guy, Brooks squeezed her hip gently, speaking close to her ear. "Want to get some air?"

"Sure," she answered breathlessly, her body hyperaware of Brooks beside her, and her brain wrapping around the fact that her life was going to be on display for the next two weeks until the end of the cruise. She'd agreed to it, of course, but it had felt nebulous and unreal at the time she'd said yes. Suddenly, it felt very real—perhaps, for a woman who'd lived a quiet life among her beloved boats—a little *too* real.

Giving Guy a sharp look, Brooks said, "We agreed to a photo spread, not having our privacy invaded. Which means questions about Miss Sorenson's bank account are completely off-limits."

"Touchy." Guy's eyes narrowed, but after a moment, he managed a smirk. "I hear you loud and clear, skipper. Well, I guess I'll run along now and look forward to seeing you two in Virginia Beach a week from Monday, huh? Happy sailing, lovebirds."

Reaching for Skye's hand, Brooks pulled her across the room to a set of French doors that led outside to a brick patio. Closing the door behind them, he dropped her hand as soon as they were outside and raked his hands through his hair.

"Damn it, what have I gotten you into?"

"Nothing I didn't agree to," she answered softly.

"I get the feeling he wants more than a few pictures."

She shrugged. "I don't have anything to hide."

Brooks cut his eyes to her, looking up sharply. *He did.* His family would be mortified to learn that he used an escort service, and suddenly—looking into Skye's wide, innocent eyes—he felt an unexpected bolt of shame, which made him scowl. He made a quick decision and mental note not to enjoy any more dates from Elite until long after the article was published in *Celeb!*. In fact, he thought, it was probably best to go ahead and close his account as soon as possible.

"Sorry," he said. "I'm accustomed to my photo being taken, but I'm sorry you'll have to deal with that sort of thing over the next couple of weeks. Hopefully he'll respect the agreement and just show up at the appointed stops. If you see him sniffing around the marina this week, call me."

"Will do," she said lightly.

He watched as she crossed her arms over her chest and walked around the patio. Finally stopping to smell a bright-yellow rose, her eyes closed, and a small smile tilted up her lips. Brooks recognized something strong and new in his gut, and it felt warm and good, but it also felt tinged with a low-grade panic. How the hell had he missed this? How had he missed that Skye Sorenson was one of the sexiest, loveliest women he'd ever seen? And now that he knew it, how the hell was he going to keep his hands off of her while they shared a small boat for a week? Pat or no Pat, petite blondes with lush breasts were his weakness. Damn it, the whole reason he'd asked Skye to join him in the first place was to avoid any chance of a romantic entanglement. And now, every time he looked at her in those stupid overalls, he'd know what was underneath. It made him nervous. It made him second-guess the entire plan.

"Skye," he said softly, hoping she didn't hear the note of self-preservation in his voice. "After meeting Guy . . . if you wanted to back out, I wouldn't hold it against you."

She turned to him, resting her palms on the brick wall behind her, her face luminous in the moonlight, her breasts heaving softly from her breathing. "No way. I wouldn't do that to you. I made a promise. Plus . . . the cutter."

"The cutter," he said, taking a few steps toward her and grinning. "Was there ever a girl who loved sailboats as much as you?"

"Nope." She arched an eyebrow at him. "Some people would call me obsessed."

Brooks shrugged dismissively. "Then they don't understand. They don't love sailing like we do."

"Sometimes I feel like the wind and the water are in my blood." Her eyes sparkled at him in the moonlight as her glossy lips turned up wistfully. "The thrill when the prow cuts through the waves, the way a sudden gust fills the sails and you hike over the side with a line in your fist and the spray in your face. That's when I feel the most alive, the most complete."

"Yes," he said, hypnotized by the beauty of her face and the poetry of her words. "Me too."

"I know. We have that in common," she said. A gentle smile reached out and squeezed his heart as he gazed at her. "When I was ten, your parents gave you the Primrose."

"I remember. I'm surprised you do."

"She was the prettiest boat I'd ever seen. Before you came to claim her, I'd sit on the dock and stare at her. Just stare." She laughed self-deprecatingly. "I got very possessive of her, I guess."

"You must have hated it when I finally took her out."

"I was worried," she confessed. "If you'd been reckless or foolish with that boat . . ." She waggled her finger censoriously, then paused, grinning at him. "That first day? Your birthday? I watched you walk down to the dock and board her. The way you checked her lines and cleats, and you were ginger with the rudder. I watched you cast off, luffing the sails until she was free of the larger boats, and then I watched you tighten the jib to get her moving. I stood on the dock and watched until I couldn't see you anymore, but by then I was just enjoying the sight because you looked so right together. I knew she was in good hands."

"In good hands," he murmured, searching her eyes, strangely touched by her story.

"That's when I knew."

"Knew what?"

"That the wind and the water were in your blood, too."

His breathing had become noticeably erratic as she spoke, and his heart thundered in his ears as he flicked his gaze to her full, glossy lips before catching her eyes again. They widened just a little before dropping to his lips and staring, lingering, resting. Her breasts rose and fell more quickly now, the tips brushing the crisp whiteness of his shirt with every quick breath, and when she looked back up at him, her eyes were dark and searching. Whether she'd meant to or not, her body had just offered him an invitation that Brooks was helpless to refuse.

"Skye," he whispered, closing the distance between them and dropping his lips to hers.

It surprised her at first—the pliant warmth of his lips suddenly pressed against hers—and she gasped softly as her eyes fluttered closed. His palm cupped her jaw gently as his other arm encircled her waist, pulling her up against the firm wall of his chest. And his lips . . . God, his lips moved slowly over hers, pursing to catch her lower lip over and over before he tilted his head to seal his mouth over hers.

Skye moaned, leaning into him, two decades' worth of simmering lust giving her permission to respond as she smoothed her fingers over the crisp white of his tuxedo shirt, her fingernails digging into his chest as she felt the first touch of his tongue against hers. His fingers tangled in her hair, his thumb gently swiping the soft skin of her cheek as he groaned into her mouth, backing her up against the brick wall behind her to press his body flush against hers. Feeling the rock-hard outline of his erection against her thigh made her arch against him, and as her tongue slid down the length of his, she shivered with pleasure.

"Skye," he murmured, peppering kisses along her jaw before taking the lobe of her ear between his teeth and pulling lightly until she whimpered.

"Brooks," she panted, leaning her head to the side to give him better access to her throat.

Releasing her ear, he pressed teasing kisses to her sensitive skin, lingering at her pulse to rest his lips against the throbbing beat there. Her nipples puckered against her bustier, the aroused peaks longing for the touch of his lips as her inner muscles clenched with need, dampening her new lingerie with a rush of wetness.

Through a fog of lust, with her skin still tickled by the brush of Brooks' hair on her chin and lips on her neck, she opened her eyes slowly and stared up at the starry sky. The North Star, bright and steady, shined overhead, and she gasped, picturing the tattoo on Pat's wrist.

"*A sailor must have his eye trained to the rocks and sands as well as the North Star,*" she quoted in a whisper, a soft sob emerging from her throat where a lump quickly formed.

"What?" Brooks mumbled, his lips still moving against her skin.

"Pat." Skye swallowed with difficulty, then pushed at Brooks' chest as her face flushed hot with guilt and shame. "I'm with Pat."

Brooks leaned up, his eyes glassy and thick as his chest pushed into hers with every panted breath. His eyebrows furrowed together for an instant, as though he was seeing her for the first time, and then he shook his head, cringing.

"I-I know. Pat. Yeah. God, I'm . . . oh, I'm sorry. Skye—"

She pushed harder against his chest, dropping his eyes as he released her to take a step back. Skye stared down at the ground, trying to figure out what to say, but words failed her, and her eyes burned with the gravity of what she'd just done. In a nutshell? She'd cheated on Pat. Cheated. She was a cheater. Just like her mother.

Turning around, she rested her palms flat on the brick wall, trying to catch her breath and figure out how the hell that had just happened. Brooks' hand was warm and gentle on her shoulder, but she jerked away as though burned.

"Skye . . . I'm sorry. I got carried away."

"That . . ." she began breathlessly, touching her fingertips to her lower lip as she turned to face him, ". . . can't happen again, Brooks."

His hand still hovered in the air near her shoulder, but he lowered it, fisting it by his side.

"It won't," he promised her gravely.

"We're just friends," she insisted, though the imprint of his lips and the soft slide of his tongue against hers would be impossible to forget. "You said you didn't even see me as—"

"I know what I said," he interrupted her with a growl. He softened his voice to add, "I don't know what got into me. I shouldn't have . . ." His voice trailed off as he raked his hand through his hair, his eyes flicking to her lips before capturing her eyes. "It won't happen again."

"I should go," she said, edging away from the wall to step around him, her heart still hammering with equal parts of desire and shame.

"Skye," he called, his face stricken as he gazed at her from across the terrace. "I mean it. I won't lay a hand on you ever again. You don't have to worry."

Even with her conscience bearing down on her, she couldn't deny Brooks' devastating handsomeness in the moonlight, or the toe-curling chemistry she'd just experienced with him, and for just a split second, she considered running back into the heat of his arms.

Cheater, sneered her heart.

Her eyes prickled with tears as she whispered, "Good night," in a broken voice before rushing back into the ballroom.

Chapter 6

Though it briefly crossed Brooks' mind to call Elite and arrange for a woman to meet him upstairs in a hotel room to ease the force of his arousal, his pledge not to use the escort service again left him with few options. He could walk back into the ballroom and find another woman to seduce, which could lead to undesirable complications, or he could stalk out of the fundraiser and drive home to Westerly for a date with a cold shower.

Adjusting his pants to no avail, he took several deep gulps of the cool evening air, surprised to hear the door behind him open again. Whipping around in the hope that Skye had returned, he was disappointed to see his youngest brother, Christopher, standing in front of the closed door with a shit-eating grin.

"So," he said, eyes twinkling with mirth, "*that* happened. Some auction, huh?"

"Just be lucky you're not the oldest, Chris. You're spared from this idiocy because you're the baby."

Christopher took a few steps toward his brother, swirling his drink in thought, his lips still tilted up. "Actually, Jess is the baby. And frankly, I don't know what you're complaining about. Whoever she is, she's gorgeous . . . *and* she spared you from a week trapped on a boat with Felicity Atwell."

"Only because I'm paying her," huffed Brooks, crossing his arms over his chest.

Chris' smile grew wider as he nodded. "Ahhh. I see. I should have known you'd rig it. Who is she?"

"Why?" asked Brooks, leaning his head to the side and staring back at his little brother with narrowed eyes.

"Like I said, she's beautiful. Every man in that room is wondering who she is, me included."

"Well, she's not for you or any of them. She's a mechanic at the marina where I moor my boats. And she has a boyfriend," added Brooks, fully aware of the warning in his voice—a warning he'd have done well to apply to himself, he thought with disgust.

"A boyfriend? Huh. Because it sort of looked like—"

Brooks cut him off. "She's doing me a favor. We're just friends."

"*Friends*?" Christopher winced. "Didn't look much like friends."

"Well, that's all we are." *Were.*

"That sucks for you," lamented Christopher, "because she's stunning."

Tell me about it.

"Wait a second. The boyfriend doesn't mind that you two are about to go away for a weeklong cruise? All alone?"

Brooks sighed, pulling Christopher's drink out of his hand and throwing it back before handing the empty glass back to his brother. He figured he needed it more than Chris.

The truth? Brooks wasn't sure.

He and Pat had been sailing out of the Chesapeake Cruising Club together for the past few years, and though he didn't know Pat very well personally, they'd crewed together a time or two, which meant they'd also shared the odd beer in the club bar. Pat was a solid sailor, but he was always talking about himself. Brooks knew all about Pat's ex-wife, his plans to circumnavigate, his boats, his life . . . He was the sort of guy who monopolized the conversation for twenty minutes, then excused himself when someone else started telling a story of their own. That said, Brooks didn't have a problem with Pat, per se, he just wasn't one of Brooks' favorite people either.

And frankly, Christopher's question led to a good point. Presumably Pat knew what Skye had going on under her overalls—a thought that made a totally irrational bolt of jealousy clench Brooks' stomach—so it didn't make a lot of sense that he'd leave her for almost two years while he circumnavigated alone. Hell, if Pat had had misgivings about Skye being pursued during his absence, he should have considered bringing her with him. Come to think of it, Brooks thought, his forehead creasing, hadn't he heard that Skye was supposed to join Pat on his trip? Hmmm. He wondered what had happened. One thing was salient, however: Pat didn't know the jewel he had in his hands, or he did and didn't care. Either way, he was a damn fool for leaving her behind.

"Earth to Brooks."

"Uh, yeah. I don't know. I don't know if he's bothered. I guess not. I'm sure she mentioned it to him."

"Huh. Some boyfriend. It would bother the crap out of me to know that my girlfriend was going away for a week with you . . . and I'm your brother. I actually trust you."

Brooks gave Christopher a cocky smirk. "Even though I'm definitely better in bed than you are, small fry."

Christopher rolled his eyes, passing his empty glass from one hand to another thoughtfully, refusing to rise to the bait. "And yet you haven't had a girlfriend in years to verify that claim."

"Who hasn't had a girlfriend in years?" asked Preston, sauntering out onto the porch and gesturing to Brooks with his thumb. "This sad sack?"

Brooks glared at Preston, who followed Brooks in birth order and was probably his closest friend.

"Speak for yourself, lonely hearts," said Brooks with an annoyed smirk. "Just because I don't have a girlfriend doesn't mean I don't see action."

Preston scoffed, then deadpanned sarcastically, "Yeah. Some action. Westerly's a regular revolving door."

"Just because I don't bring women to Westerly doesn't mean—"

"Maybe they're all skanks."

"You have a lot of room to talk, Pres. When's the last time you had a steady girlfriend?" asked Chris, pegging Preston with a dubious look.

Preston's eyes flicked to Brooks, his usual relaxed posture stiffening just a touch. For years, Brooks had assumed that Preston's reluctance to fall in love had something to do with their father's early death, but just recently Brooks had learned the truth about why Preston was so noncommittal when it came to women. That said, he'd stumbled across the information accidentally, and had sworn to keep Preston's secret.

"Pres likes playing the field," Brooks said evasively, coming to his rescue.

"Women are a lot of work," muttered Preston, his shoulders relaxing as he gave his older brother a grateful nod.

"Truth," said Brooks, his mind shifting effortlessly to Skye and wondering if the kiss that just rocked his world was going to cost him Skye as crew. He'd have to think about what he could do to win her back. He'd already promised that he wouldn't touch her again, but he had a sinking feeling it would take more than promises to win back her trust.

"Listen, I may not be interested in a girlfriend hanging around my neck, but I will say this," said Preston, his characteristic teasing smile back in place. "*She* was a beauty.

If I was the type of guy who *wanted* a lasso on his balls, I wouldn't mind if she was the one holding the rope."

"No one wants to hear about your demented sex life," said Christopher, shaking his head and turning back to Brooks. "So, I'm interested . . . how come your sailing partner *friend* just hurried across the ballroom swiping at her eyes and beelining for the exit alone after being out here with you for ten minutes?"

"Great question, Chris," piped up Preston, raising his eyebrows and leaning his elbow on Christopher's shoulder. "I noticed that too."

She was crying? Crap. If she was crying, it was *definitely* going to take a lot more than promises to get her to sail with him. Brooks shook his head, looking back up at his brothers. "I . . . damn it, I kissed her."

"Dude!" exclaimed Christopher, his age showing with his surprise. "You *kissed* her? What the hell? What about the boyfriend?"

Brooks took a deep breath and released it slowly, giving his little brother a sour look. "Obviously I wasn't thinking about the boyfriend at the time."

Preston's shoulders were shaking from laughing. "Oh, man, you're screwed. If she withdraws her bid, the auction winner will default to the next highest bidder."

"What are you talking about?"

"Fine print," said Preston, who was the most popular sports lawyer in Philly. "You probably should have read it before you let Jessica talk you into this whole thing."

"Talk me into it? I wish! I was railroaded!" yelled Brooks. "Tell me about the fine print."

"Your *friend*," said Preston, using annoying air quotes, just as Jessica had earlier, "has a week to pay. If she doesn't, she defaults, and Felicity Atwell will be given a chance to win you with her last bid."

Brooks' nostrils flared as the full meaning of this settled in his mind. If Skye didn't follow through with their agreement—which was looking tenuous at best, after the haunted look in her eyes—he'd be stuck at sea for a week with Felicity.

Christopher clapped him on the back, stifling a chuckle. "Tough break."

"Maybe grovel?" Preston's eyes were still sparkling with glee. "Sometimes groveling works." He adopted a high-pitched, pitiful-sounding voice. "I'm so sorry I kissed you, Skye . . ."

As his two younger brothers headed back into the ballroom cackling with laughter, Brooks cursed loudly, running both hands through his hair in frustration. Begging for forgiveness was not his strongest suit. In fact, Brooks purposely compartmentalized his life so that he didn't make emotional decisions that required contrition and apologies. He didn't like impulsive behavior. Impulsiveness scared him because it represented a lack of control, and Brooks much preferred a controlled, orderly existence.

What the hell has gotten into me tonight?

He grimaced as his mind flashed to Felicity's overeager smile, and groveling suddenly didn't sound so terrible. Unless, he thought, his mouth dropping open as his brain came up with an alternative solution, he could offer her something even better.

"Honey!" said Clay. "*All* the details. I want every. Single. One. How tall is he up close? What does he smell like? Was his tux Armani? No! He's Main Line all the way. I bet it was *Brooks* Brothers!"

Because Skye had never been particularly adept at making female friends—her clothes had always been unfashionable and her interests were decidedly masculine, which hadn't exactly endeared her to the girls she went to school with—she didn't have a trusted confidant to call as she climbed into her car and sped away from the Ritz Carlton. She had a cousin with whom she was somewhat close, but Tina had small children who were probably in the middle of their bedtime routine. And though she liked several of the wives and girlfriends of Pat's friends, she didn't feel comfortable calling them. When she'd glanced down at her phone to find a text from Clay asking about her evening, he suddenly seemed like the perfect person to call.

"And why on earth are you calling *me* when you should be enjoying *him*?" he finished with a huff of disapproval.

Skye sucked in a deep breath, navigating the crowded streets of Philadelphia as she headed toward the highway that would take her home. "He's much taller than me. He smells like fresh air and the sea and hot skin. His tux was black."

"Oh," sighed Clay dramatically. "Then why on God's green earth are you calling me, girl?"

The words were like a bomb about to detonate in her head. She had to get them out. "Because he kissed me."

The line was silent for a moment, as though Clay was waiting for more. "Aaaand . . . ?"

Skye squirmed in her seat, the memory of the kiss making her stomach flutter and her pulse quicken. "It was . . . it was . . ."

"Spellbinding? Mind-blowing? Toe-curling?"

All of those things, thought Skye, but she heard herself murmur, "Wrong."

"Wrong? Wrong! Honey, you're going to have to school me on how kissing an ex-Olympic hottie like Brooks Winslow is wrong. I didn't notice a ring on your finger this afternoon."

"Oh, no!" Skye rushed to answer. "I'm not married!"

"Engaged?"

"No!"

"Then I fail to see the issue."

"I'm *with* someone."

"But are you engaged or married to him?"

"No. He's my boyfriend."

"Your boyfriend?" He repeated the word "boyfriend" with hints of exasperation as Skye turned onto the highway and pressed down hard on the gas. "Okay. You ready for today's truth serum, Miss Skye?"

"Uh-huh," she said, not actually sure she was ready at all.

"If you don't have a ring on your finger, you're still looking, you're still available, and you have every right to keep your options open, girl. You're still figuring out what you want."

"But, I cheated on—"

"Cheated? Who cheated? Didn't you say *he* kissed *you*?"

"Well, yes, but—"

"And here's what I need to know . . . where was this mysterious boyfriend tonight?"

"Oh, he's circumnavigating right now."

"Circum—what?"

"Navigating. He's circling the globe on a catamaran for the next two years." She told Clay all about how she and Pat had agreed to sail together, but how he'd decided to go alone, and they had approximately twenty more months ahead until Pat made his way home.

"And what precisely are you supposed to do for two freaking years? Sit at home with your legs locked, acting like a nun? Nuh-uh. Nope." Clay paused, and Skye waited for his voice to fill the silence of her car again. "Tell me this, honey . . . did you *like* kissing Brooks?"

Skye took a deep breath, remembering the firm pressure of his lips on hers, the satin touch of his tongue, the way her nipples had hardened and her skin had ached for more of his touch. "Yes."

"Then do it again," said Clay gently. "You're not married to Pat. You're not even engaged."

"But we're in a relationship."

"Really? Because it seems to me he left you for two years. Sorry to be the homo harbinger of ghastly news, but that doesn't scream 'commitment' in my book."

Skye pulled her bottom lip between her teeth. She had to admit that she'd been having very similar feelings lately where Pat was concerned. It *didn't* feel like they had much of a commitment, or much of a relationship, for that matter.

But Brooks? Forasmuch as Skye had lusted after Brooks for years, she'd never actually allowed her mind to wander to a place of *being* with him, and she had no idea of what that looked like. For one thing, Brooks had a different girlfriend every time she saw him, and Skye wasn't exactly someone who had recreational sex. Not to mention, Brooks was her father's most lucrative account, and she didn't want any awkwardness between them. Getting entangled with Brooks—even casually, not that she knew how to do casual—had the potential of getting very messy.

"Okay, so maybe Pat isn't being a model boyfriend right now . . . but I think Brooks is, well, a player."

"Mmm. A girl can hope."

"Hope? No, I—"

"Tell me what's wrong with some hot, sweaty, ex-Olympian, casual sex?"

Skye gasped, her mind overloading with the image of Brooks looming over her, his body hard, hot, and sweaty as they . . .

"What? No! I-I don't—"

"Skye? Just breathe," said Clay, laughing lightly at the sudden panic in her voice. "Okay. I tell you what . . . take sex off the table. Just let him kiss you again. See what happens."

"You're counseling me to cheat."

"I'm counseling you to keep your options open," Clay scolded softly. "And don't be so hella serious. Have a little fun."

A little fun. Hmm.

It *had* been fun kissing Brooks . . . until it wasn't—until her conscience had ripped her a new one. And anyway, she highly doubted Brooks would ever touch her again. She'd been so upset with him, so aghast by his actions, he'd been resolute when he said he'd never lay a hand on her ever again. She couldn't imagine a scenario wherein he made another move on her. Which meant that if she ever wanted to kiss him again, it would most likely be up to her to make a move on him.

And *that* would never happen.

She sighed.

"Honey, it's closing time. I have to go. You call me again, though. I *need* to know what happens!"

"Thanks, Clay," said Skye, "I will."

As she hung up, she wondered about the gray lines that had seemed so black and white to her just a few minutes ago. Skye had always considered cheating a hanging sin— the worst of the worst. She'd seen the way her mother's pre-California affair had decimated her parents' marriage. And when her father had discovered that his wife's failed career as a singer had prompted her to take a job with an LA escort service? His pride had suffered a terrible blow. When he found out, they were still technically married, but faced with her multiple and ongoing infidelities, her father had initiated divorce proceedings immediately. That's when Skye had realized that he'd held onto the thin hope that her mother, Shelley, would someday come home. Her father had hardened after that—all pictures of her mother had been boxed and taken to the garage, her clothes given to Goodwill and most traces of her removed from their house. It was how Skye knew that her father's heart had been shattered.

Skye's definition of cheating, as a result, had always been conservative, strict, and firm. So why did it feel so much more tenuous suddenly? It wasn't just Clay's advice, which felt so tempting, but her frustrating relationship with Pat and brutal attraction to Brooks. She *wanted* to kiss him again. She wanted to do *more* than kiss him.

So, break up with Pat, her conscience urged. *Break up with Pat and you can do whatever you want with Brooks.*

Except she wasn't scheduled to talk to Pat again for another four weeks, and there were still months before their visit if she wanted to break up with him in person. She could send him a text, but that rash action begged the question: was she ready to break up with Pat?

The answer came swiftly . . . No.

Between her profession and intense interest in sailing, not to mention her total lack of feminine wiles, Skye hadn't had a lot of romantic opportunities. When Pat had asked her out, it had meant the world to her. There was a security in being his girlfriend. She had a standing weekend date, someone to sail with, someone to have dinner with, and sometimes, when one of them slept over, someone to fall asleep with and wake up next to. Before meeting Pat, she'd been lonely, married to the marina, and—aside from the occasional date for dinner with her cousin or her pop—very much on her own. She wasn't ready to give up the comfort and security offered to her by being Pat's girlfriend.

"Well, that's that," she said firmly in the dark silence of the car. "You want Pat. Your decision's made. No more kissing Brooks. In fact, no more Brooks at all."

She nodded once to her reflection in the dashboard glass, promising that she'd call Brooks tomorrow and explain that she was no longer able to go with him for the weeklong. He would understand. After what happened, she was positive he wouldn't pressure her, and she hoped that over time their friendship would find its footing again.

Her decision made, she waited for a feeling of righteous relief to overtake her, but as the miles flew by, it didn't. As she pulled into her driveway an hour later, all she felt was heavyhearted.

Chapter 7

As Brooks parked his car at the Sorenson Marina on Wednesday afternoon, he waffled between feeling excited to see Skye again, worried that she'd refuse to sail with him, and irritated that he'd brought this situation down on himself in the first place. He'd checked with Jessica and his bank to confirm that Skye hadn't used his credit card to pay for her bid before leaving the hotel on Saturday night. She'd run away from him, and the gala, without looking back . . . and if she didn't pay by Friday, Felicity would be contacted and offered the win. Brooks groaned as he checked his reflection, opened his door, and slammed it behind him.

He went over the plan in his head again.

First line of attack? Promises and reassurances.

Second? Groveling.

Last? His lips twitched. His last-ditch attempt to convince her had the potential of being a hole in one, but he wasn't crazy about the conditions. He crossed his fingers that reassurances and groveling would be enough.

Added to the general anxiety of the situation? A picture of Brooks and Skye dancing had appeared on the website of *Celeb!* magazine on Monday morning, with a short description of the gala, auction, and the excitement of Skye's winning bid. The caption under the photo? "Newly minted lovebirds, ex-Olympian, Brooks Winslow, and his charming, but mysterious, partner, Skye Sorenson, trip the lights fantastic! Stay tuned as this romance-on-the-high-seas unfolds exclusively with *Celeb!*!"

He could only imagine what Skye had felt when she'd seen it. Since she hadn't called or texted him over the last three days, despite his two voice mails apologizing to her, he assumed it hadn't been good. And yet Brooks had stared at the photo many times, gazing at her lovely face, which tilted up, smiling at his. The delicate curve of her neck haunted him, and as his eyes dropped to her breasts, pressed against his tuxedo shirt, he could almost feel the sensation of her stiff nipples brushing against his chest. The expression on his face bothered him, too—an open, bewildered mixture of lust and captivation. It made every moment with her rush back in startling detail: how she felt in his arms, how it had felt to kiss her, how much he'd wanted it, and how much he wanted it to happen again.

No. No, no, no. Promises and reassurances, Brooks, starting with this one: We're just friends and I will never make a pass at you ever again.

He took a deep breath as he opened the door to the marina shop and walked over to the counter to chat with Jack.

"Hey there, Brooks," said Jack with a tight smile.

Jack Sorenson was second-generation Swedish, and his body—tall, thick, and muscular—sometimes reminded Brooks of the legendary Vikings. His shock of shaggy, blond hair, the same color as Skye's, only added to the illusion.

"Jack. Good to see you." He offered the older man his hand, noticing Jack's expression and wondering if Skye had confided the details of their short episode on the hotel patio. Mortified at the thought, he felt color creep into his cheeks. "Cutter come in yet?"

"Yep. Got her moored at dock five."

Dock five where Skye watches the sunset. Brooks didn't know what made the fleeting thought slip into his mind, but it distracted him for a moment as he imagined her blonde hair made golden by the setting sun.

Jack was looking at him strangely when Brooks blinked and refocused on him.

"You taking her out tonight?"

"No, sir. I'm just here to see the cutter."

"Yeah," said Jack slowly. "That's what I meant."

Brooks shifted gears as quickly as he could. "The cutter! Yes. Yes, I am—I'm taking *her* out. The boat."

Jack tilted his head to the side, looking at Brooks thoughtfully before pursing his lips and crossing his beefy, tattooed arms over his chest. "It's none of my business, and she'd kill me for saying anything . . . but I'm her father, and I wouldn't feel right if I didn't speak up. Skye's a good girl, Brooks."

"Yes, sir." Brooks tightened his jaw, wondering how much of his "social life" had been witnessed by Jack Sorenson over the years. Jack's expression indicated that he'd seen quite a bit and didn't at all approve.

"She's not racy or fast. She's a *nice* girl." *Unlike the ones you bring around here from time to time.*

"I know she is," Brooks said seriously, meeting Jack's eyes.

Skye's father nodded, looking away as though uncomfortable and reaching under the counter for the key to the cutter's cabin. He held it firmly in his hand as he spoke again, "She'll make you a good crew, but . . ."

"Jack," Brooks heard himself saying. "I have no designs on Skye. We're just friends."

The older man nodded again, a good deal of the tension leaving his face as he handed the keys over to Brooks. "Glad to hear that."

"Guess I'll go see the cutter," Brooks said, bobbing his head in farewell before heading out the door that led to the docks.

Brooks wasn't sure if he should be insulted by Jack's words, but they sure didn't make him feel very good. From an outsider's perspective, Brooks knew how he looked—a rich playboy who occasionally got his rocks off with escorts on his yacht. It was, admittedly, disgusting when seen through that lens alone. Only Brooks knew that his use of escorts was a means of protection, to eliminate any possibility that his sexual needs would land him in trouble or hurt someone else.

It didn't matter that Brooks hadn't been able to stop thinking about Skye since Saturday, fairly assaulted by the power of his dreams every night. Brooks had engineered his whole life to *avoid* any meaningful romantic relationships that could lead to the emotional devastation he and his siblings had endured when his father had suddenly died. He had zero interest in any romantic attachment—*frankly, it was stone-cold terrifying to him*—and even if Brooks occasionally engaged in casual/social sex with someone from the club, he knew that Skye wasn't the sort of woman he should pursue for casual sex. She was strong, yes, but Brooks sensed an innocence about her that made her seem more vulnerable than other women. He felt protective of her. Hell, he'd have no problem pummeling the man who used her and walked away, leaving her hurt and disappointed. Skye deserved better than that. Better than him.

She *had* better than that, Brooks reminded himself. While Brooks didn't necessarily love Patrick, he was, in fact, Skye's boyfriend, and had been for quite some time. Aside from the fact that Brooks wasn't in the market for a relationship of any kind, he certainly had no interest in messing up her relationship with Pat, especially when he couldn't offer her something equally substantial in return. The truth was that Brooks had nothing to offer her but friendship and the opportunity to skipper an antique cutter. Kissing her had definitely sent a wrong—and incredibly unfair—message.

More than regretful, he was deeply ashamed of his behavior at the ball. When he thought of Skye in her beautiful dress in the moonlight, poetry pouring from her lips, her eyes wide and luminous, he wasn't sure he could've stopped himself from kissing her even if he'd wanted to, but he was still furious that he'd let his cock overrule his character. It wasn't like him, and he needed to understand why he'd given into his urges so it wouldn't happen again.

There had been other conditions at play that had weakened him, he'd reasoned and resolved. He'd been shocked by her transformation, check. He'd been drinking, check. He'd been so grateful for the way she swooped in at the last minute and saved him from Felicity Atwell, check. He reminded himself that she'd be back to her greasy-fingered, overall-ed self on the weeklong, eliminating any temptation. But just to be sure, he'd forbid himself even a sip of alcohol and thank God she wouldn't need to save him from anyone. He wouldn't touch her. It simply wouldn't happen again.

He'd do his best to erase the image of her stunning beauty as she walked down the center aisle of the ballroom: the pleased twinkle in her dark-blue eyes when he mouthed "Wow," the way her breath hitched when he jumped off the stage and approached her, the way her breasts had puckered against his chest as they danced, the low, hypnotic sound of her voice telling him that the wind and water were in his blood, the way she'd felt and tasted in his arms . . . Yes, he'd erase it all. He would. He *had* to.

Because he still needed her help. If she wouldn't crew for him, Jessica was obligated to offer Brooks and his cruise to Felicity, and he shivered when he recalled the wet, chilly unpleasantness of her saliva drying on his ear. He cringed as he made his way down the gangplank, heading for his new boat moored at dock five.

As he passed dock seven, his steps slowed until he stopped, distracted by half a dozen Optimists tied to the end of the dock, and the six little faces that looked up at their instructor. Their instructor who, for once in her life— *goddamnit!*—wasn't wearing overalls and a scrubby baseball cap.

Brooks didn't mean to stand there and ogle, but today she was wearing denim cutoff shorts and a yellow polo shirt that was an almost-perfect match to the single braid that ran down her back. Her legs were long and tan, her ass a work of art, and her feet were bare. Staring at her ankles for an extra minute, he realized that she was wearing a thin silver anklet on the left one, and for no good reason at all, that narrow strip of silver made his breath quicken, and he clenched his jaw, taking a deep breath.

He couldn't explain why he found it so sexy, except that Skye had seemed almost androgynous to Brooks for so long, this tiny concession to her femininity was a reminder of the woman he'd kissed on Saturday, and therefore, erotic to him on a level that was at once intense and ridiculous. But his whole body tightened as he imagined her ankles locked around his back with that fine chain digging into his skin, sounds from the back of her throat deep and—

"Uh . . . Brooks?"

He shook his head, swallowing, and focusing his eyes on Skye, who was staring at him as her students giggled behind her in their little boats.

Had she said his name more than once? From her slightly annoyed, slightly curious expression, he guessed she had. *Damn it.* He'd been so prepared to act like he was totally unaffected by Saturday night, and here he was, sabotaging himself before even saying a word to her.

Trying to recover, despite the uncomfortable flush in his cheeks, he raised his hand, taking a few steps down the dock toward the little group, like they were his destination all along. "Hey, Skye. Hi, kids! Having a lesson?"

Skye's brows furrowed, and she gave him a deadpan look that passed just as well for, *No, we're having a tea party*. She turned back to her students with her hands on her hips. "Do you all know who this is?"

One little girl with blonde ponytails nodded gravely. "That's Brooks Winslow. He won the 'Limpics."

"He didn't win it, dummy," said a little boy. "He only came in third."

Skye turned back around and grinned at Brooks in wide-eyed surprise, on the verge of laughing.

"Third still medaled," mumbled Brooks.

"Oh, yeah?" said the kid from his bathtub of a sailboat. "Well, it sure wasn't first."

The other children nodded, humming variations of "Mm-hm."

"Third's just third," offered another mournfully.

"Like last."

"They didn't play 'The Star Spankled Banner.' They played some other song."

"Yeah," said the little boy, narrowing his eyes at Brooks in challenge. "Third."

He may as well have spat the word "poop" for all that he respected Brooks' bronze medal.

"Well, I don't see any medals around *your* neck," pointed out Brooks, standing beside Skye with his hands on his hips and wondering how much pressure it would take on the bow to capsize the kid.

"You can bet when I win my medal, it'll be gold," said the little boy, and the other children nodded in enthusiasm and support.

"You did your best," said the little girl with the ponytails, shrugging with sympathy.

"Geez!" Brooks turned to Skye, incredulous. "I give up! Tough crowd!"

She was laughing silently, her eyes sparkling with tears of mirth, and he suddenly he felt his own chest rumble with laughter, looking down at the crew of pip-squeaks who looked back and forth at Skye and Brooks in confusion.

"Weirdest lesson ever," lamented one of them, and Skye lost it, turning to Brooks and dropping her head to his shoulder as she erupted in gales of laughter.

And yes, Brooks laughed right along with her, but he'd be lying if he said he wasn't affected by her forehead on his shoulder, a wisp of her blonde hair tickling his ear, the smell of coconut sun tan lotion an unexpected aphrodisiac.

His laughter faded as he looked down at her head, reminding himself that he couldn't have her, remembering his promise not to touch her again, and took a sudden step away from her. Without his shoulder for support, she lurched forward, falling into him, and while Brooks' arms reached out instinctively to steady her, she'd already barreled into him, her weight setting him off-balance. And *oh my God,* the dock was simply too narrow for a graceful recovery.

With barely more than a second's notice, they both fell into the murky water of the harbor, bobbing up to the surface a moment later, sputtering and spitting with surprise.

"Oh! God! Oh, no!" said Skye, taking in Brooks' soaked, annoyed face, which made more laughter bubble up inside. "I'm so s-s-s-sorry!"

Brooks leaned his head back to get his hair out of his eyes, grimacing at the slick of oil on the surface of the water. He frowned at Skye, which only made her laugh harder.

Diving under the water to escape his irritated scrutiny, she came back up with her hair slicked back and eyelashes glistening. Blinking at him, she turned back to the dock, put her hands on the planking, and hefted herself out of the water, sitting on the side. She grabbed the hem of her shirt, twisting it in her hands to wring out the water and chancing a glance at Brooks, only to find him staring at her chest with his eyes on fire. Looking down, she realized that her wet shirt was hugging her breasts like a second skin, which made a shiver run down her back and puckered her nipples into tight points.

Damn it.

Her cheeks flushed instantly. Looking up, Brooks' eyes seized hers for a hot moment before she became aware of the giggling behind her and stood up quickly, turning to her students.

"Well, I guess that's it for today," she said, forcing a smile, even though she felt unsteady and hyperaware of Brooks still in the water behind her. *Why* was he still in the water? Then she thought of his hungry eyes, and a very hard and long reason occurred to her, which just made her blush deeper. Thank God she wasn't facing him. "We, uh, we were almost done today anyway."

There were a few groans as the kids took off their life jackets and left them on the floor of the Optimists.

"Just, uh, leave your boats where they are. I'll take them back over to dock ten later."

One by one, she helped the kids back onto the dock, waving good-bye to them as they scurried toward the marina where their parents would collect them. Only when the last child entered the marina did she turn back to Brooks, who, at some point, had lifted himself out of the water and sat on the edge of the dock, his expensive shoes still submerged in the dirty water.

"So . . ." she started, uncertain of what to say. His green eyes locked on her blue, and she could feel the heat of his gaze in her toes.

She'd promised herself to leave their Saturday night kiss in the past and chalk it up to a one-time mistake. No matter what Clay had counseled, Skye was not a cheat, and until she and Pat decided to take a break, she was not available to Brooks or any other man. And that meant the following thoughts were off-limits: the memory of their kiss, fantasies of future kisses, and any other mental image that included Brooks Winslow's lips touching down on hers.

That said, she'd also sworn off overalls for a while, Brooks' words about not seeing her as a girl still smarting. It had felt sort of nice for men to look at her so approvingly on Saturday night, but she didn't need to dress like a girly-girl to add a *little* femininity to her wardrobe. She'd pulled her shorts and polo shirts from the top shelf of her closet and stowed her overalls for now. She had to admit, the change was refreshing. However, looking down at said polo shirt now, she realized it was once again clinging to her breasts like a second skin. She pulled it away from her body, looking over at the abandoned Optimists as Brooks finally stood up.

"Sorry," she said softly, chancing a glance at him.

"No," he said. "It was my fault. I moved away when you put your head on my . . . It was my fault."

His eyes dropped to her lips for a moment before he looked away, sighing deeply.

"This is awkward," she observed.

"It was bound to be," he said. "Although for a moment there, I thought we might slip past it."

Her lips twitched in amusement. "You were right. They *were* a tough crowd."

He chuckled softly, gesturing to the Optimists. "Can I help you with these?"

Say no and tell him to go.

"Sure. Why not?"

They both leaned down to uncleat a line, and Brooks' arm brushed against hers, sending a jolt of warmth down her arm, forcing her to say what needed to be said.

"Brooks?"

"Hmm?"

"I don't . . . I just don't think the cruise is a good idea," she murmured, looking down at her fingers, which held the line securely.

"I was afraid you might say that," said Brooks, handing her his line, then standing up to pull the small trailer over to the edge of the dock.

When the trailer was in place, he pulled the first little boat out of the water, positioning it easily onto the trailer bed, then pushing it a small ways up the dock before retrieving the other trailer.

"I mean, Pat wouldn't . . . he doesn't deserve that, Brooks. I feel terrible about it."

"What if I swore to you that it wouldn't happen again? That I will not make a move on you for the entirety of the cruise? I promise, Skye. I can't say my hand won't brush yours or I won't bump into you on deck. But I swear I won't, you know . . . purposely . . ." He took a deep breath and sighed, leaning down to pull the second boat out of the water.

Skye stood up to help position it onto the trailer, looking at him from across the little boat, grateful for the solid boundary it imposed between them. Did she trust that his self-control could prove as reliable a boundary?

They stared at each other in the fading afternoon sunlight, each leaning over the side of the small boat, the moment intense and incredibly intimate even though they weren't touching. She searched his sea-green eyes, lingering on his dark, beautiful, obscenely long eyelashes and ignoring the sudden quickness of her breathing.

"I promise, Skye," he whispered.

And she saw it in his eyes, the sincerity behind his words, the force and weight of his promise. It's not that she didn't see desire in his eyes. She did. But the strength of his vow outshone his longing. She felt it in her bones and knew she could trust him.

"I believe you," she said, dropping his eyes and walking to the first trailer without another word, tugging it back up the dock behind her.

The reason she turned away so quickly . . . the truth she didn't want him to discern in her own eyes was that, unfortunately, Skye didn't totally trust herself.

Yes, Brooks would keep his hands to himself.

But could Skye?

She heard his footsteps squeaking behind her, his wet shoes complaining as he followed her, dragging the second boat.

She'd thought of little else but Brooks since Saturday, reliving the best kiss of her whole life in exacting detail over and over again. Though she knew that Brooks had enjoyed the kiss as much as she, she also sensed he wasn't comfortable that it had happened. Not then, and not now. Why? Because of Pat? Because it was a mistake? Because he didn't really want *her*, but she'd been convenient and available in a romantic moment? She sensed strongly that Brooks wasn't interested in her on any serious romantic level, and it made her think about the different women with whom he sometimes spent time on his yacht. Maybe it wasn't personal. Maybe Brooks didn't want to be attached to anyone.

But why?

Did he like being alone? Did he prefer it?

She frowned as she parked the Opti on the dock, set the brake on the trailer, and pushed it gently into the water, leaning down to cleat the bow line.

For lack of any other diversion in her life, Brooks had become a fascination to her this week. She'd known him for years, yes, but she didn't really *know* him outside of the marina and their mutual passion for boats and sailing. Had there ever been someone *significant* in his life? Had she hurt him? Had she made him swear off romance and love?

Skye couldn't help wanting answers to her questions, but digging for answers would mean getting to know Brooks on a deeper level, and she feared that any additional intimacy between them would invariably lead to more kissing. And more kissing meant more cheating. And Skye was *not* a cheater like her shameful, embarrassing, disgraceful escort of a mother.

Brooks' Optimist sloshed into the water beside hers, and she looked up at him, the question in his eyes unmistakable. Would she still sail with him? Could she?

"You can skipper," he blurted out. "For the whole week." He paused, clenching his jaw before releasing it. "I'll crew for you."

Her eyes widened, and her lips dropped open in shock. She'd never, ever expected this sort of custom-made sugar to sweeten the deal. He trusted her to skipper his boat? His brand-new antique cutter? For the whole week?

A small laugh escaped her mouth, and she quickly covered her lips with her fingers. "Are you kidding?"

"Nope."

"You mean it? You'd let me skipper?"

He took a deep breath, nodding and finally offering her a grim smile. "I'm out of options. I *need* you Skye. And yeah, I trust you with my boat. I trust you more than anyone I c think of."

And quite possibly, those were the words that sealed her fate because they were neither casual, nor flippant. In fact, they were everything she'd longed to hear from Patrick and never received, which meant that they fed and soothed an ache inside of her. Patrick had neither needed her, nor trusted her skills as a sailor. But Brooks needed her. Brooks trusted her.

"Okay," she said, picking up the line attached to her trailer and giving him a quick nod as she headed back down the dock to pick up another Optimist. "I'll still do it."

He stared at her for a long second, disbelievingly, before his face broke into a beaming smile. "You will? You'll do it? You'll come with me?"

His smile was so joyful and relieved, it was utterly infectious, and she found herself grinning back. "I will."

"Thank you!" he said, opening his arms and taking a step forward like he was going to wrap her in his arms.

And, oh man, that sounded like heaven, but at the last minute, she thought of Pat and stuck her hand out, firm and straight between them. Brooks looked at her hand, his smile fading, and stepped back. He offered her a small, reserved smile, then reached up and took it, shaking it once before letting go quickly.

"Friends?" he asked, leaning down to pick up the rope attached to his trailer.

Yeah, right, she thought, but she gave him what she hoped was a *friend*ly smile and nodded.

"Friends," she agreed, taking a deep breath as he turned away, preceding her back up the dock.

Chapter 8

They ended up taking the cutter out for a test sail on Wednesday evening after hauling the remaining two Optimists from dock seven to dock ten, their conversation carefully neutral as Brooks explained the stops they needed to make en route to Charleston. He'd charted his own course a couple of weeks ago, looking at nautical maps, weather patterns, and currents, and making reservations for them at various marinas down the coast, but now that he'd turned over command of the cutter to Skye, it would be up to her to figure out the route she wanted to take. And Brooks would have to fall in line.

As he stepped down the grand staircase at Westerly on Saturday morning, the day before the cruise, the thought chafed a little—letting someone else skipper one of his boats. Then again, he thought, his expression softening, it was Skye. Not only did he trust her completely with his boat, he needed her, and he was relieved she'd given him a second chance. He was determined not to ruin it.

Peeking into the West Salon, he saw Jessica with two of her girlfriends, Valeria Campanile and Kate English, sitting at the small gaming table, staring at a poster board diagram in tense silence.

"Morning, ladies."

Three pairs of eyes—green, brown, and blue—turned to look at Brooks and offer greetings, and Jessica hopped up to kiss her brother's cheek.

"Brooks, we could use your help."

Valeria, the newish girlfriend of Stratton English, whom Brooks knew to be outspoken in a harmless sort of way, rolled her eyes meaningfully. "And this is why I tell Stratton 'No' every time he hints about proposing."

Kate, who had recently become engaged to Brooks' childhood neighbor, Étienne Rousseau, looked down at her engagement ring and grinned up at him. "And why *I'm* glad there's no more bad blood between the Englishes and Rousseaus."

Valeria cleared her throat.

"Which is great," said Jessica, grinning at her friends, "because it means I don't have to separate your men."

Valeria cleared her throat . . . again.

"Who *do* you have to separate?" asked Brooks, glancing over her shoulder at the poster board.

"Well . . . I can't have Bree Ambler with Emily and Barrett English."

"Or J.C. Rousseau," Kate reminded her.

Jessica sighed. "Right. And Betsy Story still feels awkward about Étienne. Sorry, Kate."

"She needs to get over that. It was a million years ago!" Kate shrugged. "But now that you mention the Story sisters . . . Alice Story and Étienne's brother, J.C., have had bad blood since Princeton."

Jessica nodded, then gave Brooks a knowing look. "But Cam will *definitely* want to sit near Margaret Story, right?" She turned to Kate. "Do you ever remember hearing about a *thing* between Jax Rousseau and Cort Ambler?"

"Cort?" Kate pursed her lips. "I don't *think* so."

Jess nodded knowingly, moving Cort's tiny place card away from the Rousseaus. "I do." She paused a second, looking at where she had Étienne and Stratton side by side at one of the two head tables that included the English and Winslow siblings. "Be honest. Will Stratton be okay sitting next to Étienne?" Jessica asked Valeria.

Val gave Kate a dubious look. Stratton English and Étienne Rousseau had learned to tolerate each other for Kate's sake, but they certainly weren't the best of friends.

"They're total pains in the ass," lamented Val, grimacing at the tiny place cards.

"Amen," said Kate, raising her hand for a high five, which Valeria slapped on cue.

Jessica blew out an exasperated breath, sitting back from the table and throwing her hands in the air. "I give up."

Brooks' head was positively spinning. As the oldest child of the twenty-three kids born on Blueberry Lane between 1980–1991, he'd been largely insulated from the drama.

"Okay. Wait," said Brooks, leaning over his sister's shoulder and moving the place cards around like puzzle pieces. "J.C., Jax, and Mad Rousseau with Dash and Slone Ambler at one table. Alice, Betsy, Pris, and Jane Story with Bree and Cort Ambler at another. Make sure Cam asks Margaret to be his date, so she can sit with me, Pres, Chris, and Kate at one head table. And you and Alex join Barrett, Fitz, Stratton, and Weston at the other. Done."

Silence reigned as the three women looked down at the diagram in amazement.

"Holy cow!" cried Jessica, leaping up and throwing her arms around her brother's neck. "You are the *best*!"

"You really are," said Kate, staring at the poster board in awe.

"Whoot! Go Brooks!" said Valeria, raising her hand for another high five. After he slapped her palm gently, she looked up at him thoughtfully. "So, now that that's done, we need the dirt. Who was the hottie who bid on you at the auction last Saturday night?"

Damn it! Why had he solved the seating problem so quickly? Now they were all focused on *him*. He leaned back from his sister.

"Yeah, Brooks," said Jessica in a singsong voice. "Who was the hottie?"

"Uh, well . . . she's my mechanic," he said, opting for the truth.

They all stared at him with wide eyes, as though waiting for the punchline.

"I'm serious," he said. "She's my mechanic."

"Your . . . *mechanic*? Okay. Well, that's a new one. Does she work *under your hood*?" asked Valeria, enunciating each word carefully before winking at him.

Brooks frowned at her suggestive tone, which made Kate English giggle. "I think it's kind of cute that you call her your 'mechanic.'"

"No, I don't *call* her that."

Valeria grinned at him. "But it's sweet that you *think* of her that way. Someone who's giving you a tune-up. That's a very healthy role to play in a new relationship, you know."

"But, we're not in—"

"Your *mechanic*." Jessica shook her head, grinning at him. "It *is* sweet, Val. You're right. I can't wait to get to know her better!"

"No, it's not . . ." he started saying, but they'd all turned back to the seating chart, deciding which group should sit at which table and how far away they needed to be to keep the peace.

Not one to look a gift horse in the mouth, Brooks decided to escape while it was still possible. He headed out of the room quietly, turning back at the last minute. "Jess, just a reminder . . . I'm leaving tomorrow for that cruise. I'll be gone for a couple of weeks."

"You have an appointment with Dr. Dryer this afternoon. Don't forget."

Brooks huffed softly. He *had* forgotten.

"We're all going this week," she said dismissively, still staring at the chart in front of her. "Me and the boys, too."

He grimaced. Dr. Dryer was his family's cardiologist, and each of the siblings visited his office every six months for a routine checkup that included an EKG. It only took fifteen minutes, and Brooks knew it was important, but it tied him up in knots every time.

"Fine." He sighed.

"Oh, and Brooks," she said without turning around. "Have fun with your . . . *mechanic*."

She used air quotes over her head, which made Valeria and Kate giggle, looking up to grin at Brooks before turning their attention back to the seating chart. It was all incredibly annoying.

Skye isn't my . . . my . . . anything, he thought as he walked through the labyrinth of hallways at Westerly that led to the kitchen. She'd made it more than clear on the dock that she was with Pat, committed to Pat, and other than joining him for the sail to Charleston, there was nada between them. Fine. Good. That's exactly how it should be. That's exactly what he wanted, right? Right.

Wrong.

On Wednesday, when she'd leaned on him and he'd breathed in the scent of her coconut-scented sun block as her shoulders shook with laughter, he'd had a split second when he allowed himself to dream. With those little faces looking up at her and the light weight of her forehead on his shoulder, he'd inadvertently opened the window to a whole fantasy he saw playing out in his mind like a sneak peek of heaven: this sweet-smelling girl beside him, little ones with his green eyes and her blonde hair, sunshine, sun block, and sailing. His heart had galloped from her nearness, the guilelessness of her personality, the way he felt so much better, so pointlessly hopeful, in her presence.

You can't have her, he'd reminded himself, and the whole fantasy came crashing down. God, he'd practically pushed her away.

Taking a loaf of cinnamon-raisin bread from the bin on the counter, he placed two slices in the toaster and poured himself a cup of coffee. *You going to steal her away from her boyfriend? And offer her . . . what? Hot kisses? Maybe even a week of unforgettable onboard sex? Make her fall for you . . . and then what?*

His first sip of coffee burned his throat, but he took a second sip anyway, preferring physical pain to the alternative. He knew what Dr. Dryer would say today. He'd say the same thing that Dr. Fiorello had said to his father so many years ago: Your heart sounds good. Your heart looks good. See you in six months.

Except, for his father, six months had been a cruel promise. Taylor Winslow had never even made it to three.

So, there it is, thought Brooks, closing the door on the bright and lovely fantasy of having a woman like Skye in his life. *Stop thinking about her as anything but your friend. And be grateful she's still willing to be that.*

Skye stared at the mess on her bed feeling overwhelmed. She'd have to sit on her overpacked duffel bag to wrestle the zipper shut, there were nautical charts spread out all over her comforter, and a notebook serving as her Captain's log was splayed open with scribbles she'd need to decipher.

But most distracting of all was her contact lens case, which alone wouldn't be such a big deal, but when she'd pulled it out of her bedside table, the serrated edge of a condom had hitched a ride on the black nylon of the case.

She'd dropped the case onto her pillow like it was on fire and turned away quickly to continue packing, but every few minutes, her eyes darted back over to the simple, black nylon pouch now decorated with a cheerful red-and-white foil packet that read "LifeStyles."

It taunted her, resting on her pillow, because both she and her pillow knew that she hadn't had the need for a condom in months. Even before Patrick left, their sex life had been a little thin, owing to his obsession with his trip. Her nose twitched as she counted back in her head and realized that she hadn't had sex since . . . Valentine's Day. Four and a half months ago.

God, how depressing.

No wonder she couldn't seem to control herself around Brooks Winslow.

She'd had no business resting her head on his shoulder on Wednesday evening, but she hadn't given it thought, turning to him, her whole body shaking with laughter—it had seemed the most normal and natural thing in the world. And it had felt nice to laugh with him. Really nice.

Brooks wasn't—as far as Skye had observed—a laugher. He seemed, more often than not, to have the weight of the world on his shoulders. His face serious, his eyes cast down, as though life had, at some time or another, delivered him a terrible blow that he'd just as soon not reprise.

It made her wonder again what had happened to make him so reserved.

"Or maybe that's just the way rich, handsome, ex-Olympians roll." She sighed, pulling the charts off her bed and folding them neatly.

She glanced at the notebook, picking it up and taking a closer look at her notes. She'd seen Captain's logs a thousand times, but she'd never held her own, and she felt pride as well as trepidation as she stared at it. She took a deep breath and raised her chin. Brooks was trusting her to skipper for a whole week, and she wasn't going to let him down, regardless of what Pat thought of her sailing skills.

After the *Celeb!* photos at the marina tomorrow, they'd lift anchor and sail south via the Chesapeake Bay to Gloucester Point, Virginia, not far from Virginia Beach. On Monday morning, they'd do the obligatory photo shoot for *Celeb!* before setting sail along the coast of the Atlantic Ocean, stopping in Hatteras on the Outer Banks of North Carolina where they'd drop anchor on Tuesday night for another photo shoot. It was an aggressive sail, but if she and Brooks kept the boat cruising throughout the day and didn't make any additional recreational stops, they should make it on schedule. On Wednesday and Thursday, they'd be at sea, stopping in Myrtle Beach on Friday morning before arriving in Charleston late-afternoon on Saturday for their final photo shoot. On Sunday morning Skye would fly home.

"Seven nights," she murmured, her traitorous eyes flicking over to her pillow reflexively.

Brooks had promised her the aft, or forward, cabin, which had two full-sized berths and ample storage with a connecting bathroom. This led her to assume he would take one of the two guest cabins, both of which had two twin berths. Those were smaller, much narrower, and configured like bunk beds in a really nice closet.

A man as large as Brooks would barely fit into one of the tiny guest bunks, and she couldn't imagine he'd get a very good night's sleep.

When he'd given her a tour of the boat on Wednesday evening, she'd paid close attention to their sleeping arrangements, and she had to admit she felt a little guilty that it was Brooks' boat and he'd be consigned to such a tight, uncomfortable room. It didn't seem fair, but there was no other option unless she allowed him to have the other, wider berth in *her* room that would be otherwise empty.

Share a bedroom.

Platonically, of course, but . . .

Share a bedroom.

Bad idea. Bad idea. Bad idea.

The condom on her pillow practically giggled at her, and she grimaced, fishing the deck plans of the cutter out from under her Captain's log. Because she was the skipper of his boat, she would assign their quarters tomorrow morning when they loaded their gear on board, and because Brooks respected the conventional and time-honored tradition that a skipper was in total control of a maritime vessel, he wouldn't argue with her decision.

Even if he shares the aft cabin with me, it's not like we would be sharing a bed, she reasoned, *just a room . . . and just at night.* Brooks could change his clothes in the head or in one of the other tiny cabins. But at least he'd get a good night's sleep. With a crew of two, they would require good sleep every night, and how could he be expected to sleep with his body barely fitting on one of the tiny guest berths?

She was so deep in thought, the sound of her phone ringing made her jump a foot. She reached for it, pressing "Talk" without looking at the screen.

"Hello?"

"Skye?" said a crackly voice. "Skye? Can you hear me?"

"Pat?" she asked, her heart thumping with a sudden adrenaline rush. "Is that you?"

"Yeah! It's me."

"Oh my gosh! Where are you?"

"Coast of Costa Rica."

"Pat, that's amazing!" she said, picturing Pat and his Cat bobbing on the blue of the Pacific. "You're on ocean number two!"

"Yeah, I made it."

"I bet it's *gorgeous*." She sighed enviously, never having sailed the Pacific.

"It's beautiful, Skye."

"Wow," she said softly, feeling happy to hear his voice, but a little sad that she was in Maryland, and he was so far away in Costa Rica when they were originally supposed to go together.

"Saw the article in *Celeb!*," he said.

So had Skye. And she'd rolled her eyes at the sensationalized phrase "newly minted lovebirds."

"It was silly, Pat."

"Didn't look silly. Looked like you were all dressed up and dancing with Brooks Winslow."

"Well, I was. But it's an act. It's just publicity . . . for his sister's cause."

"Modern art," said Pat, scoffing.

"It's nothing. Really," she said, her cheeks hot as her heart called her a liar.

"Do I have anything to worry about, Skye?"

She winced, pulling her bottom lip between her teeth and feeling a rush of guilt for her kiss with Brooks and her non-stop thoughts of him since last Saturday. But she couldn't help her thoughts . . . and she'd been clear with Brooks: her choice was Patrick.

"Of course not. I'm with you."

"Are you?"

Her eyes burned and she blinked quickly. "Yes! Pat, I-I'm just . . . it's hard being away for so long. I miss you."

"We'll be together in Mexico soon, babe."

"I know . . . I just . . . this is a really long time to be away from—"

She wasn't positive, but she could swear she heard the tinkling laugh of a woman in the background. Her eyes narrowed.

"Are you ashore?"

"Huh? No. No, I'm about a mile offshore."

She paused a second, listening intently, but didn't hear anything and wondered if she'd just been imagining things.

"Oh."

"That's how we got a signal."

Wait. We? Then she heard it again. A woman's laugh. No doubt this time.

"Pat? Who's with you?"

"What? No one. Just me and the Cat." A pause. Then, he whispered, "Shhh. Come on. Stop. She can hear you." Skye's mouth dropped open. Did he think he was covering the mouthpiece of the phone? Well, he wasn't. His voice was louder when he asked, "Uh, Skye? Babe? Can you hear me?"

"Yeah. And I can hear her, too," she said, steel in her tone. "Who's with you?"

He cleared his throat. "Skye . . . It's no big deal. Inga and Helmut got into a fight, and I'm just giving Inga a lift to San Salvador."

"Giving her a lift?"

"Yeah. It's nothing. She's going to fly home once we get there."

Skye nodded dumbly, the breath knocked out of her lungs. Patrick had been so resolute about her not joining him—*I just feel like this dream started before I met you. I can't shake the feeling that this is just an adventure I'm meant to enjoy alone. I think it's my destiny*—and yet Inga was on the Cat, hanging out with him, having an adventure with him, while she was home alone.

"Babe," he cajoled. "What was I supposed to do? Leave her stranded in Panama City? She came to my room after midnight with her backpack, crying, telling me that Helmut had—"

"I have to go," said Skye, furious, swiping at her eyes with the back of her hand.

"Skye . . . don't be mad. It doesn't mean anything. She's just . . . I mean, *you're* going on a cruise with Brooks. Aren't you sort of a hypocrite for pulling the 'indignant girlfriend' card?"

Yes. Yes. I guess I am.

"Well, that stops now, Pat . . . because if *you're* entertaining Inga, you can bet your ass *I'll* be entertaining Brooks."

"Wait! Skye—"

No, no more waiting! She was so sick of staying still and swallowing her hurt feelings so she didn't rock the boat with Pat. She was sick of taking the higher road and being the understanding girlfriend so that Pat could fulfill his stupid, selfish destiny. He was clearly having an onboard fling with his flavor-of-the-moment. Great. Fine. Terrific. But two could play that game.

"No! You're right. I'll take a card from *your* deck instead. You enjoy your time with your . . . your Swedish slut, Pat, and I'll—"

"Skye, I'm not fucking her," he said softly, an edge of warning creeping into his voice. "Don't . . . just don't do anything you're going to regret, okay?"

Hurt feelings made her voice low and bitter. "I *won't* regret anything."

"Come on, Skye—"

"I gotta go," she said, pulling her phone from her ear and pressing the "End" button before he could say another word, then throwing her phone down on the bed.

He was cheating on her.

He was cheating, and she knew it. She could tell. She could hear it in his voice.

And it hurt. It hurt a lot more than she would have expected.

She thought back to Inga's pretty, tanned face, flirting with Helmut before kissing him passionately in front of a stranger on a webcam. That's what Inga was comfortable doing on a webcam in front of a stranger, and Skye's best guess was that she and Pat had been at sea for at least a week. Like hell they weren't fucking.

Which suddenly made her guilt over that single, solitary kiss last Saturday seem utterly ridiculous. Reaching across her bed, she picked up the black nylon case, and without detaching the condom, she shoved it into her duffel bag with a huff of satisfaction.

Chapter 9

"How about a kiss on Brooks' cheek, Skye?" asked Guy Hunter, snapping away with his camera while a small group of well-wishers, including Jessica and Alex, Preston, Cameron, and Skye's father, Jack, stood uncomfortably on the dock waiting to wave good-bye. Well, uncomfortable except for Jessica, who raised her eyebrows and nodded enthusiastically behind Guy, miming a kiss.

Brooks looked down at Skye, who flushed pink, then shrugged, and Brooks dropped his lips to her cheek in a chaste kiss as the camera snapped again. Her cheek was soft and warm under his lips, and a faint hint of coconut made his nuts tighten uncomfortably. He ignored it. He was going to have to ignore it a lot this week, and while that might make the next few days a little painful, he had no other options.

"Nice!" praised Guy. "How 'bout another? Skye? How about you kiss Brooks?"

Brooks drew back from her, telegraphing "I'm sorry" with his eyes as she grinned dryly at him. He leaned his head down, closing his eyes as her soft, pink lips brushed his cheek.

"Thatagirl!" said Guy as they held the pose for several seconds.

Think about something else, Brooks, or you're going to embarrass yourself, he thought, feeling his dick flinch inside khaki shorts.

When Brooks arrived with his entourage at seven o'clock, Skye and her father were already on the cutter, and from the looks of things, they'd been prepping her for hours. The deck had been hosed down, the sails raised loosely and the lines recleated. He had grinned at Skye in appreciation, respecting a skipper who took her duties seriously. He had no doubt that her gear was already stowed, she'd established a Captain's log with their course, and if he peeked in the Chart Room, it would undoubtedly have a clean chart of the Chesapeake under the Plexiglas of the rectangular table.

Brooks still needed to stow his bags, then all that remained were a couple more pictures and their farewells before they pulled up anchor. They were just about ready to go.

"Brooks," asked Guy, "what have you decided to christen your new boat? How about *The Skye*?"

Brooks stepped away from Skye, giving Guy a forced grin. "She's already named *Zephyr*."

"Hey Skye, are *you* as fast as a zephyr?" Guy asked suggestively.

Brooks fisted his hands, taking a step toward Guy.

"Guy," said Jessica quickly, stepping between her brother and the cheeky reporter, "can we get you anything else before you go?"

"How about a couple shots of you and your fiancé?" he asked, waggling his eyebrows. "Hard for the world to believe that Alex English has actually been reformed. I'd love to take some photos to prove it!"

Brooks watched Alex's posture stiffen and gave his sister a look that asked, *How do* you *like it?*

Jessica slid her hand down Alex's arm, and the tension in his body seemed to ease, but he still looked at Guy Hunter with disgust.

"Sure," said Jessica. "Can we just say good-bye to my brother first? So he can get underway?"

"No problem," said Guy, flicking his eyes at Brooks' shorts. "I'll just take a few *bone* voyage shots, huh?"

Guy elbowed his way around Preston and Cameron, who were doing a good job of glowering at him, and Jessica took Skye's hands, pulling her aside.

"I hope you have a great time," said Brooks' sister, her lovely, green eyes sparkling and kind as she squeezed Skye's hands in hers.

"We will," said Skye, glancing at the cutter. She was unaccustomed to holding hands with other women and uncomfortable with so much attention focused on her. More than anything, she just wanted to get going. "I love this boat."

"I love my brother," said Jessica evenly, leaning forward to press a kiss on Skye's cheek. She whispered in Skye's ear, "You can trust him, you know."

"Can I?" murmured Skye, the words reflexive, not sanctioned.

Jessica drew back, catching Skye's eyes and smiling. "Yes. I think you can. He's good at taking care of people. He's been taking care of me forever."

But you're his sister, thought Skye, instinctively knowing that the enormous love Brooks clearly had for his sister probably didn't extend to any other woman in his life.

"Have fun," said Jessica, squeezing her hands again before turning to Brooks, who was chatting with his brothers.

Alex English, who'd been introduced to Skye quickly when the Winslows arrived, grinned at her as they both watched the Winslows engage in a gregarious group hug.

"They're a great family," said Alex, who only had eyes for Jessica.

Skye, who'd never had any family but her father and a few cousins, looked on with envy, her eyes pulled magnetically to Brooks, who was grinning at something his brother Cameron was saying. "Seems like that."

"I heard Brooks is letting you skipper."

"Yep," said Skye, looking at the *Zephyr*'s sparkling decks with pride and pleasure.

"Don't take this the wrong way, but I've known Brooks since I was a little kid, and he's not the type to let just anyone skipper his boat."

"You make him sound very controlling."

"He is," said Alex. He glanced down at Skye thoughtfully. "He must trust you. A lot."

Trust again. That seemed to be a theme this morning—one that Skye had an issue with, especially in light of Patrick's recent betrayal.

"Maybe he was just desperate," said Skye, softening the words with a small grin.

"Or maybe he thinks you're an amazing sailor."

She scoffed in her head, thinking about Pat's painful summation of her skills: *decent* crew, but *not* a racer.

"I doubt it." She looked up at Alex, shrugging nonchalantly. "I know how to sail. He needed someone to go with him. He sweetened the deal by letting me skip, and I couldn't pass up the chance. That's all there is to it."

Alex looked like he was about to say something else when suddenly, her father's head reappeared from below decks and he stepped over the bow, onto the dock, approaching Skye.

"Frig generator is all charged up. Engine looks good. Gave her a touch more oil. Remember that Marconi mainsail is canvas, Skye. She's going to luff and fill differently."

"I know, Pop," she said gently.

He wiped his hands on his overalls, looking back at the boat. "You only had a thousand liters of fresh water, so I topped you off earlier. Didn't like the looks of their VHF radio, so I added another portable. You'll find it in the overhead compartment. Chart room."

"Pop," she said, putting her hand on his arm. "It's a good boat. It's going to be a good trip."

"Oh, I know that," said Jack, clearing his throat, finally meeting her eyes. "You be careful, huh, Skye?"

"Who sails better than me?" she asked.

Jack opened his arms, and she leaned into her father's comforting warmth, as he answered, "The guy behind you ain't half bad."

Skye released her father and stepped back, her body hitting a wall of muscle. Brooks. He reached his hand around her and offered it to Jack, sandwiching Skye between them in a way that felt incredibly intimate and yet surprisingly nice.

"Don't worry, Jack. I'll get her home in one piece."

"All of her," warned Jack, taking Brooks' hand.

"All of her," agreed Brooks, pumping the older man's hand before releasing it. "You ready?"

Skye twisted her neck to look up at him. "As I'll ever be."

Brooks leaned down for his duffel and hoisted it over his shoulder, stepping on board the *Zephyr*, and Skye followed behind.

He shrugged the shoulder that held his bag. "Should I take this below?"

"Um, yeah, that's fine. Just put it anywhere. We'll work out the arrangements later." His eyes widened a touch, and her cheeks felt instantly hot as she looked away, heading for the ship's wheel. She looked back at him once there was several feet between them. "After your bag's below, untie us, huh?"

His lips spread into an unbelievably beautiful smile as he nodded slowly at her. "Aye, aye, skip."

We'll work out the arrangements later?

What did that *mean?* he wondered as he uncleated the bow and stern lines before pulling in the buoys, as Skye started the engine and backed them out of the slip, giving his siblings, Alex and Jack, a wave good-bye.

As per maritime convention, Brooks hadn't argued with her. He'd placed his duffel bag on a table in the Chart Room, awaiting further instruction from her, and then had come back upstairs to get to work. He assumed her plan was to motor out of the harbor, then raise and tighten the sails once they were in the open water of the bay. That's what he would do, though it wasn't his call. In fact, just about nothing was his call, which made a whoosh of excitement sluice through his veins, making him feel a little hot and bothered. She was totally and completely in charge of him for the next seven days. She all but owned him, and he'd orchestrated it.

Having raced large sailboats competitively for most of his life, Brooks knew that a vital component of sailing was to maintain a positive and supportive relationship between skipper and crew, but he was also a traditionalist in that he respected the ultimate authority of the skipper. And for the first time since he'd turned over the *Zephyr* to Skye, it occurred to him that he was, literally, at her mercy. If she wanted to motor all the way down to Charleston, he wouldn't raise a complaint. If she told him to sleep above-deck, he'd lay out a bedroll under the stars. If she told him to take the wheel, he'd take it without question and steer where she commanded. If she said, "Jump," Brooks would ask, "How high?"

So where exactly was he going to be sleeping tonight?

He had no idea, but the wait was going to be strangely, yet deeply, exciting.

"Looks like it's going to be a little choppy out here today," commented Brooks, walking up from the bow to midship where Skye stood behind the skip's wheel, strands of her blonde hair escaping from her braid as the wind whipped up.

She looked at the sky, where the sun was trying to break free from cloud cover. "Could go either way."

"How far do you want to motor out?" he asked.

She gave him a sidelong glance.

"I'm not questioning your plan," he said quickly, leaning against the mainsail boom, watching the intense concentration in her eyes as she steered them out of the harbor. "You're the skipper. Whatever you say, goes. I'm just wondering."

"Is it hard for you?"

"What?" he asked, the adolescent part of him distracted by the way she said "hard."

"Letting someone else be in charge? You skippered your boat in the Olympics."

"Yes, but only to third place," he reminded her with a dry grin.

She chuckled softly, shaking her head. "It's pretty amazing, you know."

He shrugged modestly.

"I'd like to hear more about it at some point," she said.

"Just tell me when."

She stared at him for a moment, seemingly lost in thought, before blinking twice and licking her lips.

"Um . . . what? What did you ask me?"

"Are we motoring out?" he asked again, forcing himself not to grin, but enjoying the way she'd gotten a little flustered. *Why? Because of the Olympics? Because he'd said, "Just tell me when"?*

Her cheeks were pink when she answered him. "I thought we'd motor past Elk Neck point, into the channel, then tighten the sails. The wind's strong today. We should go pretty fast."

Motoring that distance meant they had a little time to relax as the boat put-putted farther and farther away from the marina. Brooks leaned against the railing to her left, out of her direct line of sight, which meant she'd have to turn her head to look at him head-on.

But it gave him a great view of her profile: her braided, blonde hair, straight nose, and pouty lips. Her breasts were full and lush under her light-blue polo shirt, but her stomach was flat as a board, and the rest of her body was incredibly toned and athletic. She wore white denim cut-off shorts, which emphasized the tan on her long legs, and her feet were covered by new-looking navy, leather Top-Siders with white laces and white soles. She was also wearing that incredibly distracting anklet, which just about taunted him, reminding him of his Wednesday-afternoon fantasies. She was casual. And gorgeous. And it vaguely registered that he was ogling her, but he couldn't help it.

"You're staring at me," she said without facing him.

"Yes, I am."

Her little, pink tongue darted out to lick her lips again. Was it a nervous tic? Or did it mean more? He tried to remember if he'd ever noticed her doing it before, but up until a week ago, he hadn't thought of Skye as anything but a friend, so it probably wouldn't have tripped his radar.

"It's distracting," she said. "Can you stop?"

For a moment, he considered arguing with her, teasing her that no, he wouldn't stop staring at her because there wasn't anything else worth staring at when she was in view. But her word was law for the duration of the sail, so he turned his glance forward instead, checking out a white cruiser that motored by.

Suddenly, it bothered him that he didn't know her better. Of course he'd been frequenting her marina for years. He knew her father. He knew her boyfriend. He knew she could handle a boat like a pro. They'd sailed together a few times and shared a beer together afterward. She'd worked on his boats for hours at a time while he tinkered or relaxed, and they'd engaged in long conversation. They'd traded teasing brother-sister-style banter over the years as well, but he didn't *know* her. What did she eat for breakfast? What was her favorite movie? What music did she listen to? Did she shower in the morning or the evening? What did her body look like when she got out of the shower naked and dripping? Did droplets of water fall from her puckered nipples? And if he was there with her, would she—

"Any more questions?" she asked.

Uh, yeah. Lots.

"We're about to spend a week together, and I've known you for years, but suddenly I don't feel like I *know* you all that well," he blurted out, still staring straight ahead.

"What do you mean?" she asked. "That doesn't make sense. I've known you since I was ten."

"Yeah, that's true. We've sailed together, and we bump into each other at the marina, but I don't really *know* you. What you like, what you don't like, your favorite food, your dreams . . .". . . *what it means when your tongue wets your lips when you're staring at me . . . because you've made it clear you're with Pat and off-limits to me, but every time you do that, I have to restrain myself from grabbing you and kissing you senseless.*

He felt the heat of her eyes on his face for a long moment.

"Do you *want* to get to know me?"

Although it was completely against Brooks' strict set of rules to allow himself the intimacy of getting to know a woman personally, he couldn't help it—the answer was unequivocally . . .

"Yes."

"Well," she said, glancing at him briefly before relaxing her stance a little, "ask me something. I'll answer."

"Anything off limits?"

"I reserve the right not to answer, but . . . no. You can ask me anything."

"Okay. Umm—"

"But I get to ask too, okay? We'll go back and forth."

"Aye, aye, skip," he said, glad she was still facing forward.

He was also glad that she couldn't see exactly how wide his smile was when she said that. He didn't even know why it mattered, but for some reason it did. It mattered that she wanted to get to know him better, too.

Peripherally, Skye noticed the way his perfect lips tilted up in a smile, his cheeks tightening, his eyes lifting. Her tummy, which had been filled with butterflies since Guy Hunter had made her kiss Brooks' cheek at the dock, fluttered.

For no good reason, but probably from the mere fact that he was Brooks Winslow and he'd kissed her last weekend like the world was ending, she shivered, feeling exhilarated by the sudden rush of power the nickname "Skip" implied. And no, it shouldn't have—in any way—felt sexual, but he was so incredibly good-looking, it did. And even more? She liked it. She liked being in charge of him. God, how she liked it.

On the ruse of checking out a passing sailboat, her gaze darted to the side for a moment, then slipped to his strong thighs, lingering on the tan muscles she found there. His body was just as athletic as hers—bronze, hard, and toned. It made her breathing hitch, and she looked away from him quickly, back out at the water, wondering what he wanted to ask her.

"You can go first," she said.

"Okay . . ." He stared down at the planking before looking up at her. "We'll start small . . . What do you eat for breakfast?"

"Oatmeal, usually. With berries and almonds. Sometimes cereal. You?" It felt safer to volley back the same question for now.

"Scrambled egg white omelet with vegetables," he said. "And sometimes toast."

"White bread?"

"Multigrain," he answered. "Umm . . . how old were you when you got your first kiss?"

Her eyebrows shot up as she cut her eyes to his.

"Too personal?" he asked, a challenge in his eyes.

She shook her head. "Sixteen. You?"

"Twelve."

"Guy should have asked if *you* were as fast as a zephyr," she quipped.

He chuckled at her, nodding, his lips quirked up in an adorable combination of embarrassment and sass. "Okay . . . fair enough."

"Next question?" she asked.

He shrugged. "You go."

"Hmm. Oh! Here's one I've always wondered . . . Why don't any of your brothers or sister sail?"

He grinned at her, a relaxed, reflexive reaction, and for a moment Skye felt a spike of jealousy that the mention of his siblings should garner such a loving expression.

"They weren't encouraged, I guess. I mean . . . well . . ." His smile faded a touch, and he shrugged. "My father was a sailor. He loved getting out on the water, and he often took me and Preston along with him . . . but he passed away when I was seventeen. Pres was fifteen. Jessie wasn't even six yet. My younger brothers were thirteen and eleven—too young to really have any appreciation for the sport. Preston actually has the skills, but he sort of turned his back on it after my dad died. I think—I don't know for sure—but I think it hurts him to sail . . . like my dad couldn't sail anymore, so Pres didn't want to either. Me? I felt the exact opposite. I wanted to be the best. I imagined my dad watching me sail, and it . . . I guess it made me feel closer to him, if that makes sense."

Skye didn't know what she'd been expecting to hear, but such a deep and honest answer stunned her. In just a moment their conversation had gone from breakfast foods and first kisses to Brooks' single-minded yearning to feel connected to his late father. And thinking of her own father, how close she was to him and how much she loved him, her heart clenched.

She had a vague recollection that Mr. Winslow had been a sailor, and she knew he had passed away a long time ago, but she had no idea that he'd been the motivation for Brooks' Olympic dreams. To discover that Brooks' lifelong love of sailing and fiercely competitive spirit had been borne from his grief touched her deeply.

"I'm so sorry," she said, looking at him, ". . . about your dad."

He flinched for just a moment, locking his eyes with hers. Then he looked away, back out at the water. "Me too."

"What happened to him?" she asked.

The change in Brooks was immediate. His whole body stiffened and his jaw clenched. She watched his fingers curl around the deck railing and he shook his head, looking down at the deck. Finally, he turned to her, his eyes closed and cool.

"It's my turn to ask a question."

Her eyes widened at the change in his tone—from warm and reminiscent to hard—but she nodded to let him know she was ready.

"What's the deal with you and Pat?"

His father's heart attack wasn't something he discussed. Ever. It was something that ate away at Brooks quietly. It was a silent killer he was convinced lived somewhere inside of his own body, waiting to take him down as surely as it had his dad. He couldn't bear discussing it, so he'd changed course deliberately, distracting her with a loaded question.

She raised her eyebrows at him before turning her glance back out to the bay. They were about halfway to Elk Point now, and soon they'd need to go to work, but they had enough time for a few more questions, and this one had been burning a hole in his brain. What was someone as guileless and down-to-earth as Skye doing with a pretentious douche-bag like Pat?

"What do you mean?" she asked, keeping her eyes trained straight ahead.

"Can I be candid?"

"Why stop now?"

"You and Pat don't seem . . . I don't know . . . *obvious*."

"Ummm . . . ?"

He shrugged, glancing at her, then away. "You're not an obvious match."

"Why not?"

"I knew Dionne. You two are like night and day." In that Dionne was a bitch on wheels, and Skye was one of the nicest people he'd ever met.

"They're divorced. It's probably a no-brainer that he'd look for someone different than his ex-wife," she observed, avoiding his question.

"Okay, here's what I really want to know—"

"You already asked a question."

Brooks cocked his head to the side. "It's not a new question. I'm just rephrasing."

"Fine," she said, though the look she gave him said she thought he was cheating. He didn't care. He needed to know.

He waited until she looked back over to him, raising her eyebrows for him to get on with it. "How come you didn't go with him?"

Her tongue darted out to lick her lips before she dropped his eyes, jerking her head forward and staring out at the sea.

"That wasn't the plan," she said softly.

"Yeah, it was," he said quickly, pressing her. "It *was* the plan. The original plan. I remember, because you were excited about going. I remember one day while you were changing the oil on my Passport, you talked my ear off about it. So, why didn't you go?"

"Plans change."

"Come on, Skye."

She lifted her chin, her blue eyes cutting to his. "Why does it matter?"

"Because if you were mine, there's no chance in hell I would have left you behind," he said, his tone harsh.

Wait! What? Shit! Did I just say *that out loud?*

He heard her tight gasp and watched as her lips parted and her eyes widened. She stared at him, completely distracted from the helm.

He cleared his throat, dropping her eyes. "Sorry."

She was silent for a long time, and when Brooks looked up, she was staring out to sea, her face sad. And he hated that he'd had anything to do with putting sorrow on her face. In fact, he was about to apologize again when she finally turned, raising her eyes to Brooks.

"He wanted to go alone," she said in a little voice.

Looking back at her, Brooks flinched, reminding himself of his promise not to touch her again and restraining himself from taking the two steps that would allow him to pull her into his arms. Instead, he crossed them over his chest uselessly and felt his face grow hard.

"I hope you'll forgive me for saying so, but if that's true, then Patrick Flaherty is even more of a jackass than I ever gave him credit for."

He stared at her, wondering if she'd protest. Or admonish him. Or feel genuinely hurt on Pat's behalf. Which is why he felt like such a rockstar when she turned her lovely face back to him, licked her lips, and smiled.

Chapter 10

For most of the day they worked without time for or interest in conversation, their only goal to help the cutter achieve maximum speed. Skye barked orders, and Brooks was—unsurprisingly—the most capable, intuitive crew she could have asked for, anticipating her needs almost before she asked. In addition to keeping the sails trimmed and changing them for every tack and jibe, he had somehow found time to slip below at noon to fix them each a ham-and-cheese sandwich on wheat bread, and he'd always made sure Skye had a bottle of water in the holder by her hip.

Ten hours later, they'd practically *flown* south, slicing through the Chesapeake Bay waters by Maryland, and arrived in Gloucester Point, Virginia, by five o'clock.

Luffing the sails as they approached the marina where Brooks had booked them a slip for their first night, Skye motored into the harbor, and Brooks, who'd been below since the sails had come down, reappeared on deck with two longneck beers hanging from between his fingers.

Grinning, he offered one to Skye.

Keeping one hand on the wheel, she smiled back at him, accepting the cold bottle and lifting the smooth, green glass to her lips.

"Wait!" said Brooks. "We need to make a toast!"

Skye stopped, lowering the bottle with surprise.

"That was *fast*, Skye!" he said, his eyes twinkling and animated. "I mean, that was *racing* fast! *Excellent* racing fast."

She glanced down at her watch and had to admit that yes, they'd made damn good time. A winning race time from Baltimore to Norfolk would be nine and a half hours, and they'd made it to Gloucester Point, close to Norfolk, in a little over ten.

She looked up at him, her smile widening as she nodded. "It was good."

"I don't know what I expected . . . but you're *amazing*," he said reverently, staring deeply into her eyes. "Why don't you skipper more often? Why aren't you racing? I mean, all the time? Every weekend? We'd win every race!"

A few things happened immediately in Skye's head, all of which made her stare back at him, slack-jawed.

One. *We? "We" like, you, Brooks, and me, Skye, sailing regattas and races together?* Her heart stuttered as her mind conjured a slideshow of pictures showing her what life would look like racing one-on-one with Brooks every weekend. The wordless teamwork, the heady sense of satisfaction. She bit her lip to keep herself from sighing with longing. One look at his gorgeous face forced her back down to earth. It was only his excitement after a long, successful day of sailing that had led him to say such a thing, she reasoned. He didn't mean it. He was an Olympic medalist. He could race with anyone on the east coast, anyone in the world.

And two. She was a nobody . . . a mechanic at her father's modest marina. A *decent* crew, but—by her own boyfriend's own admission—*not* a racer.

And three. She didn't even own a boat to skipper. Yes, she'd crewed for local teams over the years now and then, but the *Zephyr* was her first opportunity to skipper a sailboat. *Any* sailboat. She didn't skipper more often because it wasn't an option unless she borrowed someone else's boat or bought one for herself.

She looked at his face, searching it for flattery, and even though he looked open and honest, she took a mental step back. He was just being kind. They'd had a good day, and he was supporting her, which was a function of a good crew member. He didn't mean what he was saying in any special way, and taking his words seriously would just embarrass them both.

She shrugged. "I don't race much. I'm . . . at the marina, you know, a mechanic. That's really what I do."

"Well, you *should* be racing," said Brooks, still smiling at her, his eyes warm and admiring, and she saw a little wonder in them, too, like he was seeing her for the first time. And then she realized . . . it was exactly how he'd looked at her the night of the auction—like she was new to him.

Skye swallowed, losing herself in his green eyes, feeling her grin fade with the hot intensity of his gaze. He was still pumped up on the adrenaline of the cruise, his hair wind-blown and messy, his face tan, his eyes wide and fascinated. His energy was riveting and exhilarating, and her tongue slipped between her lips to wet them.

His eyes dropped immediately to her mouth, his nostrils flaring lightly as he rested his gaze for a long moment before raising his eyes . . . and his bottle.

"To Skye Sorenson," he said in a husky voice, "a better skipper than most of the Olympians I know."

She blinked at him, the weight of his words heavy and wonderful as she processed them. He was comparing her to world class racers? To internationally recognized skippers? Her heart thundered, and she wanted to accept his words as truth, but his praise was too high, especially when weighed against Pat's words, which had indicated the very opposite. Brooks couldn't possibly be serious. And to take him seriously would place her in jeopardy, because she might believe for a moment that she could be more than she was; that life could be bigger than it was. The last time she'd trusted in a big, beautiful plan, she'd stood on a dock waving good-bye as Pat sailed away alone.

She dropped Brooks' eyes, a soft, embarrassed laugh escaping from her throat, as she clinked his bottle with hers. "And the fastest oil change on the Chesapeake."

He flinched, turning away from her to take a long sip from his beer. His voice was flat and business-like when he asked, "Buoys out, skip?"

"Not yet," she said, looking at him and instantly feeling terrible. He couldn't have been serious, and yet . . . it almost looked like she'd hurt his feelings. His whole face had lost its exuberant, childlike excitement, and she didn't like it one bit that she'd taken it away from him. "Hey . . . ?"

"Hmm?" He turned to look at her, his eyes cautious, lifting his beer for another sip.

"I just . . . thank you, Brooks. Thank you for saying such nice things, but—"

His forehead creased. "I wasn't just *saying* them. I *meant* them."

Her cheeks flushed. She still didn't believe him, but she sensed that his kindness was genuine, and she hastened to return it. "I'm sorry . . . You're being really nice. I have a hard time with compliments."

"You seemed okay when I told you that you were beautiful."

Her head tilted to the side in confusion.

"At the auction," he added.

"Oh. Yeah, but . . ." She shrugged. "That wasn't really me."

"What do you mean?"

"Getting dressed up like that? It wasn't me. I'm not a . . . girly-girl." She laughed self-deprecatingly. "Obviously."

"I don't know," said Brooks, shrugging with an adorable grin. "It might not be your natural habitat, but you still nailed it, Skye."

She took another sip of beer, shaking her head, incredibly pleased by his words, but wanting him to understand what she was trying to say about sailing, about being on the water, how important it was to her—it wasn't a joking matter. In as much as it could be, it was her church, her religion. It was sacred to her, and she'd prefer he treated it as sacred space too, and didn't just hand out empty flattery.

"You're sweet." She took a breath. "But this? Sailing? It's—"

"This is really you," he said softly, his eyes connecting with hers, his voice low and soft. "The wind and the water are in your blood."

Yes! she thought, amazed and a little spellbound to hear him repeat her own words back to her. *This is me. All of me. The* real *me.*

"This is practically me . . . *naked*," she murmured as an extension of her thoughts, her eyes widening as the words ricocheted around her brain in a rat-tat-tat of inappropriate fire.

His lips parted, and his eyes flashed at her, the heat in them unmistakable.

"Is that right?" he asked slowly, raking his eyes down her body.

Her fingers flexed on the wheel, her face almost painfully hot, and she was so flustered she could barely put her next sentence together. "I only mean . . . this is . . . I mean, this is the *real* me. This is as real as I get."

"This . . . the water, the wind, sailing, boating . . . this is your natural habitat."

"Exactly." She sighed, her shoulders relaxing a little.

"And it matters to you."

"A lot," she said.

"Which is *why* you should *believe* me," he said. "Because like you, I don't bullshit when it comes to sailing. Not now. Not ever. I think you know in your bones that *you* are one of the most intuitive sailors you know."

"That doesn't make sense," she murmured.

"Yes, it does." He stared at her, and she drew her bottom lip between her teeth, feeling overexposed and vulnerable in a way she wasn't sure she liked or disliked. "When you look around at other skippers, you know what you'd do differently. You quietly assess when they're doing wrong and how you'd correct it. I watched you today. It took one hour before I stopped judging your skills and just fell in line, doing whatever you asked me to do because I trusted your instincts and your experience. You're not a *good* sailor, you're a *great* sailor, Skye . . . and you know it. Maybe something shook your confidence, but you must know what I'm saying is true."

You're a decent crew, Skye, but I want to make good time and you're not really a racer.

"I don't—"

"Well, I *do*. This is my natural habitat, too." He leaned forward from the railing, taking a step toward her. "I'm one hundred percent serious, Skye. You're a fantastic skipper. I'd sail with you any day, any time. And we'd win."

His words were like honey, like water in the desert, like coming up for air and filling your lungs with goodness. She hadn't realized exactly how much Pat had hurt her until that moment, but uninviting her to go with him had been a terrible blow. It's just that she'd been so concerned with keeping the peace, she'd buried her disappointment instead of examining it. She examined it now. And somehow, by acknowledging it for the first time since Pat withdrew his invitation, she felt stronger. She didn't feel the pain of his unkindness, his selfishness weighing her down. For all that his words had hurt her, perhaps they hadn't, in fact, been true.

Brooks took another step closer, and she looked up, caressing his expression with her eyes. She searched his face—still beautiful—but found it new, too. Somehow more real, more genuine, deeper, like an intimacy that she missed had already been established between them, and she was just realizing it now.

His thick, black hair was waved and unruly, his tan cheeks cut from burnished marble, the shadow of a beard outlining his jaw with dried salt in tiny, round flecks on his chin. She could smell a hint of sweat on his warm skin, the slight scent of beer on his breath. He'd taste like beer if he kissed her right now, and she leaned closer to him, her fingers slackening on the wheel as she—

"Buoys out, skip?" he asked softly, inches from her face.

"Buoys out," she replied, pulling her eyes away from Brooks' broad shoulders as he turned away from her to get to work.

As Brooks fastened six buoys on the port side of the boat and tossed them over the side, he thought about their conversation.

Although it was clear that Skye was new to skipping—her hands were tight on the wheel, and her concentration was singular and intense, while a seasoned skipper would be more relaxed—he was serious about her intuition and skill. He'd sailed with skippers as good as Skye, but very few with better natural instincts.

Why had she protested his praise so hard? Why had she immediately assumed he was being disingenuous?

It bothered him. It bothered him a lot that Skye felt like she couldn't trust him, because . . . because, damn it, he wanted her to. He liked her. It was dangerous and inconvenient and it couldn't actually go anywhere, but he *really* liked her, more than he could ever remember genuinely liking a woman. And sure, it helped that she had a body to kill for, soft breasts that he remembered pressed against his chest, delectable lips that he was aching to taste again. But it was more than how she looked or his attraction to her—he liked who she was. She was modest and self-deprecating, low-maintenance and proud. He appreciated the way she'd had a course charted and memorized it so she didn't have to refer to her notes midsail. He liked the way she quietly and effectively took charge. He liked working with her and for her. He respected her.

And if his health, if his father hadn't . . . hell, he might actually be thinking more seriously about her, wondering how his life could mesh with that of a marina owner's daughter, and his heart tightened with longing at the very idea. He might imagine her body, naked and trembling, beneath him as he pushed into her slick heat. He might imagine telling her that he loved her, asking her to marry him, holding their firstborn on his shoulders while she pushed a stroller holding a baby. He might even imagine her eyes, still blue, but softer with age after the wind of a thousand sails, looking back at him with the sort of love that had lasted a lifetime.

If he was able to do anything about it, he might let himself imagine it all.

But he wasn't able, he reminded himself, throwing the last buoy over the railing.

He wasn't able.

Because chances were, when Skye's eyes were soft with age, Brooks Winslow, like his father before him, would be long gone.

Fifteen minutes later, tied up in one of the many slips at the York River Yacht Haven marina, Skye watched as Brooks lowered his sunglasses and lay down on the dock with his beer by his side.

"Okay with you if I take a catnap?" he asked.

"Sure," said Skye, knowing that his body must be ten times as tired as hers since he'd done a lion's share of the work today.

Since their loaded conversation about her skills as a sailor, he'd been standoffish, almost like he was avoiding her, so it surprised her a little when he added, "We have a dinner reservation at seven," his voice low and dull as he relaxed on the sunny deck.

"Dinner?"

"Yeah," he said, sitting up to take off his T-shirt, then balling it under his head. "There's a good restaurant here."

"Oh," she whimpered softly, checking out his toned chest, tan and glistening with sweat under the late-afternoon sun. He was godlike—so hard and beautiful, her mouth went dry and she had to force herself to look away. "I didn't know."

"Mm-hm. There's a swimming pool too . . . and showers . . . and Wi-Fi," he added, yawning, "if you want to go online to say hi to your dad . . . or Pat."

She flinched for absolutely no good reason.

Why shouldn't Brooks suggest she connect with her boyfriend?

Why did it bother her so much that he did?

To distract herself, she turned her attention to the marina. Skye hadn't checked it out closely after pulling the *Zephyr* into its assigned slip, but she looked up now and realized that it was bright and well kept, almost like a mini resort. And she had to admit, a hot shower sounded like pure heaven.

"I think I'll take advantage of the showers," she said.

"Go for it," he mumbled, though unless her eyes deceived her, his pecs had tensed for a moment, at odds with his lazy voice.

Taking one last look at his long, lean, muscular body, Skye turned and headed below to grab her toiletries and a towel. She walked down the polished wood staircase, holding onto the railing and making her way into the small salon that had built-in cabinetry, seating, and a table, serving as library, dining room, and living room. Noting Brooks' duffel sitting prominently on the table, she darted her glance up the stairs and winced, shaking her head and wondering if he was napping on the deck because he hadn't yet been assigned a berth.

"Shoot," she muttered, flinching with disappointment in herself.

It was unkind and unprofessional that her inability to make a quick decision for her crew would cost Brooks a decent nap. Grabbing the heavy bag off the table, she held it in front of her as she made her way down the narrow passage to her bedroom. Sighing as she looked at the made, but unused, full-sized bed taking up the unoccupied port side of the cabin, she plunked his bag down in the middle of the down comforter, then turned to the starboard side, where she'd already settled in. She sat down on the small bench built into the side of her bed and eyed his bag, hoping she had made the right choice.

To Skye Sorenson, who's a better race skipper than most of the Olympians I know.

She looked down at her lap, feeling her lips slide into a grin as she recalled his words.

He had no idea how much she would savor his compliment—likely for the rest of her life. Even when she'd bargained with Brooks to skipper, one of her key insecurities was that maybe her sailing skills *weren't* up to the task of leadership. But he'd assured her that they were, and in one wonderful, supportive swoop, Brooks Winslow had repaired the damage Pat had inflicted. He respected her skills, and she respected his opinion, and just as Jessica, Alex, and Brooks had all encouraged her, she decided to trust him from here on out. For the next seven days, they were a team. Skye grinned at his bag. A team. Two people dependent on each other, trusting and respecting each other. Maybe even—

Maybe even what, Skye?

She stood up, opening one of the dresser drawers built into her berth, and taking out a towel, then opened another drawer and took out fresh underwear, khaki shorts, and a clean, crisp, light-pink polo shirt.

Maybe what?

Pat's latest escapade with Inga notwithstanding, the more time she spent with Brooks, the more she was starting to see her boyfriend through an entirely different lens: selfish, self-absorbed, shallow, and, yes, even cruel. Perhaps she'd only been settling for Patrick Flaherty because she was flattered by his attention and tired of being alone. They had sailing in common, but when she compared Pat to Brooks, there was *no* comparison. Brooks hadn't wanted to be in the auction, but he'd agreed to it because he loved his sister. Brooks had devoted his life to sailing because of his love for his father. Brooks had allowed her—an inexperienced skipper—the chance to captain his boat, and then encouraged her and praised her effusively. Brooks, it seemed more and more, was a giver. Pat was a taker. And Skye was getting sick and tired of being taken.

Opening the top dresser drawer, she found her cell phone in the back and quickly signed onto the marina's Wi-Fi, pulling up a fresh, blank e-mail.

Hi, Pat,

Made it to Gloucester in 10 hours.
Feels good to be out on the water again.
Assuming Inga is still with you on the Cat.
I think we need to take a break.
Write back to let me know you got this.

Skye

Her finger hovered over the "Send" button as she read and reread her words. "Take a break" was essentially a soft way of saying "break up," and he'd know it. She was breaking up with him. Pat, who'd seen beyond her overalls and greasy fingers and asked her out. Pat, who'd been her boyfriend for a year. Pat, who liked having her at home waiting for him while he enjoyed Inga's company on the bright-blue waters of the Pacific.

Shouldn't it hurt more? she wondered, staring at the words. *Shouldn't it feel messier?*

The fact was, it wasn't messy.

There were no rings to return.

No leases to dissolve.

No pets to coshare.

They didn't even leave clothes at each other's places since they lived in the same town, and Pat preferred to shower and change at his own place.

And her heart . . .

Placing a palm gently on her chest, she realized that her heart—which should have ached at the idea of losing Pat— had already started and finished its aching at some point: she'd been hurt by Pat, said good-bye to Pat, fruitlessly hoped that Pat would tell her that he missed or loved her while he was so far away. None of that had happened, and now that she was saying good-bye to him, she realized that her heart had probably moved on weeks ago.

It *wasn't* messy and it *didn't* hurt, which meant that this message was just a necessary formality to let him know things were finally over.

She took a deep breath, her eyes flicking upward where Brooks Winslow napped in the sunshine. If she sent the message, she'd be single again. She'd be free to do whatever she wanted with whomever she wanted. She wouldn't be a cheater. She'd be taking a chance that there was something—someone—out there in the world better for her than Pat.

Her finger hovered for one more moment before touching down softly and pressing send.

Chapter 11

Across the candlelit table from Brooks, Skye grinned at him, her teeth white against the tan of her face, her blonde hair cascading down her shoulders in natural waves. He assumed she'd let it air dry after her shower because it looked beachy and sexy. The collar of her pink polo shirt was popped, and the edges brushed the soft skin of her cheeks, one of which was dented with a small, beguiling dimple. She was naturally stunning and he couldn't look away, but staring at her had the unfortunate side effect of keeping his shorts tented for the entirety of their dinner.

"I swear," she said, giggling as she reached for her coffee cup. "It's true."

"Never? You've *never* skippered before today? Ever?"

She shook her head, that tiny dimple beckoning his eyes like a beacon, teasing him like crazy.

"How is that possible?" he demanded, pulling his bottom lip between his teeth.

"I don't have my own boat."

"I could remedy that."

She rolled her eyes, but her smile widened just a little. "You gonna buy me a boat, Brooks Winslow?"

"It'd be a good investment if you'd race it with me. I'd make back the purchase price in prizes."

She laughed heartily then, shaking her head back and forth. "You know? You might be a little crazy . . . or a little too rich. Offering sailboats to every girl you meet!"

He laughed with her and gestured to the waiter to bring him another beer. When he looked back at her, the grin was gone, and she was holding her phone, her finger sliding down the screen as she checked her messages.

While she was away from the boat this afternoon, after his nap, he'd gone below to grab what he needed to take a shower, shocked to find his bag—which he'd purposely left in the common room so she could assign him a cabin—on the bed opposite hers. He'd looked in the other two tiny bedrooms first, then—feeling confused—he'd peeked into hers, only to have his jaw drop when he saw his duffel sitting deliberately in the middle of the bed on the port-side berth. They were *sharing* the master bedroom?

He'd leaned against the door, his eyes wide, stroking his stubbly jaw with his thumb and forefinger and wondering what it meant. He acknowledged that she could just be as good a skipper as he gave her credit for and was ensuring he had the most comfortable possible accommodations, regardless of her own sensibilities about sharing a room with him. But he'd be lying if he said he wasn't hoping it meant something more.

That Brooks was deeply attracted to Skye was a well-established fact at this point, even though his body still took every opportunity to remind him. What had really shocked the hell out of him, however, was the intimacy of their conversation this morning. For the first time he could ever remember, he was letting a woman into the sacred space with which he surrounded and protected himself. He could barely believe how forthcoming he'd been with her about his father and how much he wanted to understand her relationship with Pat, or—more accurately—find vulnerabilities in that relationship that could work to his benefit.

What benefit? he questioned as she pursed her lips at her phone, her fingers flying over the screen to type a message.

Skye wasn't someone to play with.

And Brooks had already decided long ago that pursuing a meaningful relationship with a respectable woman wasn't fair. He'd have to be a truly selfish bastard to allow that to happen, to allow someone to care for him when there was no guarantee he'd still be around five years from now.

But this growing easiness between them felt so unfamiliar to Brooks, yet so rare and special and fine, he couldn't help wanting it to continue. Tonight at dinner was the first time she'd allowed his eyes to linger on her without asking him to stop. She seemed more open, more comfortable. And their sleeping arrangements, sharing a room—God, he couldn't get it off his mind, and the anticipation was so hot and distracting, he'd found himself fantasizing about her more than once over dinner.

Suddenly, she gasped, looking up from her phone, her eyes sparkling and her sudden smile dazzling. "Oh, gosh! I love this song."

It wasn't especially familiar to Brooks, but he cocked his head to the side and listened to the '50s-style song playing softly from a speaker over their table.

What if I-I-I-I . . . I want to kiss you to-morrow?

It was sweet and soulful, and for a moment, Brooks thought about asking her to dance, about how much he'd like to hold her in his arms and feel her body pressed against his.

"Your dad likes the old stuff," he said. The radio in the marina shop was always tuned to a '50s and '60s music station.

"It only *sounds* old," she said, then sang softly, *"Don't be ner-vous, I'm so in-to you . . ."*

His heart raced as he stared back at her, mesmerized by her pretty voice and soft, pink lips mouthing words he wished were true. "But it's not?"

"Not what?"

"Old?"

She shook her head, closing her eyes and singing, *"What if I-I-I-I. . . . I want to kiss you to-morrow?"* She grinned at him, shrugging adorably. "It's Meghan Trainor."

"Meghan . . ."

"Trainor. You know, 'All About That Bass?' She's all over the radio. She's . . . amazing. I heard her sing, you know. At a bar in Nantucket . . . before she made it big."

"Oh! *Meghan* Trainor."

"Yeah!" She nodded, beaming at him. "See? You know her!"

"Nope. Actually, I have no idea who she is," he said, chuckling softly before catching her eyes. "But I think I might be missing out."

"You are," she said, sighing as the song ended. "And yes, my Pop loves songs from the '50s. My grandparents played those tunes all the time, my whole childhood."

"I remember your grandma. She used to help out at the front desk now and then."

Skye nodded, grinning sadly. "She was great. A real salty dog."

"What about your Mom?" asked Brooks. "You never mention her. How come I've never met her?"

Her face fell immediately, closing up, the pretty, happy smile from a moment ago fading quickly.

"Skye?" he asked softly, wincing because her mother must be a painful subject, and he felt obliged to extend sympathies or apologies if appropriate. "God, did she . . . did she pass away? I'm so sor—"

Her face was cautious and her tone cool when she looked up at him. "As far as I know, she's alive. She's just . . . she moved to LA a long time ago. She's not a part of my life."

"I didn't know."

"This," she said, pointing out the window beside them at the marina and boats bobbing in the evening breeze, "wasn't really her thing. She's . . . I mean . . . it's just better that she stays out there."

Skye's cheeks felt hot with shame as she imagined her cheap escort of a mother ever meeting wealthy, respectable Brooks Winslow and suppressed a cringe.

Every moment she spent with Brooks, she felt her lifetime infatuation for him deepening into something more substantial and infinitely more troublesome. Because Skye had never really considered Brooks a realistic romantic interest, she'd never allowed her imagination to envision how their lives would mesh. Now she imagined it. And they didn't. Mesh. At all.

As an ex-Olympian, Brooks was still in the news from time to time, chairing benefits and judging regattas for ESPN or NBC Sports. He wouldn't want to tarnish his reputation by dating a woman whose mother was a glorified hooker. Not to mention, Skye was a middle-class mechanic, and he was an upper-class trust-fund baby. Although she'd appreciated his reaction when she'd dressed up for the auction, she had no interest in regularly attending fancy galas, and she highly doubted a lifetime of sunsets viewed from dock ten of her Pop's marina would satisfy Brooks' well-known wanderlust.

He wouldn't fit into her world, and she wouldn't fit into his. Despite their mutual love of the water and undeniable

chemistry, Brooks really wasn't an option. It hurt her heart
to acknowledge it, but Skye believed in being honest with
herself and looked down at the table with disappointment.

Spying her phone, she frowned, picking it up for a moment,
then turning it over so it was facedown. Pat had gotten her
message and responded with anger, accusing her of sleeping
with Brooks and demanding that she call him and explain
herself. She texted Pat back that she wouldn't speak to him
again until Inga was off his boat, and since he hadn't written
back, she assumed Inga was still in the picture.

But suddenly, she wasn't anxious for Brooks to find out
about their breakup. She was fairly certain that Pat's role
as her boyfriend was the major reason Brooks hadn't made
another move on her, and it was probably for the best that
he continued to keep his distance.

For a moment, before Brooks had asked about her mother,
while Meghan Trainor's superromantic ballad was playing,
Skye had almost spilled the beans about her recently single
status, thinking maybe he'd wind his fingers through hers
on the short walk back to the boat, and pull her against him
in the moonlight to revisit their first kiss.

Now with the reminder of her mother's tawdry lifestyle
front and center, she wondered if it was better to keep the
news to herself. She and Brooks were friends. Better friends
every moment, but still just friends, and as long as they
didn't give into their attraction, that's how they'd stay. And
as much as she longed for more from him, she wondered if
it was best for them to keep their distance.

"When did she go?" he asked gently, lifting his eyes from
her phone.

"I was very little," she said curtly, folding her hands on the
table and giving him an annoyed look, even as the mantra,
Please, oh please, stop asking me about my mother, circled
in her head.

He reached for her hands from across the table. "Skye . . ."

"Do you think we could get the check?" she asked, jerking her hands back and dropping them to her lap. "We'll get gas and water in the morning, but I have a few things I still need to do before bed."

"Sure," he said, sitting back in his chair, looking confused and disappointed. When the waiter came back, he asked for the check before turning to Skye. "Not to make things more awkward, but speaking of bed . . ."

He let the words trail off and clenched his jaw, his handsome face otherwise expressionless as his eyes burned into hers. He'd found his bag in her bedroom, of course. When she'd returned from her shower, he was gone, but his bag was open on his bed, and she wondered when he'd bring it up.

She shrugged, keeping her voice crisp, though her fingers trembled in her lap. "We're getting up at six and sailing for twelve hours straight tomorrow. If you think you can get a better night's sleep in one of those little bunk beds, go for it."

"No, I'm . . . I'll stay where you put me." He searched her face. "Listen, I shouldn't have asked about your mother, but I didn't know—"

"It's fine."

"I just—"

"Really, Brooks. It's fine," she said again, her heart twisting a little as she maintained a cool tone that shut him down. "Thank you for dinner. They have great food here. You were right."

His eyes flicked to her phone, as though he was still trying to figure out what had changed so suddenly and drastically between them. She could see his mind working: *If it wasn't her mother . . .* "Who were you texting before?"

"Pat," she answered levelly. "My boyfriend."

Brooks' lips tightened into a thin line as he placed several bills in a wallet with the check and stood up from his seat.

"I'm going to get a few things at the marina store. You need anything?"

"Nope. All good," she answered, swallowing the lump in her throat.

"Great," he said, reaching for his beer and chugging the rest before placing the glass a little rougher than necessary on the table. "I guess I'll see you later."

She didn't let herself wince until he turned his back and walked away.

Stupid, stupid, stupid.

The thing about sealing yourself off from the possibility of liking someone—or God forbid, falling in love with someone—is that when your heart suddenly starts feeling something real, you don't know what the hell to do about it because you haven't had much practice falling for someone. But Brooks was learning quickly that if the object of your affection seemed disinterested in your attention—or worse, is taken by someone else—it stings like hell.

"Shit," murmured Brooks, taking a deep breath of brackish air and walking along the docks away from the restaurant, away from Skye, headed nowhere.

She wasn't reaching out to him or trying to get closer to him by letting him share her room. Her purpose was practical, not personal, and certainly not romantic. She needed him well rested for tomorrow's sail, and that was it.

For God's sake, she has a boyfriend, Brooks!

And yet, the disappointment that he felt was worse than he could have anticipated and clued him into something important: he was past the point of deciding whether or not he *should* have feelings for Skye. He already had them.

And she, it seemed, didn't. She'd been at dinner with Brooks texting with her selfish prick of a boyfriend. It was impossible for Brooks to know if the conversation about her mother or texts from Pat had put that puss on her face, but either way, her coolness at the end of dinner had hurt a little.

Damn it.

It had been so long—so fucking long—since Brooks had allowed himself to feel anything for a woman, he felt vulnerable and stupid and much younger than his thirty-five years to be infatuated with a woman who'd never given him the slightest reason to hope.

In some ways, he *was* younger than his age. Yes, he'd had to grow up quickly to be the head of his family and a pseudofather to Jessica and his brothers. He hadn't had an opportunity to date a lot in college because he was concerned with going home every weekend to spend time with his grieving siblings, and after the Olympics—once he'd been old enough and had the time to pursue a meaningful relationship—his fears for his mortality had become so significant, he wouldn't allow it.

And yet, he wanted love and stability. He *ached* for it.

No, not for *it*, for *her*.

For Skye.

He couldn't have her, but he wanted her. It was as simple and stupid as that.

Sitting by the empty pool for an hour, he traded texts with Preston for a bit, filling in his brother on the sundry details of the first day, then e-mailed Jessica to check on her wedding plans. Cameron posted something on Facebook about his renovation, which was probably bait for Margaret's dubious benefit, and Chris, who was more and more interested in Philadelphia city politics, posted a photo of himself at a Republican fundraiser with a cute brunette on

his arm. Brooks even received an e-mail from his techno-
logically challenged mother, Olivia, who lived in London.
It was a nice surprise to hear from her, since she abhorred
computers and always called instead of e-mailing. She wrote
that she was coming into town next month, intending to
stay for the remainder of the summer and help Jess prepare
for her wedding. He loved his mother very much, and since
she hadn't been to Philly since Christmas, Brooks was especially looking forward to seeing her.

He wondered about Skye and her mother. Skye had shut
down so quickly when he asked about her—her entire
demeanor had changed from cheerful and open to tight-
lipped and moody. It was bound to be painful for her, being
abandoned by her mother at such an early age. *Like losing your father suddenly to illness*, he thought sadly. *We've
both experienced the visceral loss of a parent.* He wished she
would have talked about it more.

Somewhat consoled by the virtual interaction with his
close-knit family and feeling some compassion for Skye,
Brooks finally headed back to the *Zephyr* . . . to torture himself by sharing a bedroom with the only woman on earth
that he wanted, and absolutely, positively couldn't have.

Skye had lied when she told Brooks that she had some
work to do on the boat. She didn't. He'd tied down the
sails and hosed down the deck while *she* was showering,
and she'd reconfirmed tomorrow's course and checked the
weather while *he* was showering. All that remained was to
wash her face, change into her pajamas, and read a little
bit on her Kindle before bed. She was looking forward to
sleeping onboard the *Zephyr*—for the gentle rocking of the

boat and sound of lapping waves against the sides. In fact, if not for her ninth-hour falling out with Brooks at dinner, she'd be in heaven anticipating a night on the water.

But she wasn't in heaven. Her heart was hurting. And she felt guilty as hell.

Brooks had been enjoying their conversation, their banter, their dinner . . . and so had she. But after they'd discussed her mother, when Brooks had gotten up to leave, she'd outrightly lied to him about Pat.

It made her feel terrible because it wasn't kind and it wasn't honest, and Brooks deserved her kindness and honesty. Not to mention, whatever genuine feelings she had for *any* man right this minute belonged to Brooks, and regardless of the incompatible nature of their lives, she hated that he thought otherwise.

Changing into pink terry cloth short-shorts and a scoop neck, white T-shirt, she opened the door to the head, running water over her toothbrush and frowning at herself in the small vanity mirror.

Skye wasn't the most experienced woman in the world, but she could tell that Brooks liked her. She saw it in his eyes and in the way he spoke to her, the way he watched her and smiled at her and teased her. Everything had changed since that night at the benefit, and she'd bet her life that he liked her just as much as she liked him. And here they were, trapped together on this boat for the next seven days . . . with a storm of sexual tension swirling between them.

"What if the *Zephyr* was our own little alternative universe?" she queried her foamy reflection. "And we could just do whatever we wanted . . . whatever felt right . . . just while we were on the *Zephyr*? And then, when we got home, we could say good-bye to *Zephyrland* and go back to real life? What about that?"

Spitting out a gob of toothpaste, she ran the water sparingly, filling a cup and swilling the water around her mouth before looking back at herself.

It was a terrible idea, and part of her knew it, but the larger part of her—the part that had been infatuated with Brooks her whole life and finally had a real chance with him—didn't want to let these precious days slip through her fingers without making the sort of memories that would last her a lifetime. *Zephyrland*, unrealistic though it was, certainly had its merits.

She heard footsteps on the deck above her and placed her toothbrush hastily back into the cup on the sink and slipped back into the bedroom, jumping into bed, scooting under the covers, and turning off the light over her bed so that the cabin was dim from the soft light over his pillow only.

He entered the tiny room quietly, leaning over his bed and unzipping his duffel bag without saying a word.

"Brooks?" she said softly, leaning up on her elbows.

"Mmm?" he murmured with his back to her.

"Umm . . . can you look at me?"

Reluctantly, he turned to face her, his jaw hard in the soft shadows of the room. He tilted his chin up and put his hands on his hips, a sweat shirt dangling from his fingers. "What's up?"

She sat up in bed, the covers falling from her breasts and pooling in her lap. His eyes followed her movements intently, and her tummy fluttered.

"I wasn't honest with you before. About the texting. At dinner."

"You *weren't* texting Pat?"

"No. I-I was. But not the way you think."

He huffed softly, the sound of an unfunny laugh. "You don't know what I think, Skye."

He was upset with her, which somehow made it easier for her to continue, because she was upset with herself too—for wanting him in the first place, for being a coward about her feelings, for making him suffer just because it was safer than taking a chance.

She took a deep breath and released it, holding his eyes with hers. "He's not my boyfriend anymore. Pat and I broke up today."

He looked confused at first, but all of the hardness slipped from his face and his lips parted as her words sunk in. "Wait. What?"

She nodded, licking her lips nervously and pursing them together. "It's true. We broke up. I mean, well, I broke up with him. And he's not that happy about it, even though he doesn't have a right—"

"You broke up," repeated Brooks softly, his lips tilting up just slightly, his eyes tender and understanding as they gazed at her from a few feet away.

She nodded again. "Yeah. I just . . . um, I just wanted you to know the truth."

"Why?" he whispered, unmoving, still staring at her.

"Why did we break up?" she asked, her breath hitching from the low, focused sound of his voice.

"No." He shook his head back and forth slowly, his eyes searing and intense. "Why did you want *me* to know the truth?"

There were several ways she could answer.

The safe way? "Because we're friends, and I want to be honest with you." But it occurred to her that she'd be obscuring another truth—her feelings for him—even as she was espousing her honesty.

She could shrug and say, "I don't know. I just felt like telling you," but that felt like a cop-out.

And yet the honest answer, "I finally realized Pat was a jackass because I kept comparing him to you, and I want to explore what's going on between us, even if it's only in the safe confines of this little cruise because we both know we could never work out in real life" felt way too forward.

He was still staring at her, his face soft, his hands on his hips, his eyes skewering hers as he waited patiently.

"Because it matters," she finally whispered.

"Yes," he said, nodding, the hint of a grin curving his lips, "it does."

The air between them was so charged, she almost felt dizzy. Was he going to say anything else? Was he going to cross the room and kiss her? Was he going to—

"Get some sleep, skip," he said gently.

"Sleep?" she croaked.

He nodded at her, his perfect lips spreading into a full-blown, ovary-busting smile. Crossing the small cabin in two steps, he leaned down, and those warm, beautiful lips pressed softly against her forehead in a tender, lingering, good-night kiss.

"'Night, Skye," he said softly, his breath dusting across her skin. After a moment, he leaned back, but his eyes still caught hers in the dim light.

"Good night, Brooks," she said, snuggling back under the covers.

He stood staring down at her for one hungry moment before turning and leaving the room. A few seconds later, she heard the Meghan Trainor song, "What If I?" fill the quiet of the *Zephyr,* filtering softly into her cabin from the salon.

He downloaded it after dinner, she thought, her heart clenching with tenderness, her stomach buzzing with a strong current of affection for him. She couldn't stop the smile from widening across her face as Meghan asked achingly, *What if I-I-I-I. . . . I want to kiss you to-morrow?*

Skye took a deep breath, crossed her fingers and closed her weary eyes.

Chapter 12

Popping the cap off a bottle of beer, Brooks sat down at the table in the salon and listened to Meghan Trainor croon the words to his new favorite song.

Had it crossed Brooks' mind to do more than kiss her forehead? Hell, yes. It had occurred to Brooks to tell her to move over and make out with her until dawn.

But even if she had issued an invitation to join her in bed, which she hadn't, he wasn't that much of a jerk. She'd just broken up with her boyfriend a few hours before. As much as he longed to reach for her, he was going to need a little more permission than just the information that she and Pat had broken up. Not to mention, he'd promised not to touch her. In fact, his exact words had been, *I won't lay a hand on you ever again.* He hadn't made a caveat about her single or dating status. He'd promised *never*, and until Skye indicated that his promise was no longer needed, he was determined to honor it . . . no matter how much it hurt.

And damn, it sure did hurt.

If her goal was to ensure that he got a decent night's sleep by assigning him a larger bed, sharing a cabin with her had done exactly the opposite. While she'd fallen asleep fairly quickly to the sweet lullaby of "What If I?" two hours later, Brooks' body was painfully aware that she was so close—warm, soft, and pliant under the soft duvet, her head not even ten feet from his—and her deep breaths and soft, little sleeping noises more distracting than the obnoxious music three or four boats down that didn't quit until midnight.

Finally, lying on his side and staring at the loveliness of her sleeping face, Brooks had eventually dozed off around two in the morning, and six had come too quickly. However, he had to admit that the trio of smells—coffee, eggs, and sautéed vegetables—to which he woke up made it slightly easier. Well, the smells, and the sweet, blue-eyed face that peeked around the door to see if he was awake.

"Morning!" she chirped with a smile. "You're up!"

"Mmm," he groaned, blinking at her groggily. "Do I smell coffee?"

"Uh-huh. And an egg white omelet with sautéed peppers and onions," she said cheerfully.

His Skye was apparently a morning person. Hmmm.

Whoa. Wait. What? His Skye? *His?*

He sat up quickly and frowned, shaking his head and glancing up at her. She looked beautiful in a white polo shirt and shorts. Damn.

"That sounds good," he said, his face softening as his eyes skimmed her body.

"It's your favorite," she said. "Veggies and egg whites, right?"

He couldn't hold back the smile that started small but widened as she stood there looking wide awake and pretty and young with two blonde braids falling over her shoulders. She'd made his favorite breakfast, and it caused his treacherous heart to thud with emotion. God, he couldn't even remember the last time someone who wasn't his family had done something so thoughtful for him.

"It is," he said in a raspy voice. "That was nice."

She blushed, her eyes dropping to his bare chest, where they lingered for a long moment. When she raised them again, they were dark and wide, and she wet her lips. "We have to be in Virginia Beach by ten, but I'll, um, I'll give you a minute to get up, okay?"

Get up? Parts of him were already up. And if she kept flicking her dark-blue eyes to his chest, he was going to need more than a minute, unless it was a minute in a freezing-cold shower.

"Mm-hm," he mumbled.

She turned back to the door, and Brooks had a perfect view of her pert, little ass in denim cut-offs. *Okay, then. A cold shower it is.*

She turned around suddenly, catching him ogling her backside, and her eyes widened again as she shook her head and giggled softly in surprise.

"We're, um, we're casting off in, um, thirty minutes," she finished quickly, nodding nervously and whipping around to rush back through the door to the safety of the galley.

"Skye!" he called after her.

Her face peeked back into the room, cheeks still flushed.

"You can't blame me for looking," he said in a teasing voice.

She all but nailed him with an unexpectedly sassy grin. "I don't."

Brooks slid back down under the covers and groaned.

Brooks and Skye stood side by side on the deck of the *Zephyr* posing for Guy Hunter, who looked at them from the dock below as he snapped pictures.

"So Brooks," he said with his usual innuendo, "is Skye a good . . . crew?"

Brooks' lip curled up for just a moment before he looked down at Skye's blonde head beside his shoulder. "She is. But I only know that because I've sailed with her before. On this cruise, she's my . . . that is, she's in charge. She's skipper."

"Oh-ho! In charge, huh? That how you like 'em, Brooks?" asked Guy, winking at Skye.

"Do I like them careful with my boat? Capable and smart? Sure, Guy. What's not to like?"

"How about you, Skye? Brooks showing you any tricks of the trade?"

Skye looked up at Brooks, her eyes flaring with discomfort before cutting them to Guy. "I'm honored to sail with someone as talented as Brooks."

Guy lowered his camera and put his hands on his hips, taking a deep breath then letting it out with a long-suffering groan. He shook his head, staring at the wood planking under his feet before looking back up again. "Can I be honest with you two?"

Brooks scoffed. "I doubt it."

"Very funny," said Guy, looking genuinely annoyed. "I'm really trying here, but . . ."

"Trying *what* exactly?" asked Brooks derisively.

"Trying to get a decent story," said Guy. "But you two are stonewalling me every fucking step of the way."

"Watch your mouth," said Brooks, gesturing to Skye with his chin.

"Sorry," said Guy to Skye in a surly voice.

"Stonewalling you?" asked Skye. "What does that mean?"

"No one cares if you're great sailors. No one wants to hear about your great sailing times or what you think of this boat. This is *Celeb!*, kids. Our readers want a love story. An average girl from a second-rate marina falls head-over-heels for an elusive, ex-Olympian millionaire, and guess what? He falls for her, *too*! And then they sail off into the sunset and have a dozen little, blond sailor babies. That's the story. That's the *only* story I'm selling, whether it actually happens that way or not."

Skye flinched beside him when Guy called her family business "second rate," and Brooks took a step closer to her, putting his arm around her shoulders.

"Sorenson Marina's *first* rate," said Brooks tersely. "It's the best on the Chesapeake, and I'll help Jack and Skye sue you for libel if you print otherwise, Guy."

So it didn't matter what the truth was, huh? They just wanted to sell magazines about an ex-Olympian falling in love. Well hell, doing a favor for his sister was one thing, but he didn't agree to whoring out his personal li—

He froze.

His breath caught.

And suddenly every thought in his head fled, because Skye's fingers slid down his arm slowly, clasped his palm to hers, and laced their fingers together. Eyes wide, he gazed down at her, and she tilted her head up to look at him, her sweet lips offering a small smile as she mouthed the words, *Thank you.*

"Let's just finish up, huh?" she said, looking back over at Guy, who was snapping furiously while they held hands.

"Sure, sure," said Guy. "How about a kiss and then I'll get out of your hair?"

Skye looked back up at Brooks, rolling her eyes before shrugging good-naturedly. She tilted her head back, and he leaned down, aiming for her cheek, but at the last minute Guy called her name and she shifted her head just slightly . . . so that Brooks' lips dropped flush on hers.

Her fingers, which were already wound through his, tightened, and he increased the pressure of his lips on hers, taking a step closer to her.

"That's the way, lovebirds!" exclaimed Guy, and Skye jerked back from Brooks, her fingers wiggling furiously to untangle from Brooks'.

Brooks looked down at her face, his eyebrows furrowing together as he took in her heaving breasts and flushed cheeks. Jesus. She was angry, but aroused, and she'd never looked so sexy. It almost made it worthwhile that they'd just inadvertently given Guy exactly what he wanted.

Brooks flashed his eyes at Guy. "Show's over."

"Oh, I can take a hint! You two want to be alone, huh?" Guy let his camera drop to his chest and grinned at Skye. "I can't wait for Hatteras."

He was halfway back down the dock before Brooks turned to Skye. "I'm sorry, Skye. I didn't mean to—"

Her eyes were still on Guy's retreating form, but she cut them to Brooks. "It's not your fault. I . . . he said my name and I turned my head."

"I'm sure he did it on purpose."

"He's just he smarmiest lowlife," she said, pulling up the buoys as if the faster they could cast off, the faster they could leave Guy's air space. "And this was just a big set-up. That kiss is probably all over the Internet right now!"

Brooks reached out and put his hand on her arm, stopping her. "Skye."

"What?" she snapped, then huffed out an exhaled breath, her face softening a little. "What?"

"I'm sorry I got you into this, skip. I didn't know it was rigged."

She put her hands on her hips. "You didn't force me to do anything, Brooks. I agreed to come along."

"I'm still sorry . . . and I'm . . . I promised I wouldn't touch you and—"

"Brooks . . ." she started, searching his eyes.

"It just seemed like the easiest way to get rid of Guy."

"Brooks . . ."

"But next time I'll tell him to go to hell. I promised not to touch you and—"

"Don't."

"Don't?"

Her cheeks flared red. "I didn't mind."

His heart, his stupid heart that was going to get him into a world of trouble, fluttered as he took a step closer to her. "You didn't?"

She shook her head, grinning at him. "No . . . and I'm voiding your promise for as long as we're in *Zephyrland*."

"*Zephyrland*?" He smiled down at her, dropping his hands to her hips and pulling her up against his chest.

Her hands slid up his shirt, feathering over his abs, gliding over his pecs, winding around his neck. "Mm-hm. *Zephyrland*. And you know what they say about *Zephyrland*?" she asked him with a slow, sexy smile.

He shook his head, dizzy from the way she was looking at him, but never, ever wanting to look away. "I have no idea."

"What happens in *Zephyrland* stays in *Zephyrland*."

If there was a more awesome combination of words in the entire world, Brooks didn't know what they were. Because his primary fear of getting involved with someone like Skye was that he'd end up hurting her . . . but if he understood her right, she was basically saying that she welcomed his attentions for as long as they sailed the *Zephyr* together.

It'll have to be enough, he told himself, ignoring his strong and sudden desire to stay on the *Zephyr* forever.

He looked down at her lovely, upturned face, his eyes flicking to the dimple in her cheek before capturing her eyes. "Are you sure? You want to . . . *be together* this week?"

"Mm-hm," she murmured. "In fact, right this minute? I want you to kiss me. And then we're going to cast off and sail hard for twelve to sixteen hours. And when we're done, I'm sort of hoping you'll kiss me again."

"Aye, aye, skip," he said, dropping his lips to hers.

The previous two times he'd kissed her—once in the moonlight and once five minutes ago at Guy's goading—he hadn't been able to turn himself over to the sensation of kissing her. Not entirely. The first time, he was kissing a woman who wasn't available. The second time—as short and sweet as it was—had been taken without permission.

This time, she was his . . . temporarily, yes, but *his*.

This time, he savored her.

The fingers around his neck tightened against his skin, her palms pushing his head toward her, locking her lips with his. They were soft and warm, sun-kissed and ripe, and he nipped them, sucked them, finally parting them with his tongue and groaning softly as he invaded the hot slick of her mouth. She arched against him, her breasts pushing into his chest as her tongue tangled with his, soft whimpering noises from deep in her throat reminding him of her sleeping noises, and reassuring him that in twelve to sixteen hours, they'd be back in their bedroom together again.

It was hell letting her go, but the day was wasting, and the sooner they started, the faster they'd make Hatteras. He ran his hands under her shirt, up the warm, soft skin of her back, flattening his palms just under her bra and dropping his forehead to her shoulder.

"I could kiss you all day, Skye."

She laughed softly beside his ear, then sighed. "Think of me as a carrot."

He leaned back, grinning at her. "And I suppose that makes me a horse?"

She nodded, her eyes twinkling and happy. "Yes, Brooks. You're the horse. I'm the carrot. Now, let's sail."

After nine hours without speaking—other than for whatever words were necessary to help the cutter achieve maximum speed—they were making good time, and evening on the North Carolina coast with waning sun and blue skies was a beautiful thing to behold. Turning into the Pamlico Sound, they left the rough waters of the Atlantic behind. They'd be sailing the rest of the way to Hatteras in the picturesque and protected body of water, and though they still had several hours of sailing ahead, the toughest part of today's journey was over.

"What're you thinking, skip?" asked Brooks, looking at the sky, which was still fairly light, and at his watch, which she suspected read about eight o'clock. "Another four hours?"

She sighed, nodding. Her whole body ached from standing behind the wheel, and she longed to call it a day, but Brooks had reserved them an overnight slip at Hatteras Landing, which meant he'd planned to make it there by the end of today. And if he could do it, she could do it. Not to mention, if they docked there tonight, they'd have the whole day "off" tomorrow, meeting Guy for their photo session early on Wednesday morning before setting sail for the three-day trip to Myrtle Beach. And right now? A day off sounded perfect.

"This is a long day," said Brooks, looking at her with concern. "Ridiculously long. I should have . . . We could stop, you know. I'm sure we could find a marina with a slip open for the night. Or we could drop anchor. Lots of quiet coves in the Pamlico."

"If we make it to Hatteras," she said wearily but with conviction, "we have a slip waiting."

"True."

"And a day off tomorrow," she added.

"Right again."

"Which means sleeping in."

He raised his eyebrows, giving her a look. After this morning's knee-weakening kiss, they hadn't revisited sleeping arrangements, but by the time they reached Hatteras, Skye knew they'd both be too exhausted for anything but falling into bed. Fully dressed. And falling asleep before their heads hit the pillow. By that time, they'd have been sailing for eighteen hours, with the only break this morning with Guy. *Tomorrow, however . . .*

Brooks gave her a side glance, the hopeful look in his eyes telling her his mind was in the same gutter as hers. "And what *else* are you planning to do with your free day tomorrow?"

She forced herself not to grin and deadpanned, "Oh, I don't know. Gas up. Change the oil. Check out the electrical board."

"Skye," he growled.

She shrugged, giving him a sassy look. "Maybe fool around a little."

"Good answer." He beamed at her. "And go out to dinner with me?"

"Mm-hm," she agreed, laughing softly despite her fatigue. "That sounds nice."

For two straight days they'd worked, slept, and eaten together. Today, they'd been up at the crack of dawn with fourteen hours behind them, and yet neither was itching for a break from the other. She was teasing him, and he was teasing her right back. And it felt miraculous in its own small way to *tolerate* someone in such close quarters. To want them all the more was . . . was what? What was it? What was the name for working together, for wanting each other, for teasing each other, for enjoying each other so much that there simply weren't enough hours in the day?

She sighed, the question heavy in her mind and making her heart thunder in her chest because she felt like she was standing on the very tip of an iceberg, and underneath the water was something huge and strong and beautiful . . . but intimidating and dangerous, too. Did she want it? Did she—

"You don't mind night sailing?"

She shook her head, surprised by his words, but grateful that they interrupted her thoughts. "I don't mind. Plus . . . I've got you if I get in trouble."

"You've got me," he murmured, his eyes brightening as he smiled at her in that tender way that was becoming so addictive to her. "You trust me, huh?"

"You *did* almost win the Olympics," she reminded him.

"Yes, I did. Almost."

"Did you love it?"

He nodded. "Parts of it, yeah. It was a great experience, and it gave me some amazing opportunities."

"Why do I sense a 'but?'"

"It took up a lot of my life, a lot of my time," he said thoughtfully. "And time isn't . . . infinite."

"Do you feel like you missed out on something?"

He shrugged. "I trained hard for years. Then the Olympics. The endorsements, travel, coaching and consulting, judging and reporting. Sometimes I feel like I haven't stood still in years."

She grinned, her eyes trailing slowly from his Top-Siders to his face. "You're standing still now."

"Keep looking at me like that, Skye, and I'm not going to wait until Hatteras to eat the carrot."

She chuckled, feeling light, feeling sexy, feeling happy. "You have your *whole life* to stand still! I think it's exciting how much you've accomplished. I can't wait to see what's next."

He stared at her hard for a moment before cutting his eyes away, looking up at the sails, which were full. "You mind if I have a beer, skip?"

Was it her imagination, or had his voice dipped a little? And she looked closer at him; even though his face was partially turned away, his smile was gone.

"Sure," she said.

"You want one?" he muttered, heading below, not looking back.

"No, thanks. Need to stay sharp."

She expected him to tease her or snicker at her overly cautious comment, but he didn't. When he came back up the stairs a few minutes later, he wasn't holding a beer, and for a second, she thought he'd changed his mind.

He didn't say anything as he caught her eyes, stepping behind her at the wheel without a word and letting his hands drop to her shoulders. His thumbs dug into her muscles—a mix of strength and tenderness, his fingers clenching and unclenching the soreness there, and she smelled it on his breath, the beer he must have quickly chugged downstairs.

Her eyes fluttered closed for a moment because her muscles were screaming for attention and the strong pressure of his hands felt like heaven. She whimpered softly for more.

"Am I hurting you?" he breathed into her ear.

"Nuh-uh. More." She sighed.

He chuckled lightly, his breath warm by the back of her ear. "You're tight."

"I'm the skipper," said Skye, trying not to moan. "And this boat cost a quarter million dollars."

"So did I," murmured Brooks, his lips landing on the back of her neck as she let her chin fall to her chest.

"You were worth it," she said.

"Just so you know," he said, his lips stroking her skin with every word, like he was hungry for her, like she filled some need inside of him, "I would have paid double to guarantee that you won."

"Brooks," she moaned as his hands smoothed down her arms, his fingers taking the wheel.

"Turn around," he said in a gravelly demand.

She did. She turned her back to the open water and pivoted in the tight space between Brooks and the wheel, her breasts rubbing against his chest until they were flush against him, her eyes looking into his.

His green eyes were dark and extremely intense, and every shallow breath he took made his chest slam into hers. Her heart thundered in her ears as the evidence of his arousal pushed into the softness of her belly.

"Kiss me," he said softly, and then added with desperation, "*Please*."

She leaned up on tiptoes, and he bent his head, his lips capturing hers fiercely. He sucked in a breath through his nose as she slid her hands up his chest, her fingers curling into the fabric of his shirt. He couldn't drop the wheel and touch her with his hands, but his lips, his tongue, his mouth—they claimed her, possessed her, caressed her, and owned her. It was filthy and glorious, hot and demanding. He explored the secret recesses of her mouth, growling his pleasure, then bent his elbows just enough to pull her closer, groaning when she leaned into him. She was trapped willingly, surrendering to him in a way that felt wholly organic and ridiculously right. Her history was instantly rewritten, because she thought she'd been kissed before, but she was wrong. She'd *never* been kissed like this, like life was a fleeting thing that must be enjoyed today, and the fate of everything that mattered rested on his mouth and his kiss and his strong arms around her.

His tongue grew gentle over time, sliding tenderly, hypnotically against hers. He sucked gently before drawing back and letting her lips go.

Skye's forehead dropped to his chest and she panted, the rest of her body rebelling, unhappy to be deprived of him. She was breathless and boneless as she opened her eyes slowly and tilted her head back to look up at him hungrily. Her eyes focused on his face, on the beauty of Brooks Winslow staring down at her.

And then she saw it:

Agony.

Remorse.

Sorrow.

It crossed his face like a curse, and she reached up her hand to cup his cheek, to offer him some sort of reassurance, though she didn't know his tormentor.

He released the wheel and stepped back from her, dropping her eyes. "Wind's changed. Back to work."

Chapter 13

For the remaining four hours on the Pamlico, Brooks trimmed sails that didn't need to be trimmed, cleated off lines that were already secured, and checked the radio and radar for notices that were nonexistent on such a calm night. In short, he kept as busy as possible.

When she'd said, *You have your whole life to stand still!* he'd almost choked from the sudden grief—the intense and terrible doubt that had ripped through him.

My whole life? Of what? Five more years?

He'd gone below, opened a beer, opened his throat, and let the suds slide down in ten seconds flat, the tormenting questions as loud as ever in his head: *What if I have whatever my father had? What if I let myself fall in love with Skye . . . only to leave her alone and bereft a few years from now?*

Fall in love with Skye.

Oh, God.

Fall in love.

Was he falling in love with her?

He wasn't sure because he'd never been in love before, but the feelings he had for Skye were multiplying like crazy, their friendship a cherished foundation of affection that was suddenly changing into something deeper, something dearer, something that was going to be hard to give up.

He'd launched himself back up onto the deck, desperate to touch her, to lose some of his fear and sorrow in her warmth. He'd kissed her blindly, his need for her profound, and a feeling had rushed through him as she fisted his shirt and kissed him back—a feeling so sure and so strong, it had terrified him almost as much as his fear of mortality. He'd liked and respected Skye for most of his life . . . but now? Now "like" and "respect" were morphing, changing, and growing . . . not from, but *into*. He wasn't losing them, he was deepening them, and if he wasn't careful, they *would* turn into love.

She was smart and kind, capable and fun. He was attracted to her like crazy, and grateful for her, and amazed by her. He loved the way she sailed, the way she handled his boat, the way the wind and the water were in her blood just as surely as they were in his. She was gentle and quietly ambitious, playful and fair. And yes, their lifestyles were different, but not their hearts, not in essentials, not in what mattered. And if he could have a guarantee that his life wouldn't suddenly be cut short? Oh God, he'd pursue her relentlessly. He'd wait for her. He'd change for her. He'd give up anything for her. Just to be with her. Just to sail with her. Just to hold her and kiss her and sleep beside her. Just for the honor of loving her.

Zephyrland.

He wound the line in his hands tighter, then cleated it again with a grimace.

Zephyrland.

What had once sounded so sweet now tasted sour.

He took a deep breath and released it slowly, looking up at the darkening sky. He was falling in love with her. Like a fool, he wanted forever, when all he could have was today.

They had *literally* fallen into bed last night. Their own beds. Separately, not together.

Brooks had radioed ahead to the marina for their slip number, and they'd motored into the harbor at the Hatteras Breeze Marina in the dark, parked at the wrong deck, belatedly realized it, started up the motor again, and putputted to the correct dock on fumes. Brooks had tied the bowline to the dock cleat and locked the deck hatch. By the time he entered their bedroom, Skye was already asleep.

She was lying on top of her comforter, as though she'd fallen there and the effort to actually maneuver herself under the covers was way too much work to contemplate. Her salt-flecked shoes were still on her feet, and he checked her silver anklet, reaching out a finger to touch it gingerly.

As gently as possible, taking pains not to wake her, he untied and pulled off her shoes, first one, then the other, setting them down softly beside her bed. He turned down the comforter as best he could, then scooped her body into his arms, bending to catch the corner of the duvet with two fingers and flick it farther down her bed. She moaned softly against his neck, her breath sweet and warm as he placed her on the white sheets, then drew the comforter up to her chin and turned off the light over her head.

She inhaled deeply.

"Brooks," she said softly on a sigh, her voice sleepy and deep as she burrowed her head into her pillow. "Sleep."

He caught his bottom lip between his teeth, gazing at her, wondering if her words were an invitation for him to join her. But he took a step back. As much as he'd like to wake up holding Skye in his arms, they were both exhausted and they needed sleep. And Brooks was fairly certain that if he had trouble sleeping in the same room last night, sleeping beside her would be next to impossible.

He shucked off his shoes and pulled down his jeans, trying to remember the last time he'd slept beside a woman he cared for. In college? No. At the Olympics. He'd had a girlfriend on Team USA, and though he'd felt strongly for Margo, they hadn't quite progressed to a point of love before breaking up a few months later. They were young and having fun during an extremely exciting time. But once they returned to America, Brooks with a bronze medal and Margo with none, their romance had quickly fizzled.

He pulled his shirt off, tossing it onto the pile on the floor, and slipped into bed, turning off the light over his head and letting his eyes adjust to the darkness. No, what he'd had with Margo had been fun, but it hadn't been love. He knew that now.

Turning to his side, he rested his head on his pillow, and his eyes landed on Skye as he drifted off to sleep.

Pain. Achy, terrible, muscle-cramping pain.

Ugh.

She'd definitely overdone it yesterday.

Skye took a deep breath and sat up carefully, every muscle rebelling as her eyes opened to the half-light of dawn filtering in through one partially open porthole. Hmm. Her hair was still in braids and she was completely dressed, but she didn't remember going to bed, and she certainly didn't remember getting under the covers. It must have been Brooks who'd tucked her in, and the thought made her warm inside, made her happy.

Darting a quick glance at him, her lips spread into a grin. He was sleeping on his chest, his neck turned to face her, and the sheet had shimmied down just enough to show her the upper half of his smooth, tan back. The bulge of his bicep caught her eyes for a second, and she took a deep breath, all aches slipping away momentarily as she stared at him.

What had happened yesterday, she wondered. After they kissed? Why had she seen such pain, such torment, in his eyes? And what could she do to help him? It hurt her deeply to think that Brooks was waging some formidable internal struggle, but it wasn't the first time in her friendship with him that she'd wondered about his seeming lack of intimacy with anyone other than his family. And she certainly noted—for most of their lifelong friendship—that Brooks wore a mantle of heaviness, especially when he thought no one was looking.

She thought about his history, and one blaring fact kept circling in her mind: his father had died when Brooks was very young, and following his death, Brooks had essentially engineered his whole life around proving he was the best sailor in the world; almost as a memorial to his dad, as a way to feel connected to him after he was gone.

If a measure of loss can be made by how the left-behind live the rest of their lives, then Brooks' grief must have been stark and profound. His father loved sailing, so Brooks became the best in the world. He also became—as far as Skye could tell—a surrogate parent to his four younger siblings. Her mind circled back to their conversation on Sunday, and it occurred to her that he'd cut off their conversation when she asked how Mr. Winslow had passed away. She did the math in her mind. Brooks was seventeen when he died, and Skye remembered Mr. Winslow looking young and energetic—young by anyone's standards. Had he been sick? Skye searched her memories. She didn't remember Mr. Winslow looking sick.

So how had he died?

And was his father the key to Brooks' sorrow?

And what about his revolving door of girlfriends?

Was she the next girl—indeed, the *current* girl—taking a spin in the revolving door?

It hurt Skye much more than she would have guessed, having engineered *Zephyrland* herself, to imagine that she and Brooks would shake hands and go back to a conventional friendship on Sunday. And for the first time since embarking on this whole auction-cruise journey with him several weeks ago, she had her first pinch of regret.

What she knew (and Brooks didn't) was that *Zephyrland* was a myth, an impossibility, a palatable lie that enabled what she wanted from him: intimacy.

What she knew (and Brooks didn't) was that what happened in *Zephyrland* would stay in her heart, and their friendship, she mused sadly, would likely pay the price.

What she knew (and Brooks didn't) was that she had been a little bit in love with him all her life, so the journey from friendship to love had been short for Skye. In fact, she was fairly certain she was already there.

Taking a deep breath, she closed her eyes, her weary body forcing her brain to shut down as she fell fitfully back to sleep.

"Wake up, sleepyhead." A gentle hand smoothing wisps of hair off her forehead. "Hey, Sleeping Beauty, time to wake up."

"Not ready," she complained, flipping over to her stomach, but laying her cheek on her pillow so she could peek up at him.

Freshly shaved and showered Brooks sat down on the edge of Skye's bed, moving a cup of steaming, hot coffee closer to her. Her eyebrows shot up and her frown disappeared.

"Mmmm. Coffee. What time's it?"

"Eleven, lazybones."

Her eyes fluttered open. "Why do I get the feeling you're a pro at this waking-up-sleeping-people-who-don't-want-to-be-woken-up thing?"

"Try getting four siblings up and ready for school before seven thirty every morning," he said, chuckling softly. "Pres hated it when I called him 'Sleeping Beauty.' I have to admit, you wear it better than he did."

She snickered softly, then moaned as she sat up, wincing from the effort, her muscles spent and angry.

"I hurt," she said, accepting the coffee from him and taking a sip.

"And here I thought you were a morning person," he said holding out two Advil in his palm.

She took the pills and swallowed them. "I am . . . generally."

"You sailed for eighteen hours yesterday, Skye," he reminded her. "You're bound to hurt."

"How come you look so bright-eyed and bushy-tailed?"

He shrugged. "Hot shower did wonders. Spending today with you was quite a carrot."

She gave him a look over the rim of her cup.

"I don't know. I guess I sail more so I don't hurt as much. I've done so many eighteen-hour sails in my life, I couldn't count them on both hands and both feet. Once, we went two whole days awake while circumnavigating Australia."

Skye's lips parted, her eyes transfixed on Brooks'. "I had no idea you did that!"

"Sure. The year before the Olympics, we were granted fifteen-month visas to train down under. It was . . . phenomenal."

"I bet." She sipped her coffee, the caffeine doing its job. "I think I'm a little jealous of your experiences."

He furrowed his brows. "Why? I mean, you're an amazing crew *and* a crackerjack skip. You don't have to be jealous. Why aren't you racing more?"

She rolled her eyes and sighed. "I don't have a boat. I have a job. My Pop needs me."

"Seems to me Jack wouldn't stand in your way if you had a dream to follow."

"I guess he wouldn't. But my grandparents are gone and my mo—" She paused, looking down. "He'd be all alone."

"So you're just going to stay at the marina replacing light-bulbs and cutting seaweed out of outboard motors forever?"

Skye didn't take offense easily, but Brooks' comment ruffled her feathers. "Maybe."

"Well, I think that's a shame. You have your whole life ahead of you," he said softly. "If I . . ."

His voice suddenly cut off and he sighed heavily, looking away from her and standing up.

"If you what?" she asked, leaning forward.

"Nothing," he whispered. "I just think you should do what you want. And I mean, if you want to race? I'll race with you. I won't buy you a boat . . . I already have three. You choose one to race. Just give me the date and time of the regatta, and I'll be there. I mean . . . if I can."

There it was again—that sadness, that hopelessness—behind his eyes.

"Why do you get so sad sometimes?" she blurted out. "What happened?"

He stared at her, gradually forcing his features to shift from sad to neutral and finally offering her a small smile. "I'm not sad. Not right now."

Skye sighed, taking another sip of coffee. He wasn't ready to confide in her yet. Okay. She could wait.

"Hey," he said, cocking his head to the side and grinning at her. "There are some great little shops and restaurants at

this marina. It's three times as big as the one in Gloucester. How about you take a really hot shower and we'll go get
some food?"

"Sounds good," she said, matching his smile.

He leaned forward and kissed her lips quickly, then drew
back and winked before leaving the room and closing the
door behind him. Her smile faded as she stared at the door,
wondering yet again what was hurting Brooks, determined
to get to the bottom of it the moment he let her in.

They feasted on tacos and cold Coronas at a Mexican place,
and Skye made his blood race when she pushed the lime
into the bottle, covered the top with her thumb, flipped it
upside down, then sucked her thumb into her mouth before
taking a long swig of beer. Damn, she was just naturally,
effortlessly sexy.

It pissed him off a little that he'd been blind to it for so
long.

It made him grateful that his eyes had finally been opened.

It tortured him that he couldn't have her for longer than
this week.

Visiting several hokey, but cheerful, little shops, he
bought her a silver bracelet with tiny seashells, slipping it
into his pocket before she turned his way. He didn't know
when he'd give it to her, but something about it reminded
him of the anklet she wore, and he wanted to give her something to remind her of *Zephyrland* and of him when both
were just memories.

As the late-afternoon sun warmed their skin, they strolled
the maze of docks hand-in-hand, checking out the boats
with keen eyes and talking in depth about which features
they liked and didn't like, building the perfect boat during

the course of conversation. When they finally found it—a sleek, monohulled yacht moored at the end of the eighth dock they strolled upon—they laughed and high fived.

"It does exist!" exclaimed Brooks, pulling Skye into his arms for a deep, lingering kiss that made his whole body harden.

She locked her eyes with his as he drew away, and whispered, "I love this."

"Me too," he breathed, drinking in the sight of her open, upturned face and dropping his lips to hers again.

She was limp and breathless when he finished kissing her, her body leaning into his, her breathing deliberate and ragged.

"Let's go back to the *Zephyr*," she said.

"Mm-hm," he agreed, his voice as low with desire. "Good idea."

He took her hand again, entwining his fingers with hers and smiling down at her lovely face before turning them back toward dock three.

For the next few hours, he wasn't going to think about his health or his future, he was just going to live in the moment. If she'd let him, he'd kiss every inch of her body. He was going to let himself sink into the feeling of being with someone he cared for. He was going to enjoy every second of *Zephyrland*, and nothing—no, *nothing*—was going to get in his way.

"Brooks!"

As they ambled hand in hand toward the *Zephyr*, Brooks heard his little sister's familiar voice, and his head snapped up to find Jessica and Alex standing on deck, his sister's smile brilliant as her eyes slipped to his hand holding Skye's.

"Jess? What the heck are you doing here?"

Skye tried to wiggle her hand away as they approached, but Brooks wasn't having it. If he was going to be temporarily deprived of her body, he certainly wasn't going to let go of her hand. He tightened his grip to tell her he was comfortable with their new status, and she relaxed.

"We came for dinner! Alex had business in Raleigh this morning and we thought . . . why not check on Brooks and Skye? So, we rented a helicopter for the day and here we are!" Jessica jumped off the deck onto the dock and nodded approvingly, her victorious smile beyond annoying. "You two look . . . *happy*."

"Who are you? Guy Hunter's new helper?"

Jessica giggled, leaning up to kiss her brother's cheek, then Skye's.

Brooks flicked a glance to Alex English, who stood on the *Zephyr*'s deck with a "Sorry, Man" wince on his face. Alex, who'd once been a notorious playboy before curbing his ways for Jessica, recognized an interrupted tryst when he saw one. Hell, Brooks doubted his face could look more unwelcoming, but damn it, he and Skye were about to spend the afternoon and evening making out. The last thing he wanted to do was visit with his sister and her fiancé. Did that make him an asshole?

"Jessie," said Alex gently, swinging under the deck railing and landing smoothly on the wood planks to join Jessica. "Maybe we should have called."

"Nonsense!" said Jessica, still grinning at her brother. She shifted her eyes to Skye. "How's he treating you, Skye?"

Brooks looked down at Skye's flushed face. "F-Fine. Thanks."

"Glad to hear it! Alex and I thought we'd take you two out to dinner tonight."

Conceding defeat, Brooks sighed. He and Skye were going to have to wait . . . but after dinner? He'd throw Jess in the harbor if she tried to cock-block him again. And that was a promise.

"You like her," said Jessica, nudging her oldest brother in the hip as she and Brooks stood outside the restaurant after dinner. Skye was using the ladies' room, and Alex had gone next door to get Jessica a soft-serve vanilla ice cream cone. Aside from the fact that Brooks was literally aching to be alone with Skye, it had been a perfectly enjoyable dinner. "A lot. More than I've ever seen you like someone."

"It's no good, Jess," he said softly.

"What? Why not? She's nice. She's fun. She loves sailing. Don't mess this up! She's *good* for you, Brooks."

"But I'm not good for her."

"What do you mean? You're one of the best men I know," said Jessica, placing her hand on Brooks' arm and forcing him to face her. "Why won't you let yourself be happy?"

"Jess, Dad died when I was seventeen. Why? Why did he drop dead? There was nothing wrong with him. I've talked to Mom. His heart attack came out of nowhere."

Jessica grimaced. "But we have regular screenings. We just went to Dr. Dryer. All five of us."

"And Dad went to Dr. Fiorello. Just before it happened."

"So what are you saying?"

"I'll be forty in five years."

"Brooks!" exclaimed Jessica, her eyes widening in disbelief. "You can't be serious."

"As a heart attack," he murmured, holding his little sister's eyes.

She flinched, her fingers grasping his forearm tightly. "No! You're young and healthy. You have decades of life ahead."

"Do I?" he asked, an edge in his voice. "I bet Dad thought the same thing."

"I can't believe this. Are you . . . *serious*? You honestly believe you're going to drop dead of a heart attack in the next five years?"

"I don't know. But you don't remember like I do, Jess. I saw what Dad left behind, and I'm not doing that to someone else."

"Brooks, no." She sighed, tears brightening her eyes. "You break my heart."

He pulled her into his arms, rubbing her back as he had when she was a little girl with a skinned knee. "Can't you see? I don't *want* to hurt anyone. I don't want to leave behind a wife and kids. I—"

"The only one you're hurting is yourself," she whispered sharply.

"Wow, you two are being super emo," said Alex from behind Brooks. "Everything okay?"

Jessica sniffled, then nodded, wiping her eyes with the back of her hand. "Yeah."

"Hey," said Alex, handing her the ice cream and cupping her cheek with his hand. His worried eyes scanned her face. "You're crying. What's going on, Jess? Are you okay?"

"I just . . . yeah," she said, managing a smile. "Brooks just told me something sad. Family stuff."

Alex put his arm around Jess and drew her against his side as she balefully licked her ice cream. He looked up at Brooks, sour-faced. "Quit upsetting my fiancée, huh?"

And Brooks had to admit it, for just a second, he was jealous of Alex English standing there so strong and healthy, his arm around the woman he loved, the woman he was going to marry and have babies with and grow old beside.

"Ready to go?" asked Skye, exiting from the restaurant, a cheerful smile lighting up her pretty face.

Brooks turned to her, basking in her presence, determined to enjoy what little time he had left with her this week and not let his fears take that away from him, too. "Yeah."

"Good night," said Skye, smiling at Alex and Jessica. "Thanks for dinner."

Jessica's sad eyes lingered on Brooks' face for an extra second before she looked at Skye and nodded. She looked a little dazed, like she was deep in thought and surprised to find Skye suddenly in front of her. "Oh, our pleasure. Thanks for . . ."

". . . for letting us barge in on your cruise," said Alex quickly, slapping Brooks on the back with a wink. "Come on, Jess. Chopper's ready and waiting to take us back to Raleigh."

Brooks nodded at his future brother-in-law gratefully, kissed Jessica quickly, then grabbed Skye's hand, walking back toward dock three.

"That was fun. Jess and Alex are great," said Skye.

"They are," said Brooks, trying desperately to push his conversation with Jessica to the back of his mind and stay in the moment. He squeezed Skye's fingers tighter as they approached the *Zephyr*, walking quietly and a little more slowly, until they stood on the dock beside the bobbing cutter.

Brooks looked down at Skye, his free hand cupping her cheek in the moonlight just as Alex had cupped Jess'.

"You're *so* beautiful."

"I like you, Brooks," she whispered. "So much."

"We've always liked each other," he said.

She shook her head. "No. Not like that. Not like a friend. It's changing. It's growing. I can't help it."

"What about *Zephyrland*?"

"*Zephyrland* is temporary." She wet her lips, her eyes searching his.

"Yeah, it is."

"Is that what you want?" she murmured. "Something temporary?"

This girl—this amazing, beautiful girl was standing before him, asking if all he wanted with her was a fling. And his heart ached, because being with her was so much more than a fling, but he couldn't offer her anything long-term. It simply wouldn't be fair.

"I like you, too," he said, looking into her eyes. "So much it hurts, Skye. So much more than I ever thought possible . . ." He winced, hating the next words that had to come out of his mouth. "But after this week, I can only offer you friendship. I can't offer you anything else."

She flinched, sucking in an audible breath. "Why? Is there something I don't know? Are you . . . are you married? Are you—"

"No, Skye," he said gently, the pad of his thumb stroking her soft skin, "nothing like that."

"Our lives are really different," she said softly, her voice breaking. "We wouldn't mesh, would we?"

"Aw, skip," he said gently, putting a finger under her chin to tilt her face up to his. "We'd mesh. We *already* mesh."

"Then *why*?" she asked.

And he considered telling her the truth. He really considered saying, *My father died of an unexplained heart attack when he was forty, and as forty looms closer, I'm scared it'll happen to me. I can't fall in love. I can't offer you anything real. I might not be here tomorrow.* But he knew the size of Skye's heart, and he was scared, looking into her glistening, blue eyes, that she'd say, *That's okay. I don't mind. I'll risk it.* And thinking of his mother's lonely, devastated life after his father passed away, it simply wasn't a risk he was willing to let her take. He cared for her way too much to willfully lead her down a path of suffering.

He reached for her hand and lifted it, placing it over his heart—his treacherous, time bomb of a heart. "If I could,

I'd stick around as long as you'd let me . . . but I can't. I'm so sorry I can't."

She didn't pull her hand away. In fact, her eyes softened as she took a step closer to him. "If you'd let me in, maybe I could help."

It has no name, this silent killer lurking inside of me.

He shook his head. "You can't. No one can."

She searched his eyes, then nodded. "So all we have is this week?"

"I'm afraid so," he whispered.

"Then *Zephyrland* it is," she said softly, taking a deep breath and pulling him up onto the deck with her.

Chapter 14

Skye's heart was hurting as she made her way down the deck and opened the hatch. She dropped Brooks' hand to step down the narrow stairs. She wanted much more than a few days with Brooks—she wanted this to be a beginning, and what she saw in his eyes *wasn't* temporary, fleeting, or shallow. In his face, she saw the same emotions she herself was feeling: realization, tenderness, arousal, fear . . . the first stirrings of love. She saw it all, which is why his refusal to look beyond this week confused her. He wouldn't *let* himself consider a future with her, even though he cared for her. Even though he might be falling in love with her.

Love is a risk, she thought, *isn't it?*

Love is a terrible risk even in the best of circumstances, so she forgave Brooks his hesitation and led the way forward. Despite the fact that he offered her nothing beyond *Zephyrland*, she had seen the truth in his eyes and decided to trust him, to trust *them*, and whatever was growing by leaps and bounds between them. And if that made Skye Sorenson a fool, then so be it. At least she wouldn't regret letting the possibility of love, in all of its grit and glory, pass her by.

And, of course, there was this, too:

Her body—which had maintained hot, quiet fantasies of Brooks Winslow for most of her teen years and adult life—wasn't about to walk away from the chance to be with him. To touch him, to kiss him, to feel his body pressed against hers. She wouldn't deny herself five days in his arms. Even if they said good-bye on Sunday, she wouldn't invite regret then by pushing him away now. If a week was all he could offer, then that's what she would accept. And hey, she would have a lifetime to put the pieces of her broken heart back together.

She took a deep breath as she walked through the door of their bedroom, which looked much smaller and more intimate suddenly. She turned to look at him standing in the doorway, his eyes wide and dark as he stared at her.

"We only have five nights," she said, taking a step toward him and reaching for the button on the top of his long-sleeved, cotton button-down shirt. She popped it open, letting her fingers slide down the skin of his throat to the next button.

"Yes," he murmured, his eyes transfixed on hers as his chest pushed more and more deliberately against her fingers with every button she opened.

"I'm not promising everything . . ." She wetted her lips as button number four popped open. Her fingers trailed lightly over his skin, and he groaned softly. "I mean—"

"I know what you mean," he said, his voice breathless and low. "I don't want you to do anything you're not comfortable doing, Skye."

Feeling Brooks' body inside of hers? Being joined together that intimately? She ached for it, she wanted it so much. But she didn't know how to walk away from him in five days if she shared that part of herself with him. If she could never revisit the experience, she wasn't sure she wanted those memories torturing her for the rest of her life. The only way to protect herself was . . .

". . . to hold something back," she whispered, looking up at him. And even though her sentence fragment made no sense, he seemed to understand, his eyes caressing her face tenderly.

"I know." He nodded, his voice soft and sorry.

She smoothed her fingers up his arms and pushed the shirt from his shoulders. He shrugged and it slipped down his arms to the floor.

The light filtering in from the docks outside had an effect like candlelight in the small room, warm and soft, and Skye reached out to flatten her hands on his tan, hard chest. His heart thundered under her right palm, and she bent her neck back to look up at him. His brows furrowed for just a moment, his breathing audible in her ears as his eyes searched hers.

"You've been honest with me about what you can offer," she said gently. "Don't overthink it."

He took a deep, ragged breath, dropping his hands to the hem of her polo shirt and flipping it over her head, running his hands from her shoulders down her back. His fingers paused at her bra, and he looked into her eyes. She stared back at him, neither giving permission nor protesting, and he flicked the clasp open with two fingers.

His choice made her hidden muscles clench with desire, and she whimpered softly as he smoothed the straps down her arms, the lingerie falling to the ground with a whisper, leaving her chest bare to him for the first time. He didn't look down at her breasts. Instead, he held her eyes. His fingers tightened on her hips and he pulled her against him, her warm breasts flattening against his chest. Their contact finally intimate, he groaned softly, staring at her with equal parts wonder and desire, before dropping his lips to hers.

Part of him was surprised that Skye had taken the lead once they returned to the *Zephyr*, but *all* of him was taut with arousal, and though he hated that he wasn't able to offer her better than a five-day fling, he couldn't imagine pushing her away if *Zephyrland* was still on the table.

She'd worn her hair down to dinner, and he trailed his fingers up the sun-kissed skin of her back and plunged his hands into her hair, his palms cupping her head. Her breasts pushed into his chest, the tight points of her nipples making him harder by the second, even though she had basically taken sex off the table. His tongue sliding deliberately against hers found a rhythm, a cadence, and she arched her back, pressing against him. He moved his hands to her perfect ass and lifted her easily, her arms already anchored around his neck and her legs locking around his back.

Turning around, he backed up against her bed and sat down with her straddling him intimately, his concealed erection cradled against the khaki of her shorts and pressing against her hidden heat. She leaned back a little, testing the strength of his arms that held her tightly, arching her back and pressing her breasts against his chest. He dropped his lips to her throat, trailing them lightly against the coconut sweetness of her skin, nipping and sucking, finally reaching the hollow at the base of her throat where he rested for a moment.

"Brooks," she whispered in a breathy, ragged voice, leaning back a little more, until her breasts weren't pressed against him, but upturned, with pretty pebbled nipples he was dying to taste.

"You tell me when we stop, skip. Until then, I'm going to keep going," he murmured, flicking his tongue around one stiff peak, and then its twin.

When she didn't say anything, he picked her up off his lap and twisted with her in his arms, laying her flat on her bed. Her blonde hair spread out on the pillow like a halo, and her eyes were dark blue and heavy. She panted lightly, then ran her tongue along the seam of her lips, which was Brooks' undoing.

Gently nudging her legs apart, he knelt between her knees and leaned over her body. He covered one breast with his palm, rubbing her nipple as he slid his hand slowly away and sucked the beaded point between his lips.

"Ah," she whimpered, her back arching to deliver her taut skin into his mouth.

His tongue circled the puckered flesh, sucking it gently then firmly, loving her responsiveness—how her fingers fisted in the sheets and little noises form the back of her throat filled the otherwise quiet of the small cabin.

He licked her once more, then focused his attentions on her other breast, his fingers rolling her slick nipple gently as he flicked his tongue over its twin. Her fingers shifted from the sheets, plunging into his hair, her nails razing his scalp as her back lifted off the bed. And it was so hot, so incredibly arousing, Brooks slid up her half-naked body and rested his weight on her, cupping her cheeks and demanding her lips again.

He could feel the erect, damp buds straining against his chest, his own erection straining through his boxers and shorts, pushing into her thighs. She kissed him back madly, her knees bent to cradle him, her spine arched off the bed.

She was sweet and genuine, honest and hot, and Brooks couldn't remember the last time he'd been with someone he cared about or who cared about him. He'd forgotten that touching someone, being invited into their personal, sacred space, could be so emotional, so visceral, make him feel so hungry and yet so satisfied. Her coconut sun block smell surrounded him like a spell, and the sweetness of her skin was a drug. She was everything he wanted. Everything he wished he could have.

Sliding his lips down her cheek with tiny kisses, he bit her earlobe, which elicited a gasp from her, her hands smoothing down his back and slipping into the waistband of his shorts. Flattening on his ass, her fingers squeezed, spreading his cheeks just a little, and the gathering—the incredible, increasing pressure just above his dick—tripled, making him thrust against her, wanting to feel *all* of her. He traced the shell of her ear, letting his warm breath fall over the trail of kisses and licks, and she shivered, gasping lightly.

"Brooks," she whispered, her voice breathy, her chest heaving into his with every deep breath.

"What, skip?" he murmured, nuzzling the soft, warm skin of her throat.

"I think . . . Oh, God. Brooks?"

"What, baby?"

His tongue darted out, licking her strong pulse, then kissing it reverently. Her heart was strong and healthy, and God willing, she'd live to be one hundred.

"I think we should stop," she finally gasped, sliding her hands slowly out of his pants and resting them lightly on his lower back.

Wait. What? Stop? No! No, no, no! No stopping! More, Skye! I want more!

"Uh, stop?"

"Mm-hm," she breathed, sobbing softly, a sound of frustration, not sadness. "I think we should stop . . . um, slow down."

He exhaled, resting his forehead against her collarbone, but bending his knees to move. "Are you, uh, sure?"

Yes, there was a begging quality to his voice, but he didn't care. He couldn't ever remember wanting someone as much as he wanted Skye. He had to make sure her decision was firm.

"I'm sure."

He knelt up, and she closed her legs to make room for him beside her. He rolled onto his back beside her and they both panted softly, side by side, staring at the hypnotic, watery reflections on the ceiling.

She took a deep breath and exhaled on a "whoa" sound, and despite the pain in his pants, he grinned, turning his head to look at her.

"That was amazing," he whispered, afraid to break whatever wonderful spell they were under.

"It was," she agreed. She looked over at him, then shifted to her side, glancing down at her bare breasts before giving him a sheepish smile. "Sorry."

He rolled to his side too, mirroring her, reaching out to smooth the blonde hair from her face. "Don't say sorry. You make me happy."

Her lips tilted up, but her eyes retained some sadness from their earlier discussion. "You make me . . ." She wet her lips and dropped his eyes, looking down at the thin strip of sheet between them.

"Skye?"

She lifted her eyes, and he winced to find them glistening.

"Flip over," he said softly.

Without a word, she flipped over, presenting her back to him. He pulled her close, her back flush to his chest, his arm draped over her waist, resting just under her breasts.

"Good night," he said, close to her ear.

"Good night," she said, the whisper of sadness making his heart ache and clench, and he wished harder than he ever had in his entire life that things were different.

All things considered, Skye slept well.

She'd felt sad, falling asleep in Brooks' arms last night. Every minute she spent with him reconfirmed how much she wanted him. It frustrated her beyond belief that there was something keeping him from letting her love him. *Love him.* If there'd been any remaining doubt in her mind, their heat last night had knocked it out of the equation. She'd always had feelings for Brooks, always liked him, always dreamed of him. She admired him and had fun with him. He took care of her and sailed like a god. For her, he felt more and more perfect.

And yet, the whole reason she'd created *Zephyrland* was because she might not be so perfect for Brooks. Her father was still a middle-class marina owner who lived in Maryland, and Skye was determined to work and live near her father. He needed her; he didn't have anyone else. Which led her immediately to thoughts of her cheating, disgusting embarrassment of a mother.

A few years ago, she'd called her mother out of the blue, desperate for a woman's opinion about a dating situation and wondering if Shelley had changed her ways after so many years. She dialed her mother's old number, unsurprised when it went to voice mail, but the voice—her mother's voice—purred, *"This is Bunny Lynn from Hollywood Models. Leave me a message and we'll set up a . . .* (her mother giggled) *date."* Skye's cheeks had flared, and she'd scrambled to press the "End" button on her cell phone. A few minutes later, her curiosity got the better of her.

She'd opened her laptop and typed in "Hollywood Models," her hands shaking as the website came up. She scrolled down after reading about their "VIP models" and found a photo gallery of twenty women, their faces mostly hidden, dressed in all types of revealing lingerie and some without tops on at all. She searched the pictures, but the "models" were too young to be her mother. On the bottom-left corner, she saw the words "Our Mature Ladies" and clicked on that.

Her stomach fell as a photo gallery of ten more "models" appeared, most just slightly beyond their late-20s prime.

The name "Bunny Lynn" jumped out at her in the third row, second from the right. Skye clicked on the picture and a profile came up: her mother's picture and a description that started with "Bunny Lynn is a mature lady (49 years old) with seductive, blue eyes and a bewitching smile. She is sexy, but confident, and will make your . . ." Skye had sucked in a breath, clenching her eyes shut. When she opened them, she clicked on the picture to make it larger and hide the words beneath.

Her mother's hair was blonde like Skye's, twisted up in a sophisticated hairstyle. She wore too much makeup and a gray negligee that showed almost everything underneath. She stood beside a red boudoir chair, one knee bent and resting on the chair, her face turned over her shoulder to look at the camera. She didn't look sad or ashamed of herself. She just looked beautiful.

For several long moments, Skye had stared at the picture, unaware that tears were trailing down her face until one big one plopped onto her keyboard. She wished she could have known her mother better. She wished her mother could have been happy at Sorenson Marina. She wished her mother hadn't cheated on her father and left him behind. She wished that a little girl with the same blonde hair and blue eyes had been enough incentive for her to stay.

She had taken a deep, ragged breath and closed her laptop, wiping away her ridiculous tears and hardening her heart. Her mother hadn't wanted her. She certainly didn't want her mother.

Skye turned in Brooks' arms, finding him still asleep, his gorgeous face slack and peaceful. She leaned forward and pressed her lips as softly as possible to his forehead, then slipped out of bed to take a shower and get ready for the day.

Skye was making veggie omelets again, and Brooks could already smell the freshly brewed coffee. It occurred to him for a moment that her making breakfast had deprived him of a morning make-out session, but recalling the way she'd stopped them last night, perhaps it was for the best.

Lying on his back, he placed his hand over his heart, remembering the way she felt falling asleep against him— the way her soft, warm body had burrowed into his, accepting his presence beside her and savoring it in her sleep. His heart belonged more and more to Skye with every passing moment spent with her—moments that would torture him once they were apart. And yet he couldn't give her up. Not when there were only four nights left.

The door to their room squeaked open and Skye peeked in, offering him a smile far more bright and confident than he deserved or expected.

"Morning," she said, leaning down to press her lips against his before presenting him a mug of hot coffee. He sat up, taking it from her. "We have pictures with Guy in thirty minutes, so you better get up."

He nodded, sipping the strong brew. "You're in a good mood."

"Yes, I am," she agreed, sitting down on the edge of her bed. She reached out to him, running one hand gently through his hair before cupping his cheek. "You know last night? How you said you couldn't offer me anything?"

His heart clenched, then dropped. Was she about to renege on *Zephyrland*? Take away their last few remaining days together?

Oh, God. Please don't. Please let me have this little bit of fleeting happiness.

"Skye, listen—"

"Shhh. No," she said, smoothing her thumb over his bristly cheek as she smiled tenderly at him. "*You* listen. I just wanted to say . . . it's okay. I'm not asking for anything. In fact, I think it's best that we stick with the rules of *Zephyrland*. Just have fun, and then go back to normal when we get home."

"What?"

She nodded. "Yeah. I gave it some thought. I think you're right. I didn't want you to feel bad about it, because I agree. A hundred percent."

His lips parted in surprise, and he stared back at her feeling . . . disappointed. Terribly, ridiculously, tragically disappointed.

Her words should have reassured him, should have made him breathe a sigh of relief that he could be with her romantically for the next few days and then go back to friends on Sunday, but he didn't feel relief. He felt . . . awful. Even worse than before, if that was possible. Before . . . he'd wanted her though his heart wouldn't let him have her, and she'd wanted him even though he'd taken the possibility of a future together off the table. There was comfort in mutual deprivation. They were suffering together. Now it almost felt like she was perfectly happy with a fling, and it stung, not only because he cared for her deeply and wanted her to care about him in return, but because now he was suffering alone.

"Do you, uh, do you really think we can do that?"

"I do," she said, leaning forward to press her lips to his once more before standing up. "We just need to keep our feelings out of the equation. You're not the only one with . . ." She shrugged, but her gentle smile didn't falter. "It's just better this way."

The only one with . . . what? Reasons? Secrets? Baggage? What did that mean? What was she hiding?

And better? *Well. It sure didn't feel better.*

"Okay." He gulped, staring at her, feeling upset and knowing he had absolutely no reason or right to feel that way.

"Glad that's settled," she said, heading out of the room. She turned at the door. "We can just have fun now." Then she was gone.

Brooks stared at the door. Had a tornado just blown through the room, or was it just Skye Sorenson with hot coffee and sweet good-morning kisses? Because it felt like the former. Was she playing some kind of game? He thought of her smile, her touch on his cheek. No, she'd seemed entirely genuine. Besides, Skye wasn't the sort of girl to play games.

So what had changed between last night and this morning? How come she wanted a future last night and was content with a fling today? *You're not the only one with . . .* Was she hiding something? Something that he could help her with or protect her from? His fists clenched. The idea that something in her life troubled her made him feel helpless and bothered him almost to the point of panic.

He tightened his jaw, placing the coffee mug on the shelf beside the bed and swinging his legs over the side, still frowning. He was a selfish bastard for wanting her to want him emotionally when he couldn't offer her a future, but suddenly the idea of going back to his old life was so unexpectedly painful, his eyes flared in defiance and he flinched, wondering for the first time, *Is there any other way?*

How could he go back to being friends with Skye while he shared his body with women who didn't care about him?

How would he feel when Skye found someone else to comfort and protect her? Or worse, how would he feel arriving at the marina one day to see her *kissing* someone else?

His short nails bit into his palms. He'd have to live with the knowledge that he could have had her, but he'd pushed her away. And he'd hate himself for it.

Is there any other way?

Is there any possible way to build a future with her? To offer her something real and good? An ember of hope started a tiny fire in his throbbing heart. *If there is, you have four days to figure it out.*

Chapter 15

Guy seemed to recognize immediately that Skye and Brooks weren't as standoffish with each other, and he limited his usual innuendo as they posed for pictures.

Brooks stood behind Skye with his arms around her. Skye leaned over Brooks' shoulder and kissed his cheek. They were playful and comfortable, eager to touch, catching each other's eyes effortlessly. Skye blushed and giggled when Brooks dropped his glance to her chest, remembering his mouth on her last night, licking and tasting. And when she teasingly played with a button on his shirt, she saw his eyes ignite and she knew he was recalling the way she'd undressed him.

"Well, lovebirds," said Guy, "it certainly seems like you two have turned a corner. Make my day and tell me my pep talk in Virginia Beach helped."

"Whatever floats your boat, Guy," said Brooks dryly, rolling his eyes at Skye.

"Boat humor!" exclaimed Guy. "You're really loosening him up, Skye."

She looked up at Brooks and grinned, then looked back at Guy without souring. *Maybe Guy's growing on me.*

"So, Skye . . . I've been checking into you. Just a little!" he said hurriedly, shooting a cautionary glance at Brooks.

"And I found out that you have . . . a boyfriend!" Guy took a little spiral notebook out of his back pocket. "A . . . Patrick Flaherty, right? Now, I have to know! What's Patrick going to think about all of this?"

Nope. False alarm. Guy was definitely not growing on her.

Brooks straightened, taking a step toward Guy. "Skye's personal life is off limits, Guy."

"Whoa, whoa, whoa, cowboy! You two agreed to pictures and an interview. I'm just asking a question . . ."

"It's fine, Brooks," said Skye, placing a hand on Brooks' arm, and turning to Guy. "Pat and I recently broke up. I wish him nothing but the best."

"And Pat's . . . um. Let's see, he's circumnavigating the globe right now? While the *Cat's* away . . . eh, Skye?"

"That's enough—" started Brooks.

"Guy," said Skye, skewering the reporter with an icy glare. "Patrick left over four months ago. He won't be back for another year and a half. Wouldn't you agree that's a long absence for any relationship?"

Guy shrugged. "Not if it's true love."

"I guess it wasn't true love, then," said Skye sharply, turning away from the dock. "Good-bye, Guy. See you in Myrtle . . ."

"Skye! Skye! Come on! One more question! Can I quote you?"

She didn't turn back around. She heard Brooks telling Guy to get lost as she walked to the ship's wheel and turned the key to start up the motor. "Buoys up!"

"Aye, aye, skip!" answered Brooks, hurrying along the dock to uncleat the bow line before hopping back over the deck railing and pulling in the port and starboard buoys one by one.

"Skye!" yelled Guy, cupping his hands over his mouth and yelling over the roar of the motor. "Ask . . .'bout . . . his . . . friends!"

She shook her head with wide eyes and mouthed, *I can't hear you.*

Guy raised his eyebrows and pointed to Brooks—who had his back to them, pulling buoys in from the port side—then cupped his hands over his mouth again. "Ask Brooks . . . *girl*friends!"

"Ready, skip," said Brooks, turning back around.

"Sorry, Guy!" she yelled back, making sure the coast was clear before putting the sailboat in reverse. "I can't hear you!" She spared one last sardonic look for Guy and shrugged with ennui, pulling out of the slip.

Once they'd cleared the docks and were heading out into the harbor, Brooks turned to her. "Digging around about Patrick? Jesus! That guy'll stop at nothing!"

"He's disgusting," agreed Skye, although some small part of her wondered what Guy was trying to say as they pulled away from the dock. She looked over at him. "Brooks, untie the jib? We'll let her up in a minute."

"Got it," he said, kissing her cheek quickly before heading down the deck to start unfurling the foresail.

Skye's mind swung back to Guy again. Was he saying . . . Ask Brooks about his friends? Or . . . Ask Brooks about his *girl*friends?

She shrugged, exhaling a breath and taking another, deep and strong, letting the brackish air fill her lungs, making her feel fresh and clean. She looked straight ahead, enjoying the sight of Brooks' fingers working nimbly on the lines and sighing at the beautiful expanse of glistening water beyond.

Guy was nothing but a troublemaker. Whatever he was trying to say, it certainly wasn't worth her time to listen.

By late morning, a lack of good wind and too much motoring from Hatteras to Ocracoke in the Pamlico had led Skye to leave the relative safety of the sound and venture beyond the Outer Banks for the high seas and stronger winds of the Atlantic Ocean. Despite the fact that they were heading into a portion of water nicknamed "The Graveyard of the Atlantic" due to the constantly moving sandbars and shoals, in addition to powerful storms, Brooks had sailed the seas east of the Outer Banks many times without incident. In fact, he would have made the same decision in similar circumstances, so he supported this move without misgivings as she slipped through an inlet between Okracoke and Portsmouth Island and headed out into open seas. The skies were blue, the sun was high, and Brooks cheerfully raised the jib and mainsail, enjoying the adrenaline rush as they picked up speed.

After five hours of maintaining racing speeds, however, the wind suddenly seemed to die. Looking out at the water, Brooks noted the calm, glassy surface, a chill running down his back.

Slowly turning around 180 degrees, Brooks withdrew his sunglasses and noted some dark-gray clouds rolling up from the southeast.

"Skip," he said to Skye, "I think you should go below and put on your foul-weather gear."

Skye's brows furrowed at him like he was crazy.

"It's like glass out here, Brooks," she said, looking up at the dull, luffing mainsail.

"Calm before the storm," he said, gesturing behind her left shoulder.

She turned to look. "Damn it! Where'd that come from?"

"I don't know," said Brooks. "But it's coming up fast and it doesn't look good. And we're definitely going to get nailed by it."

Skye groaned, nodding for him to take the wheel. She went below and came back up ten minutes later, dressed in bright-yellow slicker pants and a matching bright-yellow jacket. She looked up at the sky again, where the approaching storm darkened by the minute, the winds just starting to whip. Maybe ten knots. Fifteen?

Brooks reached into a bench at the stern of the boat and pulled out a royal-blue life jacket, then walked back toward Skye.

"You can't be serious," she deadpanned.

"Will it make you feel better if I wear one too?"

The wind was starting to howl, and the loose sheets and sails were shuddering as the *Zephyr* started rocking more forcefully with the increasing swells.

"You think it's going to be that bad?"

Brooks looked out at the approaching black sky, then into her blue eyes. *Yeah. Maybe.*

He didn't want to scare her, so he shrugged, "Better safe than sorry?"

She snatched the blue jacket out of his hand, struggling into it while the rain started to pelt her. He reached for the vest and clicked one of the four belts closed, then kissed her salty lips quickly.

"Now you," said Skye, her eyelashes wet as she looked up at him. "Go below and suit up."

Brooks had already taken down both sails while she changed, but they still needed to be secured before raising the storm jib. He hurried below, pulling his red neoprene pants and jacket from his duffel. Slipping them on over his shorts and T-shirt, he zipped the duffel, stuffed it into the compartment under his bed, and locked the compartment closed. He took everything off Skye's bedside table and the bathroom vanity, locking up those items as well. Then he hurried back above deck to finish tying down the sails.

By the time he was topside, the sky was looking truly mean—black with grayish-white, rolling clouds—and the water was dark as ink with stiff merengue-like peaks of white. They were definitely up to wind speeds of twenty-five or thirty knots now, and it didn't show signs of letting up yet.

No stranger to flash storms over the ocean, Brooks knew they could last anywhere from ten minutes to an hour, but while they lasted, it was hard going for a skipper and his crew. He flashed a glance at Skye, whose jaw was set with determination, her fingers claw-like around the ship's wheel.

It was cold, and the water was freezing as it whipped into his face, pin-like on his hands as he worked to secure the jib and mainsail. The wind roared through the loose sheets and sails, angry and whistling.

He fastened the storm bag to the genoa, took out the sheets, and fastened the snap-shackle to a brass ring bolted into the deck floor.

"Keep the bow end-on into the waves!" he yelled at her as he walked back from the bow and hoisted the storm jib. "Don't let them break over us!"

She arched an eyebrow and rolled her eyes at him before turning back to focus on the black, roiling sea ahead.

And despite the fact that he was on a small sailboat in the middle of a nasty storm, worried for himself, Skye, and the cutter, Brooks grinned, chuckling lightly as he looked down at the line in his hands. She was facing one angry sonofa-bitch of a storm and still had the sass to roll her eyes at him.

"Damn, I love that woman," he muttered, tying a soft shackle around the mainsail to secure it to the boom.

Wait.

What?

In the fierce howling of the storm, his brain repeated the words with soft, calm certainty: *I love that woman. I love Skye. I love her.*

His hands stilled over the knot he'd just made, trembling lightly as he stared down at the blue line holding the sail. The wind whistled sharply through the halyards, and the secured sail fluttered as the wind picked up to a good thirty-five knots.

Skye was ten feet behind him, standing at the wheel, when he turned his head slowly to look at her—to look at the woman he'd just realized he loved. And the thing is? If he'd looked five seconds earlier, he might have been able to save her . . . but if he'd looked five seconds later, he might have lost her for good.

One minute, Skye was standing at the wheel, trying to stay the course into the waves, which was not easy. The boat was being tossed in the violent sea, but when she looked up and saw the storm jib take a gust of wind, it spun the boat about, and Skye lost her footing.

She slipped across the deck, and her hip hit the deck railing with a painful thud she felt, but couldn't hear over the waves and wind. Although her wet, slick hands scrambled for the slippery, brass railing, the momentum of her body sliding across the deck made her instantly top heavy, and with the next big swell, she was catapulted over the side.

She felt herself fly into the rolling, freezing-cold sea, her body submerging and her face covered by the black water. The life vest Brooks had insisted she wear lifted her to the surface a moment later, but she came up coughing and gasping, trying to keep her nose and mouth as high as possible while cold, furious waves crashed into her face. Sputtering and shocked, she looked for the *Zephyr* and found it about ten feet away, bobbing up and down in the heavy winds and wild water. Her trembling hands slid around the front of her vest, and she struggled to clip another belt, trying desperately to keep her gaze on the boat as the waves threw her around mercilessly, casting salt water up her nose and into her eyes. She thought she saw Brooks struggle into a life vest and tie a red line to a cleat on the deck.

And then he did the unthinkable.

He ran to the railing, vaulted it, and jumped in.

Brooks couldn't remember ever feeling as horrified as he felt watching Skye get thrown off the side of the *Zephyr*. He screamed her name, watching her get tossed in the waves and knowing that the longer he waited, the farther she'd be pulled away. He also knew there was no guarantee he could maneuver the *Zephyr* close enough to her to pull her back on board—not with the unpredictability of the wind and waves—and he had no idea how long the storm would last. His only option was to tether himself to the boat, jump in, and bring her back to safety himself.

The wind, which Brooks had estimated at a top speed of forty knots, wasn't slowing yet, but it didn't seem to be whipping up faster either, as though it had hit a plateau, and the storm seemed to be moving pretty quickly, rushing north toward the shore.

He tied the knot quickly around his waist, cleated the line to the deck, and jumped.

The water felt like knives as he hit the surface—cold, angry knives stabbing his bare hands and feet and face, and he gasped in pain, struggling toward her, thanking God for her life vest and bright-yellow slicker.

The sea pushed him closer to her but pushed her farther away, and he yelled, "SWIM!" at the top of his lungs, stroking as fast as he could to get to her, hoping that her efforts would keep her from being thrown out of sight. Her eyes—when he saw them above the high swells—were frightened but determined, and with them both paddling as fast as possible, he was finally able to reach out and grab her hand, pulling her against his body.

One hand held hers like iron while the other cupped her cheek. "Are you okay? Are you okay? Skye?"

"Y-Yeah," she sobbed, gasping and coughing against his neck.

"Let's get back!"

"Okay."

"There's a line around my waist," he yelled in her ear. "Grab on!"

The line was still slightly slack, so Brooks gathered it into his hands until it was taut and began inching them back to the *Zephyr*, one hand over the other. He panted with exertion, swallowing seawater and spitting it back out. Twice he looked back at Skye, and though she looked bedraggled and exhausted, she was still holding on. Between the ungodly coldness of the water and the crashing of the waves, it took several long minutes to get back to the boat, but by the time they did, the wind had probably calmed to twenty knots, and the sky was clearing from black to gray.

"You okay?" he yelled over the crashing, gurgling water and still-howling wind.

"Yeah."

"Strong enough to climb up?"

She nodded, and Brooks held the line as steady as possible as she grasped onto the red sheet and walked up the side of the boat, hoisting herself over the side and onto the deck. She looked down, giving Brooks the thumbs-up sign, and he followed suit, using the sheet to climb up to the deck and fall in an exhausted heap beside her.

Lying on his back, Brooks panted in exhaustion, staring up at the clearing, light-gray sky. The wind was down to fifteen knots now, and he could see the brightness of the late-afternoon sun trying to break through the lingering clouds. Twisting his head to the side, he looked at Skye, whose chest heaved up and down, her breathing just audible over the waves that still crashed and lapped against the side of the boat. Sliding his hand from where it rested over his life vest, he reached for hers, lacing their fingers together.

"You scared the hell out of me," he panted softly, his nose and throat burning from the salt water he'd breathed in and ingested.

Flush against his, her shoulder started shaking violently, and it only took Brooks a moment to realize that she was crying, her whole body wracked with sobs.

"Skip," he said gently. "It's okay. You're okay."

He sat up gingerly, reached under her shoulders, and pulled her onto his lap. He wrapped his arms around her wet, bulky body, and she let the side of her head fall limply against his chest, weeping soundlessly, her whole body trembling.

"Shhh, Skye. You're okay, baby," he said again, smoothing her hood down and running his palm over her wet hair. "You're the bravest girl I've ever seen."

"I l-l-lost control of the b-boat. I f-fell overboard."

He clenched his eyes shut, the image of her falling over the side burned into his brain, and the resulting feeling—one of pure, cold terror—would be difficult to ever forget. Resting his chin on her head, he held her close, stroking her hair.

"That wasn't you. That was the storm," he said, gesturing north where the sky was black and angry. "Crazy flash storm. We didn't see it coming."

"I c-could have d-died."

"No. Impossible. I could never let that happen."

"B-Brooks," she sobbed. "Oh, God. I c-couldn't b-believe it when you j-jumped in."

"I didn't have a choice. I couldn't lose you," he murmured against her hair, kissing the top of her head, then holding her tighter.

"You could've k-killed yourself."

"Nah. I was tied to the cutter."

She took a deep, shaky breath, burrowing closer to him.

He realized that although she was still crying, she was shaking and stuttering, in part, because her body was very cold from the water and her drenched clothes. He looked up at the sky. Not as furious, but still gray, and the sun wasn't going to be warming them up anytime soon. Though he didn't see another storm rolling in, the rest of the afternoon and evening could very well be overcast and windy. Overcast would be chilly, but windy could be good.

He did a quick calculation in his mind. That squall was too short to have thrown them much off course. They were probably still about three or four hours from Beaufort, but with good wind, no more. If they could both change their clothes and get the sails unfurled again, they could be there by dinnertime.

"Skye," he said. "You're soaked and cold. You've got to change."

"W-What?"

He looked down. "Your lips are blue, baby. You've got to go below and change."

"Y-You trying t-to get me n-naked?"

In spite of everything . . . the storm, their recent swim, their soaked clothes, and the hours of sailing still ahead, he grinned at her, then laughed softly.

Damn, I love this woman, he thought again, just as he had right before she was thrown overboard. Only this time, his heart swelled with gratitude for the fact that she was still alive, still breathing in his arms after such a terrible scare.

"I'm crazy about you," he blurted out, kissing her head.

She froze in his arms, stiffening as the words left his mouth, sitting awkward and heavy between them.

"Wh-what?" Leaning back, she twisted a little bit to look into his face, her blue eyes uncertain, but hopeful. "What d-did you say?"

He recalled her words from this morning, *We just need to keep our feelings out of the equation.*

Well, that was impossible. He wasn't going to be able to do that.

Cupping her cheek with his hand, his heart pounded from the force of his feelings. "I'm crazy about you, Skye. It's true."

Taking her hands in his, he stood, pulling her up with him.

"Go below and change," he said, pressing a quick kiss to her lips. "I'll start getting the sails unfurled."

"Thank you for saving my life." Her eyes were glistening, and she swallowed, flinching like it hurt a little bit. "And me too, Brooks. I'm crazy about you, too."

Then she turned and headed downstairs.

Arriving at the Olde Beaufort Yacht Club in Beaufort, North Carolina several hours later after an uneventful evening, they pulled into their designated slip, and Skye cut the engine, her body limp and weary. Her jeans and sweat shirt were damp and uncomfortable, her hip ached like crazy, her throat and lungs still burned from the salt water she'd ingested, and she was physically and emotionally drained. Brooks cleated the bow line to the dock securely then jumped back on the *Zephyr*, walking purposefully down the deck to her.

"Pack a few things in a bag," he said, catching her eyes before lowering the mainsail.

"What? Why?"

He looked back at the Yacht Club for a minute—a bright-white, hotel-like structure on the harbor—then gazed tenderly at Skye. "Because I got us a room for tonight. After today, you need a hot shower, a hot meal, and a decent bed."

She gasped softly in surprise and gratitude, tears filling her eyes as her knees nearly buckled with relief. There was literally nothing Brooks could have offered her that would have sounded better.

"Thank you," she sobbed softly.

He stopped what he was doing, shimmied around the mast, and pulled her into his arms.

"No more crying, skip," he said gently.

She leaned into him gratefully, letting his solid strength support her and protect her and take care of her.

He's good at taking care of people.

Jessica's words from several days ago swam in Skye's head, and she sniffled softly, realizing how true they were, realizing that no matter how bad of a match she was for him, with her floozy mother and middle-class background, she had fallen in love with Brooks hook, line, and sinker. She wanted him to take care of her . . . even if it was only for today. Even if he *couldn't* offer her forever.

She bent back her neck and looked up into his face, letting her eyes zero in on his lips. He lowered his face, his mouth finding hers, his lips strong, but soft, moving gently, taking her upper lip between his, then releasing it. His tongue parted the seam of her lips, coaxing hers to meet his, to tangle, to slide and dance and be happy that they'd both survived today. His arms tightened around her, and she moaned softly, running her hands up his back, into his hair, her fingers spreading into the thick, dark strands.

She had always loved Brooks Winslow a little. But now? Now the image of him leaping off the side of a boat into dark water to rescue her would be burned into her head for the rest of her life.

Now she'd love him forever.

"Skye," he groaned. "Go pack a few things. I'll finish up here, and we can go to bed . . . uh, to, uh, up to the hotel."

She laughed softly against his chest. "Bed sounds good."

He dropped his chin to her head and groaned again. "You're killing me."

"No," she said tenderly, repeating the words he'd said when he scooped her into his arms after rescuing her from the sea. "Impossible. I could never let that happen."

He blinked at her, staring down into her eyes like they were a lifeline or his last hope for something he longed for. It only lasted a second before he blinked again, sighing as he released her. "Grab me a change of clothes too?"

She nodded, pulling away from him. "Will do."

An hour and a half later, Skye murmured softly beside him in their king-sized bed, her back against his chest, as a warm breeze blew in off the ocean from their open balcony door. It was only nine o'clock, but his girl was winded.

They'd secured the *Zephyr*, then walked hand-in-hand to the Yacht Club, checking in quickly and taking the elevator up to their room. While Skye showered, Brooks had ordered them both cheeseburgers, fries, and cold beer. And while Brooks showered, Skye had tipped the waiter and set up their dinner on the balcony.

As much as they touched and kissed easily when they passed each other, or whenever else they felt like it . . . and as much as they wanted to touch and kiss and do a million other things to one another, they both recognized—in the manner of seasoned athletes—that their bodies needed sustenance and rest before they could be used to exertion again. After dinner, Skye crawled onto Brooks' lap to watch the sunset, and by the time it had sputtered into the sea, she was sound asleep.

As gently as possible, Brooks stood up and walked from the balcony back into the room, carrying her in his arms. He placed her on the bed, turned down the sheets, and gently pulled her under them. Then he shucked off his jeans, turned off the light, and got into bed beside her, pulling her small body against his.

He was in love with her, but he had no idea what to do about it.

No matter how it had started, this wasn't some one-week affair that he could walk away from on Sunday. He loved Skye as a friend, and he'd always be grateful for her friendship, but now he loved her as a woman, too. As a heroine, as a muse, as a partner. He didn't want to fall asleep without her body next to his, or wake up to omelets and coffee alone. The idea of being with any other woman made his stomach turn over, and the idea of her with another man made him want to kill someone.

But his heart.

His beating heart, half made by his father, could give out at any time.

He thought about Jessica's face outside the restaurant at Hatteras. She'd been so insistent that his fears were crazy.

That with regular care, Dr. Dryer would catch any threat to their lives. And yet, Dr. Dryer didn't know what to look for. No one did. As far as Brooks knew—and he'd asked both Dr. Fiorello before he died and his mother—no one knew what condition had ultimately stopped Taylor Winslow's heart and ended his life.

Brooks held Skye tighter, and she sank back into him, her breathing deep and smooth.

He'd heard of a place in Princeton, New Jersey—the Princeton Longevity Center—which offered full-body scans, coronary artery scans, and full cardiac angiography that would show exactly how his heart was pumping. Yes, it would cost a great deal, which really didn't matter to Brooks, but more, it would take a commitment to his preventative health that he hadn't considered thus far in his life. He had travelled the world and enjoyed his freedom knowing that one day he'd probably go quickly into that good night, like his father. Although he'd known that very expensive, private facilities like the Princeton Longevity Center existed, he'd never settled down long enough to look into a comprehensive plan to stay on top of his heart.

In order to show up at Princeton for a battery of tests every month, he'd need to settle down nearby—in New Jersey or Philly—and change his entire lifestyle. He kissed the back of Skye's neck. For the first time in his entire life, "settling down" not only felt possible, but he longed for it. Holding this sweet woman in his arms, his heart throbbing with love for her, it even felt vital. And maybe, just maybe, if he was as proactive as possible, he might stay safe. He might deserve the love of a woman like Skye. He might even find a way to let himself love her.

But then, out of nowhere, his brain conjured an image of his father—smiling with a cigar in his mouth one moment, then clutching his chest and collapsing the next. Brooks winced, the heaviness which had always plagued him returning quickly after a short burst of hope.

Even if Brooks went to Princeton regularly, even if he changed his whole life to try to get ahead of whatever had buried his father, in the end . . . there were still no guarantees.

Chapter 16

Skye wasn't on the *Zephyr*.

She knew this because she'd become accustomed to the gentle, rocking motion of sleeping on the cutter. And she wasn't rocking, wasn't in motion. She was warm, snuggled under soft, sweet-smelling covers, and something was pushing—not unpleasantly, but insistently—against her backside.

Eyes still closed, she grinned.

Brooks.

Her eyes fluttered open, and she looked down at his tan, muscular arm slung over her waist, anchoring her to him. He said he couldn't offer her anything, but he'd saved her life yesterday with little thought for his own safety. He told her he was crazy about her, and she'd responded in kind.

Regardless of his protestations, in her heart she didn't believe that things would end between them in two days. She understood that Brooks had reasons for being cautious when it came to commitment, but his actions yesterday proved that he cared for her deeply, and for Skye, it was enough. She wasn't going to hold back anymore.

Her heart brimming with love for him, she turned in his arms, her nose almost touching his, his breath warm on her lips.

"Good morning," he mumbled without opening his eyes, pulling her closer so that her breasts were flush against his chest, and his nose nuzzled hers.

"Good morning," she said, pushing her hips forward just a touch, so that his erection poked at her softness.

His eyes opened, sea-green and dark, skewering hers as he leaned away. "Don't tease me."

She moved her hips again to cradle him, and then threw one leg over both of his. "I'm not."

"You're not?" he asked, rolling her to her back and shifting his body to cover hers.

"Nope."

He searched her eyes, his breathing quick and shallow as he hardened like stone against her, pulsing and strong. "Just to be clear . . . you're *not* teasing me."

She shook her head, her cheeks flushing with heat as she met his eyes. "I'm not teasing you. I've always wanted you. But after yesterday, I—"

He dipped his head to kiss her lips, then pulled away, cocking his head to the side, his eyes sparkling but slightly confused. "Always?"

"Always," she admitted, feeling naked even though she was still wearing pajamas. She grinned sheepishly, pulling her bottom lip into her mouth. "Since the day I watched you sail away on the Primrose."

"You were only ten," he said, a slow, sexy smile spreading across his face.

"And you were perfect," she said.

"I was a cocky teenager."

"No," she said, smiling back at him. "You said hi to me even though I was just a little kid, and the way you handled that sailboat?" She sighed dramatically.

"All this time?"

"Mm-hm," she murmured.

"What about Pat?"

"I was lonesome." She shrugged, looking away for a moment before meeting his eyes again. "And you didn't see me as a girl."

"That's because I'm an idiot, skip."

She laughed softly, nodding. "True."

"Forgive me?"

"Forgive the man who jumped into a storm to save my life?" She didn't expect her eyes to brighten with tears, and she blinked to hold them back, managing a smile for him. "Hmm. Let me think it over."

"I'm going to figure it out," he said in a rush. "Give me a little time, okay?"

"Figure what out?"

"You and me," he murmured.

She gasped quietly, cutting her eyes to his, rocked to her core by his words. Though she suspected that he cared more deeply for her than he let on, she hadn't expected this. Her heart throbbed with love and relief, and her eyes swam with tears of hope and happiness.

"Don't say that if you don't mean it," she whispered.

"I mean it, skip. I want us to be together. I just . . ." He reached up to cup her cheeks with his hands. "I'm weak and selfish, but God help me, I *can't* let you go."

He lowered his lips to hers, parting them insistently and finding her tongue, a bolt of lightning shooting from his mouth to his groin as the velvet softness slid against his. He groaned, his hands skimming down her throat, caressing her shoulders, finally bracketing her breasts from either side as he kissed her. Her hands were tangled in his hair, her nails razing his scalp, then relaxing as their kiss deepened, and he pushed his hips against hers, almost shuddering when she arched her back to meet him.

He wanted her, but even more, he *needed* her. Like the wind and the water, she was a part of him, and he needed to belong to her. The feeling was exhilarating and even a little frightening, because in the whole of Brooks Winslow's adult life, he hadn't shared his body with someone he cared for . . . with someone he loved. Coupling with Skye wouldn't be about meeting a physical need before exchanging cash and saying "good night." No, being with Skye this morning was about love and trust and committing to a different kind of life so that he endeavored to deserve her. Being with Skye, he hoped, was just the beginning of something that would last for the rest of his life, however long that turned out to be.

Leaning back from her, he knelt between her legs, and she sat up, quickly pulling her T-shirt over her head and throwing it to the floor. Both bare chested, Brooks still wore his boxers, and Skye had on a skimpy pair of soft, pink shorts. She reached for the waistband of his underwear, holding his eyes, her chest heaving lightly with her breathing. His eyes dropped to the dusty pink points of her breasts, which moved up and down slowly, tantalizingly, teasing him with their soft sweetness.

"Take these off," she whispered, her eyes dark and heavy as she looked up at him.

Slipping his thumbs into the waistband, he pulled, but the material caught on his erection, and Skye reached forward, her hand slipping into his boxers, her fingers wrapping around his length as he pushed the boxers to his knees.

"Ohhh," she gasped on an exhaled breath, looking down at the hard, throbbing erection in her hand. Wrapped around his width, her fingers barely met, and he cut his eyes to her face to read her expression. Was he what she wanted?

She wetted her lips as her thumb swiped over the ruby head of his shaft, making smooth, slow circles that made his breath catch and hold, the muscles in his chest tight, wondering what she'd do next.

Raising her eyes to his, she smiled, placing her free hand flat on his chest and pushing him back. "Lie down."

He leaned back, his head resting at the very foot of the bed as she pulled his boxers down his legs. Kneeling there with those lovely, teasing little pink shorts still hiding the part of her he most wanted to see, she said, "Close your eyes."

And though he wanted to keep them open, her hand still curled around the base of his sex started to move, and there wasn't anything she could ask that he would deny her. Clenching his eyes tightly shut, he tried to breathe as she bathed her hand in his precum and used the slickness to rub up and down his erection. He groaned, throwing one arm over his eyes while the other still lay on his chest. When he felt her hair brush against his abs and across the back of his hand, he tensed in anticipation, holding his breath, and then almost bucking off the bed when he felt the hot, wet warmth of her mouth surrounding him inch by inch.

He reached for her head, caressing her golden hair gently as she sucked his entire length into her mouth, massaging him gently, swirling her tongue around the slick knob, and then taking him deep again. He felt the gathering, the sharp, thrumming, tightening throb building low in his center and tensed his muscles to slow down his reaction, but he cared for her so much, and she was milking him with every suck, every stroke.

"Skye . . ." he gasped, lowering his arm and opening his eyes. There were stars in the frame of his vision as he stared at the ceiling before looking down at her blonde head. "Skye, you have to stop, or I'll . . ."

Her lips dragged up his length, and she looked at him, her lips red and glistening, her eyes tender.

"It's okay, Brooks," she said gently, then—still holding his eyes—she took him deep again.

It was her eyes.

It was the intimacy of her sweet eyes holding his while her lips skimmed down the length of his cock.

He bucked off the bed and came with a roar, his sex tensing and pulsing into her mouth as she swallowed his essence, his hands buried in her hair, his decimated heart overflowing with the kind of love he swore he'd never, ever allow himself to feel.

Still shuddering with aftershocks, a laugh started deep in his belly and sailed up to his lips, where it released in a soft, joyful sound of surrender. Skye slid up his body, her tight nipples dragging against his skin until her face hovered over his—so beautiful, his eyes acknowledged that there was nothing else in the world that could compare.

He smoothed her hair away from her face and pulled her lips down to his, tasting himself on her tongue, which made him twitch and harden, though so recently spent. He kissed her with passion and with gratitude for her kindness and patience, her selflessness and sass. He loved her heart and her soul, and was desperate to love her body as thoroughly and intimately as she had just loved his.

Slipping his thumbs into her waistband, he pushed insistently, and she wiggled them over her ass and down her legs, kicking them off. Brooks rolled her over, onto her back. He wanted to see her—all of her—to drink in the sight of her naked body on the bed, to memorize the curves and dips and valleys, soft hips, slick core, waiting heat.

She was a contrast of colors—tan legs, tan arms, tan face and neck, with snow-white thighs and belly. He grinned at her because this wasn't the body of a sunbathing beauty, but of a sailor; someone who wore shorts and T-shirts and worked for a living, and he loved it because it was so perfectly her. On her flat, soft belly was a tan birthmark, about the size of a silver dollar, in the shape of an almost-perfect cloud. He swiped it gently with his thumb, and then lowered his lips to kiss it gently.

"You have a cloud on your tummy," he said, grinning up at her.

She nodded. "Mm-hm. My body's the sky."

"Your name."

"That's how I got it."

"I love that."

"I'm glad," she said, tilting her head to the side and smiling down at him.

His eyes darkened, giving her the same command she'd given him, "Close your eyes."

Brooks kissed a trail from the little cloud to the neat patch of white-blonde hair between her thighs. He leaned forward, between her legs, pressing soft, sweet kisses to the smooth skin of her thighs, moving closer and closer to the heat at her core. Spreading her lips with his fingers, he gently nuzzled her clit, his erection throbbing from the honey-tangy scent of her sex, as he lapped at her clit. She gasped, whimpering softly as he licked her in soft, long strokes, and then circled the stiff nub of pink flesh with his tongue. Her hips bucked and she moaned, her fingers curling in the sheets on either side of his head as his tongue moved faster, then slower, in long strokes, then short sucks. Her breathing changed from shallow to panting, and she whimpered his name, her hand landing on his shoulder.

He reached for her hand, lacing his fingers through hers as she tensed, her hips rising off the bed and her muscles clenching before her body exploded into waves of shuddering, trembling pleasure. She gasped, then exhaled long, a light "ahhh" sound, like music in his ears as her fingers tightened around his, and he licked her softly one last time before sliding up the length of her body to look at her face.

Her neck was bent back, her eyes closed and eyebrows furrowed, her bottom lip caught between her teeth. Brooks was stunned by her responsiveness to him, her trust, and her release. Dropping his lips to hers, he kissed her longingly, gently, easing her lip from her teeth so that he could love it as her body jerked and trembled lightly under the weight of his body.

He was hard and hot, and God, how he wanted her, but he thought of her words two nights ago. . . *hold something back.*

As much as he wanted to make love to her, he didn't want to pressure her into giving him something she wasn't ready to offer.

He reached back for the pillows, plumping them then laying back, and Skye scooted up to lay beside him, her head heavy on his chest, near his heart. He reached down and pulled a sheet over them, stroking her hair gently while a warm breeze blew the curtains away from the French doors that led to the balcony.

"Brooks?" she said.

"Mmm?"

"That was . . . amazing."

He laughed softly, dipping his head to kiss the crown of her head before leaning back again. "I agree."

"We can . . ." Her voice trailed off, and she shifted slightly, her hand on his chest, her breasts heavy, crushed against his pecs as she looked up at him. "Do you want to . . . keep going?"

"Do you?" he asked, looking deeply into her eyes.

"Part of me does," she answered.

"But maybe part of you's not totally ready?" he asked, caressing her cheek.

"I . . . I want to be ready," she whispered. "But there's something going on in your life that you're keeping from me, that wants to keep us apart. I just wish I knew what it was."

He tightened his jaw, dropping her luminous eyes for a second before looking back up at her. It was time to be honest. He loved her. She deserved to know.

"My father died when I was seventeen," he said.

"I know. I'm sorry."

"It was sudden," he continued. "One minute he was fine, the next an ambulance was taking him to the hospital. He was dead before they even got there. A cardiac arrest."

"Oh no," she said, pressing her lips to the space over his heart. "Brooks, I'm so sorry."

He swallowed, because the toughest part was still to come. "We don't know why."

"What do you mean?"

"We don't know the *cause* of the heart attack. My dad was in good shape. He drank whiskey and smoked cigars, but he ran three or four miles a day, and he sailed every weekend he could. He ran a major foundation, but my mom says that he wasn't unduly stressed. Before his cardiologist, Dr. Fiorello, passed away a few years ago, I tracked him down and spoke to him about my dad. He said that nothing had ever shown up on an EKG. In fact, my father had only visited the doctor two months before the attack for some vague chest pains that the doctor diagnosed as irritation of the pleura, a totally benign condition."

"Surely there are more medical records? Some way to find out what happened?"

"As far as I know, an autopsy was never done. I . . . honestly, after talking to Dr. Fiorello, I felt like I'd hit a wall. My mom has no idea what happened. His death certificate lists 'Cardiac Arrest' as the reason he died. Do you know how many causes there are?"

"No," she murmured.

"Thousands," he said, then repeated, "Thousands." He paused for a moment. "And any one of them could be hiding inside my body, too."

"Oh. Oh . . ." she murmured, finally understanding his deepest fears. She took a deep, audible breath, leaning up on his chest to look into his eyes. "Brooks. No, love. No."

"Yes," he insisted, feeling bleak and miserable. "He was only forty. That's only five years away."

"But you take care of yourself."

"I try." He shrugged. "I eat well. I exercise. I don't smoke. I drink a few beers a week. Yeah. I think I do."

"And you're under a doctor's care?"

"Yes, but—"

"And your tests come back negative for heart problems?"

"Yes, but so did my dad's."

"You can't live like this," she said gently, reaching up to cup his cheek and look deeply into his eyes.

"I do, skip. I *do* live like this."

Her eyes glistened with tears, and he hated it. He hated making her sad, and he hoped she didn't feel sorry for him or think he was some crazy hypochondriac, because he wasn't. He was a realist. His father had died for no reason and it tormented him.

"That's why . . ." she murmured. "That's why you can't offer me a future?"

"Because I'm not even sure I have one," he answered, wincing, pushing her head back down on his chest so her eyes couldn't search his face anymore. He felt too raw, too exposed, even with Skye, whom he trusted, whom he loved.

"You do, Brooks. I promise you do."

"You can't promise that."

"Tell me this," she said gently, wrapping her arm around his chest and settling her cheek back over his heart. "When you asked me to be patient while you 'figured it out,' what did that mean?"

"Well, I thought that maybe I could look into more regular, top-of-the-line screenings. There's a place in Princeton I haven't checked out yet because I've been travelling so much over the past decade, but they use really high-tech imaging. And I thought maybe . . . if I settled down and really committed myself to preventative care, well, maybe I'd feel like less of a selfish bastard about asking you to be with me."

"I see," she said softly.

"Do you?" he asked.

"Mm-hm," she murmured in a hushed, broken whisper. She sniffled before speaking again. "I see that you are exceptional. I see that you're one of the most thoughtful, caring, responsible people I've ever met, ever known. Despite how much you want me, you'd push me away before you'd let me fall for you and get hurt. Is that about right?"

"That's about right, skip."

She leaned up on her arm, pushing her gauzy, blonde hair from her face and fixing her sky-blue eyes on his sea-green.

"But there's a fault in your logic."

"What's that?"

"I've *already* fallen for you," she said softly, her eyes bright and tender.

She dropped her lips to his, kissing him passionately, tangling her tongue with his, her breasts crushed against his chest. And his arms wrapped around her like iron bands, refusing to let go of the sweetness she brought to his life, and he vowed that whatever it took—hell, he'd *move* to Princeton if he needed to and get screened every day—he'd do it . . . just for the chance to be with her.

"Me too," he whispered in her ear before letting her pull away. "You're not the only one falling, Skye."

Her eyes widened with her smile, and she giggled softly before kissing him again.

When she drew back, her smile faded just a touch, and she reached up to cup his jaw. "You know? Your beard's very scratchy."

"I'll shave."

"But I think your heart," she said, covering it with her palm, "is strong."

"I hope," he whispered.

"You're going to be okay, love," she said, her eyes drinking in his face, and he felt the calm certainty of her words.

"I promise I'll do my best to figure this out, Skye."

She nodded, laying her head back on his chest and tightening her arm around his chest.

"I trust you," she said simply, pressing her sweet lips to his treacherous heart.

Several hours later, pointed south and headed for Carolina Beach, Skye felt different. New and vulnerable, desperately in love, excited and worried. Grateful for the blue skies, sunshine, and wind that kept Brooks busy and the *Zephyr* moving steadily forward, she had time to think about all that had happened between her and Brooks this morning.

Aside from the fact that Brooks was a more skilled lover than the handful of other men she'd been with, there was something special about their intense make-out session— something she sensed neither of them had experienced before. For Skye's part, she realized that she'd never actually been in love with Patrick or with anyone before him. She knew this because what she felt for Brooks was so much larger, so much more vital and visceral than anything she'd ever felt before. Maybe because she'd had him in her sights for much of her life, but more, she believed, because they'd been friends for years. She was attracted to Brooks, unbelievably turned on by him, and her heart absolutely belonged to him . . . but she was also comfortable with him. She wasn't self-conscious lying under him, his tongue doing wicked things to her sex. For the first time in her life, she'd lived in the moment entirely. She'd given him her heart, and somewhere along the way, she felt as though her soul had entwined with his as well.

Two things that lived separately and yet together: a brook and the sky, the wind and the water that coursed through both their veins. You needed both to sail. You needed both in tandem to achieve perfection.

Lying together after Brooks' painful admission about his father's tragic death and his subsequent fears, they'd shared the moment in comforting, respectful, loving, mutual silence. She hated that he carried such a heavy burden, but she was deeply touched by how desperately he'd wanted to protect her from forming an attachment to him. It made her love him all the more.

Her phone buzzed in her shorts pocket, and it surprised her since they weren't that close to shore, but she fished her phone out and glanced down at it, hoping for a text from her father. She bit her lip when Pat's name flashed on the screen. Swiping across it, she opened his text:

> Saw a recent update on the *Celeb!* website.
> So I guess we're really over.
> Fine with me—I'm having a blast with Inga.
> Why don't you ask Brooks about his "girlfriends," Skye?

She stared at the bitter words for a couple of seconds before deleting the message and shoving her phone back into her shorts. She snorted. Leave it to Pat to try to make trouble. She should have known that she couldn't break up with him without his ego demanding a severance. Well, screw him. She and Brooks finally had a chance at something real. Pat could go to hell.

. . . ask Brooks about his girlfriends . . .

But as much as she tried to forget the words, they circled in her head, much as they had when Guy said something similar.

Chewing on her bottom lip, she couldn't deny that the message bothered her. What girlfriends? The women she'd seen him with at the marina? Did Pat object to Brooks dating several different women at the same time? She didn't see anything wrong with that as long as he was up front about playing the field.

But. Oh. Wait. Was he playing the field with her?

No. No! They hadn't actually had a conversation about commitment, but Brooks had shared his deepest concerns, his most personal secret. He had said, *I want us to be together.* That was enough, wasn't it? He was serious about her, right? If he was actively with someone else—this "girlfriend" that Guy and Pat kept mentioning—he wouldn't have made a move on Skye . . .

. . . would he?

"Everything good, skip?"

Brooks climbed up onto the deck from the galley where he'd made them ham-and-cheese sandwiches. He held one just out of reach, presenting his lips for a kiss first, and she complied, grinning at him when he finally backed away and offered her the sandwich.

"Can I ask you something?"

"Anything," he said, chewing his sandwich as he looked at her from the deck railing where he leaned back, the bright sun making his thick, black hair shiny like lacquer.

"You knew Pat and I were together . . ."

"Yeah. Of course."

". . . and then we broke up."

"Thank God."

"Well, I've seen you . . . you know, with women, from time to time. Dates. At the marina."

"Uh-huh," he said, lowering his sandwich, his smile fading.

"And I guess I just wanted to be sure that . . . Are *you* free? I mean, are you with anyone else right now?"

His shoulders relaxed. "You mean . . . do I have a girl-friend back at home?"

"Yeah."

"You mean . . . other than you?"

Her face, which had been curious, but mostly blank, suddenly burst into a smile, and she chuckled softly, staring back at him in wonder. "Me?"

"Yeah, you." He took another bite of his sandwich, grinning at her.

"*I'm* your girlfriend," she said softly, staring up at him, her sandwich forgotten by her side as she tried to process this miraculous news.

"Damn, I hope so," he said, still grinning. "Because if you're not, there was this hot blonde in my bed this morning, and she was doing some pretty amazing things with her mouth on my—"

"I am!" she said, cutting him off, her smile hurting, her cheeks flushed as she conjured a very vivid mental image of exactly what they'd done together.

"In some ways, I'm a bad deal," he said, flinching briefly before blinking the worry away. "But I'm going to figure things out for us the best I can." He paused. "And yes. You're my *only* girlfriend, Skye."

She laughed softly, and he threw his sandwich overboard, crossing to her in two long strides, pulling her into his arms and landing his lips flush on hers.

He tasted like ham and cheese, salty and loving and perfect, and she tossed her own sandwich in the water with his so she could wrap her arms around his neck and kiss him back long and hard.

Patrick Flaherty was a troublemaking jackass. And clearly, he had no idea what he was talking about.

Chapter 17

They spent Thursday night in Carolina Beach and left for
Myrtle Beach on Friday morning after a night on the *Zephyr*
that included more mind-blowing oral sex in Skye's little
bed and not nearly enough sleep for either of them.

Brooks was waiting for Skye to give him a sign that she
was ready to move forward in their physical relationship,
but since she seemed content to enjoy one another without
making love, he was forcing himself to be patient.

But he couldn't lie . . . it wasn't easy.

Last night, with her naked body pressed against his, the
tangy scent of their mutual orgasms surrounding him, he'd
clenched his eyes tightly shut to try to stop his cock from
hardening. Finally, he'd had to slip out of bed and take a cold
shower. As he pulled on some boxers, she turned around
and opened her eyes, one eyebrow arching up.

"What are you doing? Come back to bed."

He'd sat down beside her, in the C of her body, leaning
down to press his lips to her forehead. "You know I adore
you?"

"Mm-hm." She'd sighed, closing her eyes.

"I need to sleep in my own bed."

Her eyes had jerked open.

"Why?"

"Because I'm not going to get any sleep pressed up against you. I want you too bad."

"Oh." She pouted, furrowing her brows in protest. "Well, let's just . . ."

"No," he said, stroking her hair off her face, smoothing it onto her pillow. "Not *let's just*. We're not *just* doing anything. We're not *just getting it over with*," he said, employing Jessica's incredibly annoying air quotes. "When you're ready . . . *really* ready, you tell me, skip, and I'll make it happen. Deal?"

She nodded. "Deal."

"Get some sleep," he said tenderly, kissing her forehead before slipping into the bed across the room from hers.

In theory, he understood why she wasn't quite ready yet. They'd only kissed for the first time a couple weeks ago . . . and in a very short amount of time she'd broken up with Pat, confessed her feelings for Brooks, and started an incredibly intense emotional and physical relationship with him. He didn't blame her for needing a little time before she shared her body with him completely.

So reasoned his mind.

His cock? Which was semihard almost all the time lately? It wanted her so badly, he was distracted by the force of his desire for her. Even now, standing behind her as he checked on the rear halyards, he was far more interested in *her* rear, pert and round in tiny, little denim cutoff shorts that were probably custom-made to torture him. He grumbled, looking up at the waning sun. A couple more hours until Myrtle Beach and their second-to-last photo shoot with Guy, this one at sunset.

Guy worried him a little. He didn't like how he'd asked Skye about Patrick with such confidence, a cat-and-mouse smile playing on his face. He'd made it clear to them in Gloucester Point that he'd do whatever it took to get a good story, even fabricate one of his own. But clearly he was digging around, trying to find something salacious *and* real, and Brooks shuddered when he thought about Elite Escorts. What a story that would make: "Ex-Olympian Uses Escort Service." He'd arranged for a nondisclosure agreement with outrageous penalties, so he doubted that Elite would ever legitimize any rumors about him. Not to mention, no one could prove what Brooks and the various employees of Elite had done together in the privacy of his boat. He didn't worry about legal prosecution, but the court of public approval would be brutal. Aspersions would be cast on his name . . . and on anyone else with whom he was, legitimately, intimate.

At the very least, it would be a small scandal, and though he wasn't a large enough celebrity for things to get really uncomfortable, it could certainly affect his relationship with his family . . . and Skye.

And that's what bothered him the most.

His mother and siblings would forgive him quickly and knowing them, take every opportunity to defend him publicly. But Skye? What they had was too new for him to bank on her understanding, let alone standing by him.

God, he'd been so shortsighted to use escorts, but then, his plan hadn't ever been to have someone significant in his life. At the time, it had made sense. Now? Now, he just hoped it wouldn't be a stupid decision that ended up breaking his own heart.

A few hours later, with the setting sun behind them and the smells of sun block and cotton candy wafting over to the marina from the midway at Myrtle Beach, it felt like a party, though Guy still did his best to ruin the light mood with his endless smarm.

"So, Skye . . . safe to say that you dumped Pat for Brooks?"

"No comment," Skye replied.

"But you and Brooks are a couple?"

She peeked up at Brooks, and he nodded, letting her know he was comfortable releasing that information.

"We are."

"So you really *are* lovebirds," said Guy, scribbling on his little notepad. "Lovebirds at sea!"

Brooks cleared his throat meaningfully, and Guy looked up. "A few more pictures?"

"Anxious to . . . *go below*, eh?"

Once this interview was over, Brooks might start looking into Guy and make a little trouble for him. He was sick and tired of Guy's cheap and leading comments, and frankly, Charleston couldn't come quickly enough.

"Okay, kids. How about one real kiss, huh?"

Brooks looked down at Skye, who grinned up at him, winding her arms around his neck. Though Guy's camera clicked like crazy, Brooks let himself settle into the kiss and enjoy it, plunging his tongue into Skye's mouth and hardening on contact when she slid against his, stroking it with increasing pressure, arching into Brooks as he tightened his arms around her.

"Whoa! Whoa! Whoa! Is it hot in here, or is it just me?"

Brooks leaned back abruptly, breaking off the kiss, finding Guy looking up at him with a thoughtful expression. "Where'd you learn to kiss like that, Brooks?"

He hadn't looked down at Skye since kissing her, but she dropped her forehead on his chest.

"Here and there."

"It's almost like you were trained by a . . . *pro*."

Brooks flinched, his eyes flaring. "I don't like your insinuation."

"Aw, it's just conversation, cap. Speaking of which . . . how come you don't have any long-term girlfriends, Brooks?"

He knew. Shit and fuck. Guy knew about the escorts.

Brooks looked down at Skye, who was clenching her jaw, staring at Guy with venom. He knew enough about the way her mind worked to know what she was thinking: she knew about Brooks' dad, she knew that he was reticent to make a commitment, and she thought he'd conducted his personal life in a noble way. She had no idea that the women she'd seen him with had been paid to keep him company.

"That'll be all, Guy," said Brooks, ice in his tone.

Guy smirked at him. "You sure? You don't want to comment?"

"I'll comment!" snarled Skye. "You've been tasteless and insulting since the moment we met you at the auction . . . and I think we've borne it with class. But we're done, Guy. No more. It's over. Don't come looking for us in Charleston. This is the last pound of flesh you get."

Guy cut his eyes to Skye and they flared for just a moment before his lips turned up in a Cheshire-cat grin. He nodded. "I guess I can take a hint."

"I doubt it," she said crisply, detangling herself from Brooks' arms and stomping over to the hatch and down the stairs.

Guy watched her go, looking amused, then looked back up at Brooks.

"How much?" asked Brooks.

"What's that?"

"How much do you want?"

Guy chuckled, an unpleasant, overconfident sound. "How much are you offering? I know you gave her a quarter million to bid on you. Your privacy's got to be worth double that."

"You don't have any proof. I was discreet."

"You were. I only have hearsay. Her ex, Patrick? He does not like you, Brooks. Not at all. He was happy to tell me as much as he could about your . . . ah-hem, *personal* life."

"Pat and I weren't that close. You don't have anything concrete."

"I have tales of escorts at Sorenson Marina," said Guy softly, looking up at Brooks from under hooded eyes, playing distractedly with the lens of his camera. "I don't know what you did with the girls because I can't track them down, but Pat mentioned all those anonymous blondes coming and going. Luckily, I was able to track down a couple of cabbies more than happy to chitchat about a few drop-offs and pick-ups at the Sorenson Marina. Sort of your very own little whorehouse, huh?"

Brooks held onto the deck railing and swung under it, landing squarely on the dock in front of Guy. "I should pound your face in."

"You don't want to do that," said Guy, stepping back and having the good sense to look a little worried.

"Oh, I think I might."

"Nope. You were on the right track before, chum."

"Money," said Brooks. "You want money. What about *Celeb!*?"

"You give me enough money, I'll find another job in a few years after I travel the world."

"A bribe."

"A trade," said Guy.

"My reputation for your . . ."

"Comfort," said Guy.

"You don't have anything but a few cabbies and a jealous ex-boyfriend. Maybe I'll take my chances."

Guy flicked his eyes to the *Zephyr*. "You do that. I'm sure Skye and her father will be very understanding about what you were doing at their place of business."

It's not that Brooks didn't have the money. He did. It was the principle of it. It was paying money to a snake so he wouldn't do something snakelike. He looked down at the dock, knowing what he had to do. If he wanted a chance with Skye—a *real* chance—he needed to protect her, and her father, from Guy splashing their business all over *Celeb!*'s website and magazine.

"How much?"

Guy grinned. "Half a million."

"You're insane," said Brooks, turning back to the Zephyr.

"Two hundred thousand. In cash," Guy quickly amended.

"Fifty thousand," said Brooks. "In a bank check."

"Made out to cash."

"No," said Brooks, feeling dirty, wanting to get back on the *Zephyr*, take a shower, and pull Skye into his arms. "Made out to *you*. I don't want any further misunderstandings."

"By tomorrow at five."

Brooks narrowed his eyes. "That's twenty-four hours."

"Yeah. But you're Brooks Winslow." Guy smirked. "You can send it to me at *Celeb!*."

"Fine," said Brooks. "Now get out of here, and don't ever show your face to me or her again. Not unless you want the beating of the century."

"Got it, cap. Nice doing business with you."

"Fuck you, Guy," said Brooks, climbing back onto the deck of the *Zephyr*, his gut churning as the reprehensible reporter hurried away. "Fuck you."

Just as Brooks was about to head downstairs after Skye, his phone buzzed.

"Now what?" he bellowed, taking his phone out of his pocket. A picture of Jessica's smiling face greeted him as his phone continued to buzz. He took a deep breath. "Jess, I'm a little busy."

"How busy?" she asked.

Her voice wasn't teasing or playing. Brooks stopped walking toward the stairs and turned around, worried at her tone. "Why? Are you okay? Jess, is everything okay?"

"I need to talk to you. I need your attention for a good fifteen minutes. Uninterrupted."

"Um . . . okay. Give me a sec."

He needed to be sure Skye was all right after their unsavory meeting with Guy, but when he got downstairs, he could hear the hum of the shower. As much as it would have been nice to join her, he went back on deck and sat down on a bench in the stern of the *Zephyr* where he stored the life vests.

"Okay. Go ahead," he told Jessica.

"I've been worried about you. Our conversation in Hatteras . . . it really bothered me."

"I'm sorry, Jess, but I can't help the way I—"

"Brooks, shut up and listen to me, okay?" She paused, and when he didn't interrupt her again, she continued. "When I got home, I went up to the attic and looked around. Dad's desk was boxed up, and most of his papers are still up there, did you know that?"

"No."

"Yeah. They're all there. And I . . . I found something."

"What?"

"An envelope. Unopened. From the radiology department at Kindred Hospital."

"Did you open it?"

"I did. I asked Mom about it first, and she didn't know anything about it."

"And?"

"Two months before Dad died, he'd gone to see Dr. Fiorello. He'd been having chest pains."

"Yes," said Brooks. "But the EKG was normal. Dr. Fiorello diagnosed is as an irritation of the pleura."

"Right, but apparently Dad's pain continued and worsened. My guess is that he was ignoring it because he'd already been told by his cardiologist that he was fine. A week before his heart attack, he went to the ER. Probably at lunch time because they have him coming in around noon with chest pains and leaving several hours later."

"They found something?"

"No," said Jessica. "Actually, the letter from the radiology department said his chest looked fine. He got the letter the day after he died."

Brooks released the breath he'd been holding. Another dead end.

"But I went to Kindred yesterday and I had them pull the x-ray. It was still on file, which was amazing, but I guess they keep those records for a long time. I immediately called Dr. Dryer, and he managed to fit me in this afternoon."

Brooks' own heart started beating faster. Jessica had found something significant. He could hear it in her voice.

"Brooks . . ." she started. "Brooks, there wasn't anything wrong with his heart. That's why his EKG was fine. That's why they missed it on the x-ray. Because they were too focused on his heart."

"What did they miss?"

"The very faint outline of a partially calcified abdominal aortic aneurysm wall."

"Jess . . . English, please."

"The pain he felt in the weeks before he died? That was the aneurysm expanding. He didn't actually die of a heart attack. The heart attack was ancillary. He died because his aortic artery had a ruptured aneurysm. Mortality is over ninety percent if it bursts."

Brooks bent his head, tears burning his eyes as he remembered his father suddenly clutching his chest and falling to the slate patio at Westerly.

"You sure, Jess?"

"I am. Dr. Dryer was ninety-nine percent certain, even all these years later without an autopsy. After checking out the

X-ray, he said there was no way Dad would have survived the aneurysm for much longer. Once the walls calcify, especially in tandem with chest and or abdominal pain, treatment must begin immediately. In the absence of treatment . . . well, you know. You were there."

"What caused it?"

"Top cause is smoking. And you know how much Daddy loved his cigars."

A swift image of his father smoking his evening stogie suddenly flitted across Brooks' mind, and he clenched his eyes shut, trying to swallow the lump in his throat.

He heard the sound of footsteps and looked up to see Skye staring at him from a few feet away. As their eyes connected, her bright smile faltered immediately and her eyebrows knitted together in concern. She rushed to him, sitting beside him.

"Is everything okay?" she whispered, gesturing to the phone.

He nodded, taking her hand and weaving his fingers through hers before looking back down at his lap.

"But Brooks," continued Jessica, "here's what you need to know: first of all, abdominal aortic aneurysm only occurs in about two percent of the population. And yes, they can go undetected without symptoms, but a CT scan has nearly one hundred percent sensitivity for aneurysm, and it's useful in preoperative planning and endovascular repair. And there's even this new procedure since 2003 that actually fixes the aorta, so even if they found one? You could have it fixed before it ever got close to rupture. You could get a CT scan twice a year if that made you feel better, but Brooks . . ."

"Yeah, Jess?" he choked out, feeling profoundly grateful for his smart, sassy little sister whom, Brooks felt, was giving him a second chance at life.

"You're going to be okay. And you know what else? So are Preston, Cameron, Christopher, and me. You can stop worrying now, not just for you, but for all of us. Brooks," she whispered, her voice breaking, "you can stop being the dad now."

He cleared his throat, but it still felt thick, and he blinked his burning eyes.

"Be happy, Brooks," she begged him passionately. "Let Skye in. Let her love you. Give yourself permission to love her back."

"Jess . . ."

"You're going to live a long life, big brother. Why not live it with someone you love?"

Brooks' fingers tightened around Skye's as he took a deep, cleansing breath.

"Jess, Skye's here. I'm going to go."

"Of course. You okay?"

"I owe you one, Jess. I-I don't know how to thank you."

She laughed softly, but a second later, Brooks realized it wasn't a laugh. It was a sob.

"My dad died when I was six. Six years old. But you came to every recital, every art show. Every time I needed a dad, my college brother showed up. When I needed someone to talk to, someone to give me advice and direction, someone to make me feel safe, you were there for me. You're walking me down the aisle in September, and that feels perfect to me. And of course I'm sad I lost my father at such a young age, but you were the best dad I could have asked for, Brooks." She paused, sniffling. "You don't owe me anything."

"I love you, Jess," he said softly, deeply moved by her short speech.

"I love you, too. Be happy. Please, let yourself be happy now," she said before saying good-bye and hanging up.

Chapter 18

When Skye got out of the shower, she was surprised that Brooks wasn't waiting for her in their bedroom. Part of the reason she'd taken a shower in the first place was the hope that he would come and join her. When he wasn't sitting on their bed with a sexy grin and nothing else, her disappointment faded, and she got dressed quickly, feeling a little worried.

He wouldn't have gotten into a fight with Guy, would he? She'd left in a huff, furious with Guy for mucking around in their personal lives. Why didn't Brooks have long-term girlfriends? He had his reasons. Good reasons. And the thought of Guy poking a blade into that wound made her see red.

When she'd finally climbed up the stairs and seen Brooks across the deck on his phone, head bent forward, she'd felt relieved—one of his siblings was probably calling; they'd called frequently during the cruise to ask for advice or check in with Brooks. It wasn't unusual. But then he'd raised his head and looked up at her. And his face . . . his beautiful face was so raw with emotion, it had twisted her heart. She'd rushed to him, her heart only slowing down when he nodded that everything was okay, but she was anxious to find out what had upset him so terribly.

"I love you, Jess," he said softly, adjusting his fingers through Skye's and squeezing hers gently. A second later, he let the phone fall from his ear to his lap.

He didn't look up—his shoulders were still hunched and his head hung down—but rather than pressuring him to talk to her, Skye gave him a few minutes to pull himself together. She'd seen many faces of Brooks Winslow over the years, but right now he looked exhausted and undone by whatever news he'd just received. She promised herself quietly to be there for him, to love him and comfort him, no matter what Jessica had just shared with him.

"Is-is everything really okay?" she finally asked softly.

He looked up at her and nodded. "Yeah. Actually, yeah. Yeah, it is."

"Can you tell me?"

"That was Jess. My . . . um . . . well, she figured out how my dad died."

Skye's lips parted in surprise, but she wasn't sure what to say. On one hand, it would upset Brooks to learn what had prompted his father's heart attack, bringing back vivid and painful memories, but on the other hand, that knowledge could release him from his self-imposed prison. She tried to gauge her reaction on his face, but he wasn't giving much away.

"He . . . his aortic artery had an aneurysm. And I guess when it erupted, he immediately went into cardiac arrest."

"Oh," murmured Skye, still holding his hand, searching his face carefully.

"It was right there on an X-ray," said Brooks softly. "If someone had just seen it . . ."

She nodded, squeezing his hand. *If someone had just seen it*, maybe his father would still be alive today. "I'm so sorry."

"Me too," said Brooks.

"But at least you know," said Skye gently. "At least you know what happened."

"Yeah," he said, as if processing this thought. "Now I know."

The barest hint of a smile brightened his face, making him look almost boyish in the dying light of the setting sun—so golden and young and hopeful, it was like watching the weight of the world slip away from someone's shoulders, and she felt her own lips respond by tilting up in a small smile of her own.

"It's over." He sighed. "For years, I've been waiting to . . . sorry, but it's true . . . suddenly drop dead. And I'm not going to."

"No," she said, grinning at him. "You're not."

"I have . . . years."

"Mm-hm," she hummed, laughing softly. "A whole life."

"A *whole* life."

Suddenly, his eyes focused on hers intensely, darkening as he stared at her. Their thighs touched on the bench, and she felt his muscle flex, as if testing the strength of his body, and he raised her hand to his lips. Holding her eyes mercilessly, he kissed her skin, sending tendrils of pleasure up her arm and little shivers of longing down her spine. A small moan passed through her lips, and she felt her nipples tighten under her tank top, muscles deep inside her body clenching, trembling with readiness as she stared back at him.

He bent his head, his dark hair eye-level to her as his tongue flicked out over the skin of her wrist, followed by the whisper of his breath, cool and teasing, sailing over her damp flesh. She whimpered, arching her back a little and pulling her bottom lip into her mouth.

"You want me?" he asked.

"Yes," she whispered.

"You're ready?"

She nodded.

"Then say it," he demanded, raising his head so that his deep-green eyes could skewer hers.

She licked her lips, pursing them together. "I want you."

"Are you sure?" he teased, turning her hand over and running his tongue slowly over the delicate skin of her inside wrist before dropping his lips to her racing pulse. "I was going to take you out for dinner in Myrtle Beach . . . to see the sights."

"I don't want dinner," she murmured in a trembling voice. "And the only thing I want to see . . . is you."

Her breath felt hot on her lips, and her body felt wired, humming like a piece of finely tuned machinery ready to be used, ready to do what it was born to do. Give and receive. Love and be loved.

"The wind and the water," he said, standing up and pulling her to her feet. "Skye and Brooks." He stared at her lips, then dragged his eyes to meet hers. "We were always supposed to be together, weren't we?"

She nodded, unable to speak, letting her smile say what her voice couldn't as she gazed at him tenderly.

"And you knew it before me," he whispered.

"Yes," she said softly. "The wind and the water are in our blood. I *always* knew."

Brooks pulled her below, tugging her hand gently down the stairs, through the galley and the short passage that led to their room. The setting sun shone gold through two portholes, bathing them in soft, warm light.

He reached for the edge of her top, and she raised her arms as he drew it over her head. Her breasts were bare underneath, two proud, exquisite, pink peaks waiting for his hands, his fingers, his lips. His blood rushed and his sex hardened, thickening, throbbing, yearning for the wet heat of Skye surrounding him.

Smoothing his palms down the bare skin of her sides, he pushed her shorts and panties over her hips, falling to his knees before her to slide them down her long, tan legs. She leaned forward, resting her hands on his shoulders as she stepped out of them, and Brooks looked up at her, at the blonde-haired, blue-eyed beauty of the woman who offered herself to him. Reverently, his hands glided back up her legs as he stayed focused on her face, gilded like a goddess in the golden light.

"Now you," she whispered.

He stood at her bidding, reaching behind his neck and pulling his T-shirt over his head, then slipping his fingers into his shorts and boxers and pushing them, with a soft whoosh of fabric, to the floor.

He took a deep, ragged breath as her eyes dropped intentionally to his fully erect cock and widened just a little. She'd seen him before, of course, and she'd loved him with her mouth, but she'd never welcomed him into the soft sheath of her body, and he wondered if she had any misgivings.

"I'll be gentle," he promised.

Her eyes jerked to his, dark and languid, and she stepped forward until the soft skin of her belly just grazed his ruby head.

"I never said I needed gentle," she whispered, her tongue swiping over her lips.

Her words were so fucking sexy, he lost it, reaching for her, his hands under her arms to lift her onto the bed behind her. She lay back, shimmying up until her head hit the pillow, and he followed, his knees between her parted thighs, his hands plumping the perfection of her breast, and his mouth landing on her sweet skin without permission.

He sucked and lapped at her aroused flesh, turned on like hell as her fingers landed in his hair, twining through the strands, pulling to the point of pain as she whimpered and arched against him. Running his tongue along the valley of coconut-scented skin, he sucked the bud of her other breast between his lips, flicking his tongue as she moaned. Her fingers became forceful, pulling his head away from her breasts, and when he looked at her, she leaned up, smashing her lips into his, their teeth clashing, their tongues plunging into each other's mouths. Brooks braced his hands on the sheets beside her head, and his cock slipped into the valley of her clit, finding it warm and slick.

He sucked on her tongue, sliding slowly against the tight bundle of nerves, then withdrawing, and she let her head fall back, her neck taut and exposed as she panted beneath him. He dropped his lips to the wild, fluttering pulse in her neck, licking it as he pushed his hips forward, massaging her clit slowly, and pulling a breathless moan from her.

"Again," she demanded in a low, ragged voice, her eyes closed.

"Only if you look at me," he volleyed back, drawing his hips back in a slow, languorous motion and then pausing.

"Please," she panted, opening her eyes.

They were dark and fierce, heavy and hungry, and Brooks realized that his heart—which he'd only just learned would pump strong and true for the rest of his life—didn't belong to him anymore. It was hers. And so was his body. And so was his soul. It was all hers. For the rest of his life. And when she said, *Again*, he'd give her what she needed. And when she said, *Please*, he'd just about fall to his knees in gratitude that she wanted what he could give her. And when she said,

"Love"

he would love her any way and every way she wanted.

He slid back and forth across her clit with increasing speed and pressure, and she arched her back off the bed, her ankles skimming up the back of his legs to lock around his waist as he pumped forward and back. Her fingers dug into his shoulders with increasing pressure, and her breathing was fast and ragged, interspersed with the sexiest fucking noises he'd ever heard in his entire life. He started to pant, to sweat, his own body tightening to an almost unbearable point of arousal. And just then, when he wondered how much longer he could hold on, she cried out, her fingers raking down his back and making him flinch with the sharpness as her muscles started shuddering beneath him, her whole body trembling and shaking.

Her face, so familiar and so beloved, stunned him as she climaxed. A flush pinked her tan skin as she licked her glistening lips and let them fall open, slack with bliss. It was so fucking beautiful, he blinked, his body stilling, the sheer magnitude of his feelings, dormant for so long, sucking the air from his lungs.

She opened her eyes slowly, the pale lashes fluttering as she looked up at him, a small, kittenish smile tilting up her perfect lips, and he stared at her, resting his weight on his arms.

"Thank you." She sighed.

"I love you," he responded, the whispered words coming out of nowhere and surprising the hell out of him. He thought about taking them back, but even if they were premature, they were true, so he let them linger.

Her eyes widened, then flared to life, all traces of languor disappearing as she searched his face. He cocked one eyebrow at her, refusing to look away, though he felt his cheeks heat and knew they were turning red.

"You do?" she asked.

"I've never felt like this before," he answered. "Like I don't belong to me anymore. Like I belong to you." He winced, dropping her eyes. "I'm not saying it right."

"Yes, you are," she said softly, running her hands up his back and letting her palms land tenderly on his cheeks.

"We've been friends for so long. I've always had feelings for you . . . it's not that big a leap to go from like to love. Not when you realize that the person you're with is the *only* person you want. You know?"

"I know," she whispered, blinking at him.

He realized her eyes were glistening with tears, and he leaned down to kiss her.

"I'm sorry if I'm freaking you out, skip," he whispered against her lips.

"You're not freaking me out," she answered, tightening her legs around his back and kissing him again. "You're making my dreams come true."

The ten-year-old version of herself that had watched Brooks Winslow sail away from the dock on the Prim so many years ago grinned at her knowingly. And she felt laughter bubble up inside of her as she looked up at him. He was going to be okay, and he loved her.

Still on a cloud from her recent orgasm, she took a deep breath, his chest pressing into hers, his heart beating just above hers, his eyes waiting to find out if she returned the precious feelings he'd just shared.

"I love you, too," she said softly, ignoring the whisper in the back of her head that insisted she should tell him about her mother, that he deserved to know the bad and the ugly before they could truly share the good.

But Brooks was her lifelong wish, her heart's deepest desire . . . and he finally loved her. So she was silent, reaching up to draw his lips to hers. He kissed her passionately, deeply, the feelings of his heart manifested in the tenderness of his touch, the patience of his straining body. And though she delighted in his tenderness, she no longer required his patience. She peppered kisses along his jaw, pushing her hips against his.

"I want you, Brooks," she whispered into his ear, her teeth catching his soft lobe and biting, her sex slick and wet, her muscles tightening with anticipation. "Now."

"Me too," he groaned as her legs unlocked and she slid her feet down his legs. He leaned up, kneeling between her thighs and then slipping off the bed. "Let me just get a . . ." He stood in the middle of the room with his back to her, then turned around slowly, desperation widening his eyes. "Fuuuuuck."

She sat up, trying to figure out what had just happened. "What?"

"I don't have protection," he practically sobbed. "I . . . fuck, I promised I wouldn't touch you, so I purposely didn't pack any."

She didn't mean to smile. She didn't. But his erection was so incredibly long and hard, and he looked so frustrated and furious he couldn't use it . . . and she knew something he didn't.

Leaning up on her knees, she grinned at him. "It's a good thing one of us decided to come prepared."

His eyes flared and he stared at her, disbelievingly. "Did you . . . ?"

"A good sailor is always prepared for any and every circumstance," she said.

"Skip . . ." he started, advancing on her with lust doubling in his eyes.

"Will you grab my little black nylon bag from the head?" she asked, pointing to the bathroom.

Had a man ever moved as fast as gloriously naked Brooks Winslow darting through the bedroom doorway and back? He offered the little pouch to her with two hands, like a golden chalice. She unzipped it, pushed everything to the side, and there on the bottom, lay the flat, red-and-white foil packet that had so tormented her a week ago.

"Voila!" she exclaimed, pinching it between two fingers and holding it out to him.

His eyes, which were somehow tender and demanding, patient but determined, loving and passionate and hungrier for her than any man she'd ever known, seized hers and held on.

"You do it, skip," he said. "I want you to touch me. I want to feel your fingers on me."

"Someday soon," she said, scooting to the edge of the bed on her knees and ripping open the packet with her teeth, "we won't use one of these. And then I'll feel you, *all of you*, as you slide inside of me."

As she fit the condom over his head and rolled it slowly up the length of his sex, his breath hitched. She actually *heard* him stop breathing.

"Promise?" he gasped.

"Yes." She sighed, edging back on her knees to make room for him on the bed.

He climbed back onto the bed, kneeling in front of her, mirroring her. And without a word, she placed her hands on his shoulders to brace herself and straddled his thighs. His chest pumped back and forth into hers as his breathing turned raspy and shallow, and his hands landed on her hips to steady her as she reached for his penis with both hands. She raised her hips, positioning herself over him, looking deeply into his eyes, and then lowered herself slowly, inch by thick inch, gasping from the fullness, feeling her muscles stretch and adjust to take him, finally sighing to the point of a whimper when he was buried to the hilt inside of her.

His breath was jerky and hot on her lips as she flattened her feet on either side of him for leverage and lifted a little, moaning when his hands on her hips pushed her back down onto his hardness.

"Skye . . ." he groaned.

She arched her back, pushing her pelvis down, her nipples taut against his chest as she took him even deeper. She clenched her muscles to squeeze him tightly as she lifted her body up and slid back down. His breath caught and held, his eyes fluttering closed instinctively, then opening—dark and heavy—to look at her as he slowly exhaled.

Wrapping one strong arm around her, his other hand dipped between their bodies, skimming over the skin of her belly to find the hidden nub of flesh that throbbed between them. As she rose up again, his thumb pressed down on its target, and she let her head fall back as the divine pressure gathered in her belly.

"Skye," he said. "Tell me again. Tell me that you love me."

Back bowed, she lifted her body as high as she could, until the tip of his sex almost slipped from her body. He was panting, fast and rough as he stared up into her eyes, pressing the pad of his thumb into her clit, sustaining the pressure as the tremors began deep in her core.

"I love you," she gasped as her muscles went slack, letting gravity take over.

Her convulsing muscles sucked him forward as Brooks drove deep inside her body, impaling her on his sex then rocking into her again and again. A gritty, strangled sound escaped from his throat, and his arm tightened like iron right before he groaned with pleasure, his sex pulsing in fast, hot waves inside her body.

Small tremors still rocked their entwined bodies, and Brooks held her close, dropping his lips to her shoulder. His voice, thick with the sort of emotion that told her Brooks Winslow would love her for the rest of her life, rumbled gently across her skin like distant thunder and said, "I love you, too."

Chapter 19

The morning light filtered through the portholes, gray and dreamy, reminding Brooks that this was his last day of sailing with Skye . . . for now. Based on the way things were progressing between them, however, he hoped that there were many, many more cruises ahead in their future. In fact, he couldn't imagine anything better than a life spent on the water with Skye Sorenson.

He held her more tightly against him, marveling at the soft swell of her hips, the way her breasts rested heavily over his arm, the coconut-scented skin of her neck, the softness of her hair. How many times had he passed her on the docks of Sorenson Marina without any clue that under her greasy overalls and banged up ball cap was the sweetest, most sexy woman in the world? And how blessed was he to finally know?

Leaning forward, he nuzzled her neck, kissing her softly, not really wanting to wake her but sort of wanting to talk to her, to see her smile, to make love to her before they had to leave for Charleston. He was supposed to spend a few days in Charleston having the *Zephyr* outfitted for new brass fixtures, but he reconsidered now. Maybe he'd ask his contact at Classic Boats to take care of it and send him pictures via e-mail if he required Brooks' input. He was anxious to return to Maryland with Skye and solidify whatever was happening between them. He didn't want to risk that a few days apart in the real world would make her reconsider their fledgling relationship.

As for *his* feelings . . . he closed his eyes and rested his forehead against her neck. Before Skye, he hadn't woken up beside another human being in almost five years, and he'd never—not in his entire life—woken up beside a woman with whom he was in love. His strong heart fairly throbbed with love for her. With gratitude. With devotion. And it should have scared him, but it didn't. It was like Skye was made for him so long ago, such a fated part of his lonely life, his soul recognized and welcomed her without flinching.

"What're you thinking about?" she asked softly.

"You," he whispered against her skin, pressing kisses to her neck. "I'm sorry I woke you."

"You didn't," she said, sighing. Her breasts swelled against his arm as she took a deep breath, and he felt a fierce and sudden pang of gratitude for something as elementary as her skin pressing gently into his, that he was the man allowed to experience such blessed intimacy with this woman.

"What were *you* thinking about?" he asked, pressing his hips against her backside.

She turned in his arms, and he opened his eyes. For some reason, he'd been expecting her to make some sweet or sassy little rejoinder inviting him to make love to her again. But her face read differently. Not quite upset, she was definitely ruminating about something. He leaned back a little, pulling her closer so their chests touched, not to make a move on her, but to remind her that he was a safe haven for whatever was on her mind.

"What's going on?" he asked, a sudden pinch of worry making his heart race a little. Did she regret last night? Was she going to—

"I need to tell you something," she said, biting her bottom lip and looking uncertain.

"Anything. Go ahead."

"A few days ago you asked about my mom."

Now he was really lost. They were lying naked in each other's arms—whatever he'd expected next, talking about her mother wasn't it. It occurred to him that whatever she wanted to say must be very important to her . . . or very troubling. The last time they'd briefly talked about her mother, in fact, she'd shut down pretty dramatically. Brooks braced himself, gently rubbing her back, but making eye contact with her to let her know he was listening carefully.

"Yeah. I was curious about why I'd never met her."

"I told you she was in LA."

He nodded. "Yeah. And that she left when you were little, and it's best that—"

"That she's not a part of my life."

"I remember."

She dropped his eyes, looking down at where their chests collided, and she eased back just a little before looking up again. "She's, um . . . my mother's an escort. A call girl."

Honestly, he had no idea what to say, but his own history with escorts made him instantly concerned that she was going to tell him that she knew about his extracurricular activities. And then he chased away that thought by telling himself it would be okay because she'd told him she loved him last night . . . which would mean she loved him in spite of his sordid sexual history.

But she surprised him again. Or didn't. Or shouldn't have. Because by now, he should have known that Skye Sorenson was one of the most selfless, thoughtful, amazing women God ever created.

"You're . . ." She swallowed, licking her lips like she did when she was nervous. "You're a public figure . . . and I would understand that dating me could be a liability. If the press ever found out about her, and . . . and splashed her name, and profession, all over the place . . . and you, and me, and—"

"Skye," he said gently, pulling her back against his body. "Skye, stop."

He understood now. She was telling him about her mother to give him an "out," and his heart clenched from the goodness of her, and he silently promised himself never, ever to take her for granted.

"Do you want to be with me?" he asked.

Her head jerked up and down as her eyes searched his face uncertainly.

"I don't care what your mother does for . . . work. I'm sorry that she's hurt you, Skye. I'm so sorry for that. But her choices have nothing to do with us."

He didn't realize she'd been holding her breath until she exhaled heavily, leaning forward to rest her forehead on his chest and burrow against him. "Thank God. I was worried."

"Why?" he asked, rubbing her back tenderly.

"It's so disgusting," she murmured without looking up. "Humiliating and shameful. My mother has sex for money. And the men—the men she must meet, who . . . do that. Creepy perverts cheating on their wives or doing degrading things they can't get any self-respecting woman to consider doing. It makes my skin crawl. It makes me sick to my stomach to think of a man like that."

His blood ran cold, and his own stomach threatened to bottom out as he listened to her words. *The men . . . creepy perverts . . . cheating . . . degrading things.* He held onto her tightly, tightening his jaw, his heart clenching with worry.

He hadn't thought of himself as creepy or perverted while using Elite Escorts, nor had he ever pressured an escort to have sex with him or asked degrading things of her. Sometimes, they'd just end up talking all evening if the chemistry wasn't there. Other times, they'd end up fucking, but it was always consensual and respectful, and Brooks was always concerned with the comfort of his partner. Not that he could tell Skye any of this—not that it would matter. She had a firm idea of her mother's profession. He doubted anything could persuade her that he was still a good guy if she ever found out he'd been known to frequent escorts himself.

When he was silent, she sniffled softly against his chest, leaning back to look at him with stricken eyes. "Brooks, I . . . I understand if—I mean, you didn't sign up for this. We could go back to—"

"No!"

He had been zoning out, concentrating on her words and his past actions, worried about the two ever colliding, but now he focused on her face with fierce intensity, tightening his arm around her waist and pulling her back against his chest.

"No, we're not going back! This doesn't change anything, Skye. Nothing. My heart is yours." He pressed his lips to her head, a litany of *Please don't ever let her find out. Please don't ever let her find out*, circling in his own. "It's *yours*. I swear to you, your mother's life choices don't change that for me. Not at all. Not even the tiniest bit."

"You're amazing," she sobbed softly, looking up at him with wide eyes as a small, tentative smile tilted her lips up hopefully. "You're sure you don't mind?"

"I mind for you, but not for me."

"And you still want me? In your life?"

"Of course I want you in my life," he said, losing himself in her bright-blue eyes. "Skye, you're *all* I really want in my life."

"What if it comes out someday—"

He shrugged, because there was no way to reassure her that it wouldn't. But he could reassure her of his support.

"We'll deal with it then, but it still wouldn't change anything between us. I love you."

"I love you, too," she murmured, a tender, relieved smile covering her face as she rolled him to his back, slid up his hard chest, and pressed her lips to his.

There'd been a possessive, almost combustible quality to their lovemaking this morning. So intense, in fact, that neither of them had remembered protection until the last moment, and Brooks had barely pulled out of her body in time. He'd been so hungry for her, yet incredibly tender afterwards, cleaning the evidence of his climax off her stomach with a warm towel before pulling her into his strong arms and holding her tightly.

Skye was so relieved that there were no more secrets between them, her heart felt a new lightness, watching him with a mix of pride and wonder as he worked, her insides tingling with latent pleasure as his muscular back flexed while he tightened the jib rigging. Her mind skated effortlessly to the touch of those same fingers on her breasts, smoothing downward, gently parting her so that his tongue could explore the most intimate, secret parts of her. With trembling hands, she tightened her grip on the ship's wheel, surprised to look up and find him staring at her, a knowing grin on his handsome face.

"I'd love to know what *you* were just thinking about," he said, rounding the mast to stand in front of her with his hands on his hips. "Looked like something I'd like to be thinking about too."

She felt her cheeks flush with heat, but held his eyes, grinning up at him. "This morning."

"Mmm," he said, moving to stand behind her, his arms encircling her waist. "You were amazing, skip."

She leaned back into him, forcing herself not to close her eyes and loosen her grip on the wheel. "I wasn't the only one there."

"Are you saying *I* was amazing, too?"

"Maybe."

He dropped his lips to the side of her neck, his hair tickling her jaw. "What happens next?"

She straightened a little. This particular conversation had never gone very well with Pat. She'd always wanted a solid commitment, and he'd always been elusive: *We'll see what happens. Don't rush things, Skye! Let's just enjoy the moment.* She was determined not to make the same mistakes by pressuring Brooks.

She shrugged. "We'll see what happens."

"Hmm," he mumbled, his lips abandoning her throat. After a moment he spoke again. "Nope. I want more than seeing what happens. I want to chart a more solid course than that."

He wasn't looking at her, so she let herself grin as wide as she wanted to, but forced herself to hold back the joyful chuckle that bubbled up inside. "Oh?"

"Yeah." He laced his hands together over her belly, resting his chin on her shoulder. "I mean, if you do too."

"Why don't you tell me what you have in mind," she suggested.

"Simple. I want us to be together. I don't suppose you want to move to Haverford?"

Move? To Haverford? Her heart soared from the feeling of belonging, of being wanted, of how right it felt to be with Brooks, but she forced herself to look logically at his suggestion. Leave her father and Sorenson Marina? Leave Havre de Grace? Her lips twitched. She wasn't ready to give up her whole life. Not quite yet.

"My dad . . . and my job . . . and—"

"Okay . . . Wednesdays," he said.

"What? Wednesdays? What does that mean?"

"Every Wednesday you come and stay overnight with me in Haverford . . . aaaand, I'll come stay with you on the weekends until I can find my own place."

"Oh. Your own place?" she asked, the idea making her so instantly sad, she was happy the wind was blowing into her eyes.

"Yeah, I mean . . . I don't want to assume anything," he murmured.

"Like what?"

"Like calling it *our* place," he said softly, close to her ear. "Even though that's what it'll be."

She closed her burning eyes for just a second, and then blinked a few more times when she opened them. His words were so sweet—so unbelievably, incredibly sweet and perfect to her ears—she almost wanted to weep.

"So we'll just call it my place until you're ready to move in."

She didn't say anything. She was too overwhelmed with emotion. He wasn't leaving. He wasn't shoving her to the side and leaving her like her mother or Pat. He was staying. He was going to change his whole life so he could stay with her.

"Okay with you, skip?" he asked, his voice low and tender.

"Okay with me," she whispered, afraid to speak louder, afraid to break the spell they were under as the sun started to set and the miles between here and Charleston whooshed away by the moment.

"And Mondays, Tuesdays, and Thursdays will just suck for a little while," he said, pouting. "But I can't move just yet.

My sister's planning her wedding, and I have commitments in Philly, and—oh, shoot, I have to call a client out in San Diego."

"San Diego?"

"Yeah. I was offered a consulting job. A yacht club out there wanted me to spend a couple of months with them, get them in shape for a regatta this fall."

"Oh," she said, trying to be brave as she imagined Brooks waving good-bye to her as Pat had. *Don't be selfish. Don't rock the boat.* "Well, you should take it if you—"

"Take it?" He sounded surprised . . . and disappointed. "Huh. You want me to take it?"

She shrugged, uncertain of what to say. Her heart screamed, *No! Please don't go halfway across the country without me.* But her heart cautioned her to temper her expectations.

"I could, but . . . I mean, I'd prefer to stick around this summer and spend some more time with you. Maybe even get a few races in together."

And that's all it took.

Her heart. Literally. Burst.

She turned in his arms, tilting her face up to his and winding her arms around his neck. "Take the wheel."

He did.

"Thank you," she said passionately, her voice breathy and her eyes still burning a little as she stared up at him.

"For what?" he asked.

"For asking me to bid on you. For letting me skipper. For falling in love with me. For wanting to stick around." She pulled his face down to hers, arching her back and sighing as he stepped forward to trap her more tightly against him.

"Skip, you've got it all backwards," he said gently, his eyes caressing her face with such profound tenderness, her breath caught. "I won *you*. I got to crew for *you*. I am the luckiest man on earth because you love me back, and my life just got a million times better because you *want* me to stick around. *I'm* the lucky one, Skye."

"Call it a draw?" she suggested, tilting her head up to his.

"Done," he said, kissing her senseless.

They motored into the Charleston Pointe Harbor and Marina around six o'clock in the evening, and despite Skye's declaration that the interviews were over, Brooks was surprised that Guy wasn't already waiting for them, lingering at their slip to take his final pound of flesh.

Brooks threw the buoys over the sides and cleated the bow line, then drew his phone out of his back pocket, searching for messages. Sure enough, there was an e-mail from Guy dated today at five o'clock:

> I guess you made your decision.
> No need for more pictures.
> I've got my story.
> Enjoy Charleston.

His eyebrows furrowing together, Brooks quickly opened his sent mail file, looking for the e-mail he'd sent to his accountant last night. Not finding it in the file, his heart sped up and his mouth went dry as he noticed an unsent message in the outbox folder. *Oh my God.* It hadn't sent. The message hadn't sent. The check hadn't been cut. The money hadn't been sent.

He'd been so distracted with Jessica's call and making love to Skye, he hadn't confirmed the transaction. Frankly, he hadn't even thought about it again.

He flashed worried eyes at Skye, who turned off the ignition and withdrew the key, holding it out to Brooks.

"So," she said, "how about a little dinner on our last—Oh, wait a sec." She pulled her phone from her hip pocket and Brooks had the sudden, insane urge to rip it from her fingers and throw it in the water. "It's my father!" Offering him a broad smile, she held up a finger asking him for a minute and pressed the phone to her ear. "Pop! Hey! We just made it into Charles—What?"

Her face—so bright and cheerful a moment before—fell. She cut her eyes to Brooks, then turned her back to him, walking to the bench at the stern of the *Zephyr* where he had talked to Jessica last night.

"No, he didn't," she gasped. "No. I . . . Oh, Pop, I'm so sorry."

Brooks rushed to her, sitting beside her. But she didn't look up at him. In fact, she slid away from him—just a little bit, but enough to sting.

"What else does it say?" she asked in a small, broken voice.

Her neck was bent, and she was shaking her head back and forth. "Oh God. Oh, Pop. I-I don't know how they found out about her. No, of course not. I'd never mention her. Pat is the only one I ever told. I'm so sorry. I shouldn't have ever . . . Wait." Her voice changed, suddenly cracking like a whip, shock infusing it with disbelief. "What did you say?"

Now she looked up at Brooks, blinking, concern etched into her worried face. "*Brooks?* You're *sure* it says that?" She paused, listening to her father. "I don't believe it. Because it's not possible. No, Pop. I *know* him. It's a lie. You have to understand. This reporter was the worst, smarmiest, most disgusting . . . he'd make up anything to—"

Suddenly, her eyes widened with dismay, and what Brooks saw there decimated him.

"*Wh-What?*" she gasped, her eyes searching Brooks' face, looking at him like she didn't know him, or maybe like she *did* know him, she just didn't know he was capable of breaking her heart. "You . . . *You* saw him?" She was almost panting, she was breathing so fast, so hard. "No, Pop. You could be wrong," she insisted. "Couldn't they just have been . . . ?" She swallowed, clenching her eyes shut and pulling her hand away with a jerk when he reached for it. She stood up, giving him her back and walking over to the deck rail. "Girlfriends! I just thought he had a lot of . . . girlfriends."

Brooks dropped his head, trying to suck in a clean gulp of air, but he was unable. It wasn't difficult to piece together the conversation he was listening to, even though it was one-sided.

Guy had found out about her mother being an escort from Pat, who'd also shared his suspicions about Brooks' use of escorts. He'd used the information to embarrass her and get even for her breaking up with him and shattering his fragile ego. *God, what a fucking bastard.*

And Skye's first instinct had been to defend him, which made Brooks feel like the worst scumbag who ever lived.

He recalled Jack's face when he warned Brooks that Skye was a "good girl, a nice girl." At the time, Brooks had known what Jack was saying. Jack had noticed the taxis and the blondes. And he was on the other side of the phone right now reassuring Skye that everything Guy wrote was true.

His head still hanging, Brooks didn't realize she'd hung up the phone and crossed the deck to stand before him until she said softly, in a dazed, heartbroken monotone, "It seems that Brooks Winslow's technique of charming escorts has worked on fresh-faced Skye Sorenson . . . which shouldn't be a surprise, as Sorenson's mother, who can be found under the name Bunny Lynn, is an escort herself."

Brooks took a deep breath and looked up at her, her devastated, pleading eyes breaking his heart in half.

"Skye . . ." he started.

"My mother," she said, licking her lips and shaking her head as she looked over his shoulder at the setting sun behind him. "Guy wrote about my mother."

"Skye," he said again.

"No," she said softly, slowly. "You don't talk yet." Her blue eyes, usually so warm and open, were cold and hurt. "I told you all about her this morning. You didn't think to mention to me that you, yourself, use escorts with some regularity? So often, in fact, that my father—and Pat, apparently, since he was Guy's source—knew all about it?"

"It's in my past."

"*Your past?* I *saw* you with one of those women a few weeks ago!" she cried, swiping her angry tears away with the back of her hand.

"It doesn't matter. It's still in my past. It was in my past the very first night I kissed you, and it will always be in my past, because it will never, ever again be a part of my present or future. You're my present, Skye. You're my future." Brooks stood up, reaching for her shoulders, unable to bear the pain on her face, but she pulled away from him, putting her hands on her hips and staring back at him.

"No," she said, shaking her head, her eyes profoundly sad. "You're not my present or my future. You're one of the men I was talking about this morning. You're the disgusting, perverted, anonymous man who takes what he wants and leaves."

He flinched, swallowing the lump in his throat and finding his voice. "That's not true. I'm not those things. And I'm not leaving."

"You don't *do* commitment. You do temporary, remember? No wonder you loved the idea of *Zephyrland*!" she sobbed. "No wonder you found my mother's profession so easy to forgive!"

"Skip . . ." he said, letting his hands hang uselessly by his sides. "Let me explain. Please."

"I *never* wanted to be like my mother," she raged, her hands in small fists by hers. "And now, splashed all over the Internet, it says that I am. It says I'm *exactly* like her. You frequent escorts. My mother's an escort. There's a picture of us kissing. Bam! I guess that makes me—"

"The woman I love," he cried, feeling desperate, feeling scared that he was really and truly losing her. "The amazing, wonderful, beautiful woman I love." He reached for her face, relieved when she didn't pull away. He cupped her cheek, holding her eyes, frantic to get through to her. "You're *nothing* like your mother. You're nothing like—"

"Like those girls who visited you at the marina?" She stepped back, shrinking from his touch, looking at him brokenheartedly while tears still fell down her cheeks in streams. "Because I look like them, Brooks. Don't I? Blonde hair. Blue eyes."

He searched her face and nodded. "Are you asking if you're my type? Yes, you are, Skye. You know that."

"Well, you're not *my* type," she said, raising her chin as her voice shook, making the words breathy and uncertain. "Not anymore. You're *not* the man of my dreams. You're the man of my nightmares . . . and I need you to leave me alone."

She gave him one last devastated look, then turned around and ran below.

Chapter 20

Brooks stood quietly on the *Zephyr's* deck, trying to get his head around what had just happened and darting, with precision, to one terrible question: Had he just lost her? Had he really just lost her after everything they'd been through?

It sort of looks that way, he thought, his stomach clenching with pain and his heart throbbing as he looked at the hatch that led downstairs. Should he run after her? Should he try to talk to her? Try to explain? Try to reassure her?

No. Not right now.

He'd grown up with a mother and a sister. When a woman was as upset as Skye, she needed a little time and space, and the least he could do was give it to her. Checking his back pocket for his wallet and phone, he slipped under the deck railing onto the dock and walked slowly toward the marina, feeling heavy and worried and . . . incredibly pissed off.

His first call? To Preston, who was an in-house lawyer for the Philadelphia Flyers.

"Brooks! How's the cruise go—"

"Go to *Celeb!*.com."

"Okay . . . what am I looking for there?" asked Pres, his fingers clicking on the keys of his ever-present laptop.

"You'll know it when you see it."

There was silence on the other end of the phone for a moment as the website loaded and Preston took a look at it. Then, "We'll sue the bastards, Brooks. This is libelous bullshit."

"Unfortunately, it's not," answered Brooks quietly, his jaw tight.

"It's . . . not? Skye Sorenson's mother is an escort?"

"Yeah."

"Well, we'll just sue them for the shit they said about you! You don't use . . . Wait a second. You don't use escorts, Brooks, do you?" Brooks was silent, heat seeping into his face as he imagined Preston's eyes flatten with understanding and disappointment. "Oh. Well . . . can it be proven?"

"It'd be hearsay at best. I have a nondisclosure agreement with the agency. Not to mention, I'm not even close to their most high-profile client. They deal in discretion. I'm confident there aren't any pictures or a paper trail."

"Okay," said Preston, keeping his voice both professional and carefully neutral. "We could certainly sue, then . . . but do you want my honest advice?"

"No. Lie to me."

"I know you're pissed, but don't be a dick."

"Yes, Preston. I want your honest opinion."

"Well, no offense, big brother, but you're an ex-Olympian, not a movie star or a supermodel. I honestly believe that this will blow over in a day or two when one of the Kardashians decides to save the whales. My honest advice is to ignore it completely. That said, however, I might skip town for a few weeks if I were you and give it a *chance* to blow over. You know, just so that there aren't any photos of you looking pissed or reporters bugging you for a sound bite."

"I want to sue someone!"

"I wouldn't," said Preston with finality, level-headed about legal and PR matters, as always. There was a long pause before he spoke again. "Can I ask you something?"

"What?" snapped Brooks.

"Why the hell were you using escorts?"

"I didn't want romantic entanglements. I didn't want to get involved with anyone."

"So you paid for it?"

"It wasn't always like that."

"You *didn't* always have sex?"

"Not always. Not if we didn't click. Listen, I wanted to date, I wanted to meet women, but I didn't want for the women I spent time with to ever get the wrong idea. It seemed like the perfect solution: date escorts, never get attached, never raise expectations, never get hurt, never hurt anyone else."

"I get it. You *know* I get it. Romance is messy. Big time. But, here's what I don't get, bro . . . I'm looking at these pictures on the *Celeb!* website, and it looks like you *are* involved with someone."

Brooks had walked to the end of his dock, the end of the main dock, and into the resort area. There was a tiki-style bar with a thatched roof set up poolside, and Brooks pulled out one of the stools and sat down, looking up at the bartender. "Scotch. Double. Rocks."

"Now you're drinking? Great."

"Shut up, Pres."

"So? Skye?"

"Yeah." Brooks sighed. "That happened."

"What happened?"

He took a big gulp of Scotch, wincing as it burned his throat. "I fucking fell in love with her."

"Whhhhoa. *What? In* love?" He could practically hear Preston recoil through the phone. Preston had been burned by love . . . badly. So badly, he had the scars to prove it and swore he'd never go near it again. It wasn't a surprise when he demanded, "Have you lost your mind?"

"No," Brooks said tersely, taking another sip. "I love her. I didn't mean for it to happen, but it did, and now that it did . . . she's it for me, Pres."

"You mean like . . . *it* it?"

"Yeah. The whole nine yards. Ring, wedding, kids. All of it. Except now it's really fucking messy. Her mother, my indiscretions. She didn't sign up for this."

"Does *she* love *you*?"

"She said she did last night."

"You think she's the kind of girl who can turn off her feelings when the water gets rough?"

Brooks thought about this for a moment. "No. I don't, but she never wanted to be like her mom. And I cheapened her. Being with me did that to her. I don't know if she can forgive that."

"Can I submit to you that *you* didn't cheapen her . . . *Celeb!* magazine did," said Preston gently. "Anyway, Brooks, there's one surefire way to change the perception of a woman's reputation in the press, and that's to give her the right title."

"Title?"

"Wife," said Preston softly, an acidic bite in his usually level voice.

Wife. Brooks' heart clenched with longing. *Right.*

"Like she'd marry me now," said Brooks, throwing back the rest of the Scotch, then tapping the rim of the glass to request another. *Like she'd marry me.* The words circled in his head. *Marry me.*

A slideshow of Skye Sorenson played in his mind . . . little Skye waving to him from the dock of Sorenson Marina . . . teenage Skye always hanging out at the marina while he was training during college . . . Skye, the best boat mechanic he'd ever met, telling him stories while she worked on the Passport's electrical board . . . Skye walking down the aisle of the Ritz Carlton hotel in a knockout dress and the sweetest smile he'd ever seen . . . Skye's lips, her eyes, the way her words resonated in him . . . her hands on the ship wheel, her hands on his body . . . I love you, I love you, I love you . . .

Marry me.

"She'll say no," Brooks whispered.

"Yeah, you're right. Why would she want to marry an ass-hole like you?"

Brooks scoffed. "What a good idea to call my little brother for some guidance."

Preston sighed heavily. "You want guidance? You know how hard it is for me to say this, but . . . put a ring on Skye's finger or at least offer it to her. Then take that job in San Diego and take her with you. Come back for Jessie's wedding. And while you're at it, stop making your life so god-damned complicated."

"You make it sound so easy."

"It *is* easy." Preston paused, and Brooks thought about the secret Preston had somehow kept to himself for the last few years. Brooks *knew* this was difficult advice for Preston to offer, which made it all the more meaningful. When his brother spoke again, his voice was soft and a little sad. "Will you marry me . . . four words. Two seconds. The worst she can say is no."

Brooks winced. The worst was pretty bad.

"I gotta go, Brooks. I can't—" Preston cleared his throat, and when he spoke again, his voice was all business. "We're signing a new player today, and I've got last-minute contract negotiations up the wazoo. Hope it all goes well, huh?"

"Yeah. Thanks, Pres."

"Anytime."

Brooks placed his phone on the bar and sipped his second Scotch more leisurely.

The worst she can say is no. He bit his bottom lip, feeling young and stupid and way out of his depth. It was a terrible risk to ask her to marry him.

Did he love her? Yes. He loved her more than anything.

Did he want to spend the rest of his life with her? Hell, yes.

By proposing, he'd be offering her the protection of his name, publicly declaring that she was nothing like her mother—that he loved and respected her and that whatever they were doing together wasn't temporary, but permanent—and that he *wasn't* just taking what he wanted and leaving, as she'd tearfully accused him. *She* was what he wanted . . . and if she'd let him, he'd stay forever.

Could he bear her rejection? He thought about this for a moment, sipping his drink, watching the sun set over the water. Yes, he could bear it because he wouldn't accept it. She'd fallen in love with him. There might be disappointment and anger in the equation now, but there was definitely love, too. He wouldn't give her up. Even if she said "no" today, he'd keep asking. He'd ask her every day for the rest of his life if he had to—he'd prove to her that he was the man she wanted, that he'd never repeat the mistakes of his past, that he wasn't going anywhere, that when he told her he loved her . . . he meant forever.

Brooks knew something about persistence, about training, about reaching near-insurmountable goals. He knew about deciding what he wanted and working his ass off to get it. Skye Sorenson was what he wanted. And he'd do just about anything to have her.

"Hey," he said, pulling out his wallet and sliding a fifty to the bartender. "Call me a cab? I need to get into Charleston."

Since she'd hurried downstairs and locked the bedroom door behind her, Skye hadn't really stopped crying for more than a few minutes, and by this point, her eyes were raw and burning. At some point, she'd taken off her clothes and pulled on her pajamas, collected her things, and packed her bag. Lying in the bed she'd shared with Brooks several times, she looked at the prebooked airline tickets sitting on top of her duffel bag. She'd stopped crying long enough to arrange for a cab to be at the marina at seven o'clock in the morning, and she'd leave the safety of her room at six-fifty so she could avoid an awkward farewell with Brooks.

"Brooks," she murmured, her voice breaking, and a fresh stream of tears slid down her cheeks.

For years, she and her father had dreaded anyone finding out about Shelley's profession. It was a family embarrassment about which they rarely spoke, but this? Having it splashed all over the Internet? This was way beyond Skye's worst nightmares. Not only did the whole world know her mother was a whore, the article had painted her with the same scarlet brush. Like mother, like daughter. It was so frustrating, so unjust and painful that she turned on her side, staring at the cabin wall in the dim evening light, her head cradled on her bent elbow.

I swear to you, your mother's life choices don't change that for me. Not at all. Not even the tiniest bit. We'll deal with it then, but it still wouldn't change anything between us. You're all I want. I love you.

His words from this morning resonated in her head, tears plopping on her arm as she recalled how safe and loved they'd made her feel. He'd been ready to shoulder it with her if the news ever came out. But finding out that the women with whom she'd seen him at the marina were also escorts? It had knocked the wind out of her sails. It had disappointed her so terribly, she could barely look at him.

Thinking about him with those women in their short cocktail dresses with fancy hair and high heels made her stomach churn. It hurt to think about it. It ached. It was sordid and dirty. It was everything she hated about her cheap, cheating mother.

Her mother, who had abandoned her and chosen a life of servicing anonymous men over being a loving mother to Skye. Her mother, who had gone to Los Angeles and left her behind.

Why would Brooks want to be with a woman like that? Was that what he wanted?

She sniffled softly, thinking about Brooks and what she knew of him, who he was.

He'd had to deal with the shocking loss of his father as a teenager. He'd become the male head of his family and risen to the challenge, helping to raise his younger siblings. And as forty loomed closer, he was anxious that he, too, would meet his father's fate.

After this week, I can only offer you friendship. I can't offer you anything else.

And so they'd embarked on something temporary that had turned into something real.

I want us to be together . . . I'm weak and selfish, but God help me, I can't let you go.

He had fought against wanting her. He had tried not to raise her expectations. He had tried to keep her at arm's length. Why? Because he didn't think he had anything substantial to offer her.

I'm a bad deal.

Because he didn't want to hurt her. And suddenly it all clicked in her head, and her heart swelled with sympathy and understanding. He'd paid for company, and likely for sex, to avoid making an attachment, to avoid romance or commitment. He'd paid escorts for their time and company in order to keep himself an emotional island.

"Brooks," she said softly, taking a deep, ragged breath as she recalled the way he'd jumped off the side of the *Zephyr*, into black, churning water, to save her. He loved her. She didn't doubt it. She couldn't.

But it hurt terribly to realize that he wasn't perfect . . . to see him get knocked off that shiny pedestal she'd kept him on for most of his life. Rich, handsome, Olympic athlete, natural-born sailor Brooks Winslow was just a man. A man who'd made mistakes. She was angry with him for that. She was furious with him for destroying the near-perfect man she thought she'd fallen in love with.

The soft knock on her door, followed by a wiggling of the doorknob, made her sit up in bed, frantically wiping the tears away, even though he couldn't enter the room. She stared at the door like it was a snake. Though her heart had softened since their fight, she was not ready to see him. Not yet.

"Skye?" he asked softly through the door, knocking again. "Can I come in, Skye? I need to talk to you."

"Go away."

"I won't go away," he said gently, his voice quietly and patiently resolute. "If you won't let me in, I'll just talk to you through the door."

She was silent and heard him slide down the door and take a seat on the floor. His body blocked the light now, and his voice was lower than it had been before. She sank back down into the bed, but the sheets still smelled of him, and of her, and last night's lovemaking, and her eyes burned with fresh tears.

"Skye . . . I thought I was going to die. That's what I *truly* believed. Which meant I didn't have the right to love someone or let them fall in love with me. I saw what it did to my mother, my brothers and sister. I didn't want to do that to someone else. So yes, I paid for companionship, and there were times that companionship led to sex. I'm not proud of it. But I can't change it. I was lonely, but I didn't want to raise someone's expectations. I didn't want to hurt anyone. That's the truth. I swear it."

She'd already figured this out, but it reassured her to hear him articulate it. Taking a deep breath, she clenched her fingers in the sheets of the bed, licking her dry, salty lips. He'd been lonely and made a choice he thought could offer him strings-free companionship now and then. Could she really blame him for that? Hadn't she stayed in a crappy relationship with Patrick for the exact same reason? She hadn't wanted to be alone. At least for a little while, it had been better to be with Pat for the wrong reasons than alone for the right ones.

It took her a minute to realize that he hadn't spoken again, and she sat up, her eyes darting to the strip of space under the door where his body still blocked the light, and she sighed with relief. *Keep talking to me, Brooks. Please keep talking. Please be my hero and save us . . .*

"I asked you to do this cruise with me because we were friends. Good friends." He scoffed quietly. "I didn't—we've agreed I was a jackass, right?—but I didn't see you like I do now. You were just my sailing friend, Skye, helping me out of a jam, and then . . ." He paused, and she swung her legs over the side of her bed unconsciously, holding her breath, hanging on his next words. "When you showed up at that auction just in the nick of time, saving me, looking so goddamn beautiful, I . . . You know what? You were *still* my friend. You were someone I already cared for and trusted. But suddenly, in an instant, you were everything I'd tried so hard to avoid. The wind to my water. The light to my dark. This *beautiful* girl who I already cared for. And then I kissed you . . . and you were all sweetness and softness. Skye, I swore I'd never use another escort again after that night. I closed my account because I wanted to be a different man, a better man. I couldn't have you, but it was hell not to think about you. Part of me wished I could go back to being your friend . . . but I couldn't. I saw you teaching those little kids how to sail, and *all I could see* . . . all I wanted *in the entire world* . . . was you."

Her feet touched the floor, and she stepped soundlessly across the room to the door, lowering herself as silently as she could and kneeling on the hardwood floor, desperately needing to be closer to him.

"And then we started sailing. And I *still* fought it . . . for me, for you, for Pat . . . no, fuck Pat. For *you*. I didn't want to fall in love with you, but I was already a lost cause. I didn't want *you* to fall in love with *me*. But, you did. *We* did. So fucking fast. Like that lifelong friendship was a fuse just waiting for the match that would turn it into love. Boom."

She saw fireworks in her head because, yes, *boom!* That's exactly what it had been like.

"Skye? Are you listening?"

She nodded, swiping away her tears, but stayed silent.

"Yesterday? When I found out about how my father died, my sister said, 'You're going to live a long life. Why not live it with someone you love?' I was holding your hand when she said that, and I squeezed it so tightly, because *you're* the someone I love, Skye. You're the *only* person I want to live a long life with, because I see what that life would look like, and I want it so fucking badly, it aches. I want to live on the water, and race with you, and make love to you, and make babies with you, and damn it, Skye, I want a *life* with you. A *whole* life." He groaned softly, muttering something softly under his breath before continuing. "Yesterday was the best day of my life . . . but if I lose you, yesterday's news doesn't matter because I don't want to live a long life without you."

Leaning forward, she rested her forehead on the door as rivulets of tears coursed down her face and silent sobs made her shoulders shake. He wasn't perfect, but he was hers. And she wanted him.

"Have I lost you? Have I lost you, Skye?"

"No," she whispered, her voice small and broken.

"What?"

"No," she said, her resolve to stay angry at him weakening by the second. She felt such a profound tenderness for him in knowing that he'd tried so desperately not to fall in love with her, but lost the battle so soundly. So had she. She flattened her palm against the door, imagining he was doing the same. "No, you haven't lost me."

"Skye?" he asked, his voice pleading. "Please open the door. Please let me talk to you face to face."

"No," she said quickly, wiping her tears away. His words were beautiful, and yes, she understood why he'd used escorts and would eventually forgive him for it. But it didn't fix everything. She was still deeply humiliated by what had been written about her, and at least some of it she laid at his feet.

"Why?"

"Because the whole world thinks I'm a whore, Brooks. Because I know you're the same man you were this morning, but you're different too. And I want to trust you, but I—"

"You *can*," he said softly. "I'm the *exact* same man I was last night, this morning, two hours ago. I made some bad choices out of fear and loneliness, and I can't go back and change them, but they're in the past, Skye. I can promise you that."

She believed him. She hoped she wasn't a fool, but she believed him.

"And I can't do anything about you being mad at me or at *Celeb!*, but you are *not* a whore, and I'm going to make sure the world knows it." He paused again, and she leaned her ear against the door. "Are you going to let me in?"

"Not yet," she said, even though her curiosity was piqued. Was he going to sue *Celeb!*? Go beat up Guy Hunter? How exactly was he going to repair her crippled reputation?

"Fine. Then I'll do this here."

Do what?

"This morning, you said you never wanted to be like your mother. And this evening, after you talked to your dad, you said that I was someone who takes what he wants and leaves." Thinking of how he'd let her skipper his boat, how he'd saved her life, how he'd loved her so tenderly, her words from this afternoon—spoken out of hurt and anger— seemed petty and wrong, and she winced, almost interrupting him, but he continued before she had a chance. "But you're nothing like your mother. And I'm not going anywhere without you. And if you'd just . . . Skye, can you *please* open the door?"

The sudden click of the lock surprised him, and he backed up, shifting to one knee to look up at her. Her eyes were red-rimmed and her cheeks were puffy. The last thing Brooks had ever wanted to do was hurt Skye or make her sad, and it twisted his heart to know that he'd inadvertently accomplished both.

"You're *nothing* like your mother," he repeated, holding up the small, black velvet box in his hand. "And I'm not going *anywhere* without you."

Her shoulders gave her away. Her face was trying very hard to stay cautious and unforgiving, but her shoulders trembled, and she wet her lips, flicking her eyes to the diamond engagement ring, and Brooks had some satisfaction in watching them widen.

She took a deep breath and cut her eyes back to Brooks. "What's that?"

"You've never seen one of these before?"

Her lips trembled, but she battled like crazy to keep herself from smiling. "What makes you think I'd marry the man of my nightmares?"

He reached for her hand, a tremor of relief racing through his body when she curled her fingers around his instead of pulling away.

"I'm the same man I was yesterday."

She raised her chin and shook her head. "Nope. Yesterday you were the man of my dreams. You were perfect."

"Skip?" he said, still holding her hand, still holding the ring box open. "I was never perfect."

"To me you were."

"And now I'm not."

She flinched just slightly, and he had his answer. It hurt him to know that he'd taken such a fall in her estimation. It made him certain that kneeling here on the floor before her was foolishness.

But she still held onto his hand, and her face softened as the seconds ticked by, and like Preston had said . . . Brooks had nothing left to lose.

"I'm not perfect, and frankly, I don't want to be the man of your dreams. The only man I really want to be . . . is your husband."

Her fingers tightened around his hand as she sucked in a little breath and held it, fat tears slipping over the rims of her eyes.

"Skye Sorenson, I love you like crazy. You're the only woman I've ever loved, and you're the woman I'm still going to love on the day I die . . . many, many, many years from now."

Tears slicked down her face, and her tongue darted out to lick them away.

"I told you once that I was a bad deal, but you told me you loved me anyway." He took a deep breath, locking his green eyes on her blue. "Please say you'll be my wife," he murmured, doubt coursing through him. She was sweet and she was forgiving, but this was a bold move, and he knew it . . . and he hoped and prayed with everything he was and everything he would ever be, that Skye Sorenson would take another risk on him and bid on Brooks Winslow once again.

She finally let out the breath she'd been holding and dropped his eyes so she could look at the ring.

"Promise to always let me skipper?" she asked, sitting down on his bent knee and perching there.

A slow smile started to spread across his face. "Always."

"And I always get the forward cabin," she said.

"Mm-hm," he murmured, grinning up at her, his face just inches from hers. "But I'm going to share it with you."

"And you're going to sell the Passport," she said, arching an eyebrow as she referred to the yacht he'd used to meet women now and then.

"We can burn it if you want, baby."

She was losing her struggle to stay mad at him. He could see it, and it made his heart so goddamn hopeful, if she didn't say yes—

"I'm still going to wear overalls sometimes."

"That's fine," he said, "because I'm going to take them off of you at the end of every day."

"I like working at the marina."

"Luckily, I *do* have a thing for sailing, even though I often come in third."

"If I ever fall in black water again, don't risk your own—"

"I'm coming in after you, skip. Every time. No argument."

She stared at him for a long time, her blue eyes so soft and focused, he didn't know how much longer he could bear it.

"I love you, Brooks," she finally said, wetting her lips and laughing so softly, he only knew it was a laugh because it matched the stunning smile spreading out across her face.

"I love you, too," he whispered, overcome with the sheer force of his love for her.

She held out her free hand, which trembled, and said, "Yes."

"Yes?" he gasped.

"Yes," she said, the sound soft and joyful, and his heart thundered with victory as he tore the ring from its little velvet bed and slipped it on her finger.

"You're going to marry me," he said, gathering her into his arms and standing up. He looked down at her lovely, upturned face, so damned grateful for this woman and the future she'd just promised him. "I swear you won't regret it, Skye. I may not be the man of your dreams anymore, but I'm going to try like hell to make your dreams come true."

And in his eyes, Skye saw the truth.

She wasn't at all like her mother. She was loved and respected. Protected, desired, and wanted. She was worth fighting for and worth staying for, and she'd never be left behind.

Relaxing into the safe in the harbor of Brooks Winslow's strong arms, she remembered the little girl who'd stood on the dock of her father's marina in the setting sun and watched him sail away, whispering just loud enough for the wind and the water to hear, *I'm gonna marry you someday.*

Drawing back just enough to look into his beloved eyes, she grinned at him, "You already have, Brooks. You already have."

EPILOGUE

Two months later

With her bare feet propped up on the metal deck railing, Skye Sorenson looked out over the golden sand of La Jolla to the glistening, blue Pacific. She hadn't expected to love San Diego quite so much, and she had to admit that she was a little sad that she and Brooks would be moving back to Havre de Grace on Sunday. It had been a heavenly eight weeks at their little villa by the sea, helping Brooks train the Pacific Pointe Club sailing team during the day and having him to herself every night.

He'd been right, she thought, slicing another piece of apple and slipping it between her teeth. The scandal about her mother had died down quickly after the press had gotten a look at her ring; it had taken all the wind out of their sails, and Brooks' lawyer had taken care of any further character assassination of his future wife. Skye Sorenson—*almost*—Winslow was off-limits; either that, or the press seemed to recognize that there was simply no dirt to dig up on Skye, and as quickly as her name had appeared, it disappeared.

As for her mother . . . there was some speculation about Brooks meeting Skye through her mother (ridiculous) or using her services at one time (again, ludicrous). But when they failed to find any record of Brooks spending time in Los Angeles over the last ten years, that rumor faded quickly, too.

Because no escort service came forward to claim an association with Brooks, Guy Hunter's entire article hinged on the comments of a jealous ex-boyfriend and two cabbies, one of whom had been arrested for DUI twice and couldn't seem to remember at which marina he'd dropped off and picked up his fare.

Patrick, who had sent Skye an apologetic text she hadn't answered, was probably somewhere near California now. She looked out at the water. She didn't know. She didn't care. She'd never forgive him for the information he shared with Guy Hunter, though she grudgingly understood that it was his feeling of rejection that had probably goaded him into it. Perhaps he'd drop off Inga in Sweden, she mused . . . and hopefully he'd decide to stay there for good.

It probably helped that they'd left the east coast within a few days of the story breaking, with her father's somewhat dubious blessing.

He'd pulled her aside once she and Brooks returned to Maryland together.

"You're engaged to him? Are you crazy, Skye? How could you get engaged to him now that you know who he is?"

Feathers soundly ruffled, she'd looked at her father squarely and answered, "I got engaged to him because I know *exactly* who he is. You can generalize him into someone who spent time with escorts now and then, but he's more than that. Much more than that, Dad, and you know it. He had his reasons . . . and those reasons are . . . well, they're not a part of him anymore. But I am." She'd softened her voice and given her father a small grin. "And besides, I'm in love with him."

"I never had a problem with Brooks Winslow," her father had answered. "Except for the girls. He's a damn good sailor, pays his bill on time, and he's brought a lot of business to this marina over the years. But marriage, Skye? Are you sure?"

She'd caught sight of Brooks, stepping onto the dock after checking on the Prim, his dark hair thick and shiny in the late-afternoon sun. The tan, muscular arms that held her so gently, so tenderly, flexed as he checked the bow line. Those strong arms had pulled her out of black water and delivered her to safety. They were going to hold her children one day. They were going to hold her when she was old and gray.

"I'm sure, Pop," she'd whispered, her heart full and certain. "Can you manage without me for a few weeks?"

"If you're happy, I'm happy, Skye. I can manage."

Her father's business hadn't been affected at all by the article, and with no one to interview or harass—and much more interesting people in the world to pursue than an ex-Olympian and his mechanic girlfriend who were planning a quiet wedding sometime soon—the story faded almost entirely.

Almost, because Skye had had to reconcile her own feelings about Brooks' anonymous lovers, which—despite her deep feelings for him—hadn't happened overnight. It had taken at least *five or six* nights, all spent with his body worshipping hers, his vows of love and fidelity unceasing, his plans for their future bright and not the least bit overwhelming, because he would be standing right beside her, her partner and lover, every step of the way. She understood how lonely he had been, because she'd been lonely too. And she had also learned this: finding the right person didn't mean finding a perfect person. Brooks had made mistakes, and she had too. And they'd make ten dozen more before their life together was through. And that was okay. That was just fine. That was a life she—

"You ready, skip?"

She turned to find Brooks standing just inside the sliding glass doorway between the living room and outdoor porch, his hair wet and skin smooth after a shave and shower. He'd gotten tanner during their time in California, and his green eyes sparkled as he smiled down at her.

"If we hurry, we can catch the sunset," she said, grinning at him as she set her apple and knife on the table beside her.

"My woman loves a sunset," he said, closing the door and offering her his hand.

She took it, standing up on bare tiptoes to press her lips to his as he pulled her against his chest. "That's not all she loves."

He laced his fingers through hers, leading her down the steps to the warm sand and asked, "How'd I get so lucky anyway?"

"You were in a jam. And I was your friend. And you asked me to bid on you."

"What a story," he said, squeezing her fingers.

"If we ever write our story," she said, keeping her voice as calm and level as she could, "let's call it 'Bidding on Brooks,' okay?"

He stopped walking, chuckling softly as he pulled her back against his chest and rested his chin on her head. His arms held her tightly, keeping her warm as the sun neared the horizon and they watched it sink slowly, closer and closer to the sea.

"Who'd want to read our story, anyway?" he whispered softly into her ear, biting the lobe in a way that made her lean her neck to the side, wanting more. Always wanting more.

Skye reached for his hands and slid them just a few inches lower, and then laced her fingers together, resting them over his. "Our daughter . . . or son."

It took him a second before he gasped next to her ear, and she beamed, giggling softly—as softly as she could—so she'd still hear the hiss when the sun hit the water. Once it was gone, she turned in his arms, looking up at him expectantly. His hands reached for her cheeks, cupping her face so tenderly, it made her want to weep.

"I'm only eight weeks along," she said, smiling up at him. "Remember that morning in Myrtle Beach?"

He nodded, searching her face with such pure and undiluted love, she felt a tear slip down her cheek.

"I thought I would die alone. But you've given me everything. You. Your heart. Your love." His eyes glistened with tears, dropping briefly to her still-flat belly before finding her eyes again. "A family."

She smiled at him. "*Our* family."

"*Our* family," he repeated softly, "with a mother who stays . . ."

". . . and a father who lives."

He took a deep breath and nodded, his eyes brimming and glistening, full of gratitude and wonder.

"A father," he murmured, and then, in a stronger voice, "I'm going to be a father!"

Joyful laughter erupted from his throat as he tightened his arms around her, swinging her around and around on the sand.

And Skye Sorenson—*very, very soon to be*—Skye Winslow, laughed joyfully right along with him.

Because this is the life she'd longed for, and it had suddenly and gloriously arrived—with full sails and gentle lulls, sunny skies and flash storms, blue seas and black waves . . . the wind and the water running through both their veins and binding them together forever.

THE END

The Winslow Brothers continues with …

PROPOSING TO PRESTON

THE WINSLOW BROTHERS, BOOK #2

THE WINSLOW BROTHERS
(Part II of the Blueberry Lane Series)

Bidding on Brooks
Proposing to Preston
Crazy about Cameron
Campaigning for Christopher

Turn the page for a sneak peek of *Proposing to Preston*!

(Excerpt from *Proposing to Preston,* The Winslow Brothers #2 by Katy Regnery. All rights reserved.)

Chapter 1

Two years ago

"Oh, my dearest darling . . . when I say that I love you with all my heart, I mean that my heart is a canyon, a cavern with hidden recesses, perilous cracks, and dark corners. And yet somehow, your love, like the sweetest and brightest light, has found every secret part of me and claimed them all as your own. Yes, my heart belongs to you, my darling, but only because I have given it to you freely—shredded, doubting, and hard, though it was—it comes to you warm and vibrant now, made whole by the force of your love, the warmth of your light."

Preston Winslow shifted uncomfortably in the narrow, stiff theater seat, unable to look away from the young woman on stage who delivered the saccharine-sweet speech like a Tony depended on it. Her costume was a white lace, high-necked Victorian dress that he suspected was quite a bit tighter over her voluptuous breasts than Victoria herself would have approved. Every time the actress gasped dramatically for breath, her flesh pushed provocatively against the straining fabric. After almost two hours of watching her breasts instead of this godawful play, Preston's seat wasn't the only thing that felt uncomfortably stiff.

"I have used you and abused you, been fickle and frivolous and flighty. But now I know, my darling. Now I see. It was—ever and always—you! Pray, tell me that there's still time to win your affection, sweet Cyril. Tell me that I haven't lost my heart's dearest wish: another chance to deserve your love!"

Cyril, who was doing as poor a job of ignoring, um—Preston glanced at the program—*Elise Klassan's* knockers as he was, lifted his glance quickly from her bosom and focused on her face.

"My dear Matilda . . ." he began, straightening his glasses and tuxedo bow tie. Preston really couldn't care less if Cyril and Matilda lived happily ever after, so it was strange that he held his breath as he waited for Cyril to give her his answer. "If you were the last woman on the face of the earth, I could not be troubled to give you the time of day."

Cyril took one last lascivious glance at Matilda's rack, then turned on his heel and exited to stage right. *Good riddance*, thought Preston. Any man who'd give up a chance to fall asleep beside those epic ta-tas—even in a high-necked Victorian nightdress—was a complete moron.

Sliding his eyes back to Elise Klassan—um, *Matilda*—Preston sat up, leaning forward, moving, almost unconsciously, to the edge of his seat.

Her face.

Oh, God, her face.

It was like watching a silent, slow-motion movie of a derelict building filled with dynamite. One moment it's standing upright, then the slow collapse, the dusty-clouded demolition, the complete destruction. And suddenly it didn't matter that the play had been terribly written and he'd been dragged to it by his on-again, off-again girlfriend, Beth, who snored lightly beside him. Preston sat helplessly, staring at Elise Klassan's desperation with a sympathy that felt profoundly . . . real.

Her face crumpled in agony, but not all at once. First blank, as though processing Cyril's rejection, her brows furrowed a little, and he saw her lip quiver. Her eyes fluttered, like they were trying to stay open, then she closed them tightly, as though the mere action of keeping them open was too painful to bear. Her hand rose slowly to her throat, flattening above her heaving chest, and the theater was so silent, he could hear his sharp gasp as a solitary tear rolled down her cheek.

"Cyril," she murmured in a lost, broken voice that sounded nothing like Matilda, and Preston's lips parted, transfixed on her sorrow.

She took a deep, jagged breath, her body swaying listlessly for a second before collapsing to the stage with one hand still on her chest and the other flung over her head.

Preston stared at her for a long moment, then lifted his eyes, his gaze darting around the stage to see if someone was coming—if stupid, pretentious Cyril was coming back to tell her that it wasn't too late and he was a jackass for letting her go. But no one came. She just . . . lay there. Unmoving. Dead? Oh, God, was she dead? Preston's heart clutched as the lights faded slowly to black and the curtain silently closed in front of her. He stared at the slightly rippling red velvet, wondering when it was going to reopen, wondering when he was going to have one last glimpse at Elise Klassan's lovely smile as she took her bow.

He waited, staring, breathless, but nothing happened.

Finally, the house lights came up, and there was a weak smattering of applause from behind him, filling the small theater with lackluster approval, and the fifty or so patrons in attendance stood up, mumbling about the show, shrugging into their coats, and shuffling from their seats to the aisles.

Beth started beside him, yawning loudly and sitting up. "It's over?"

Her voice jerked Preston's eyes away from the stage, and he stared at her like she'd appeared from out of nowhere.

"Thank God." She sighed, plucking her tan pashmina wrap from the back of her seat and wrapping it around her shoulders. "Sorry, Pres. I had no idea it would be so . . . *bad.*"

He had an overwhelming urge to tell Beth that it *wasn't* so bad—even though, by and large, it *was*—because he'd been riveted by Elise Klassan. He shifted his eyes back up to the stage, focused on the curtain, as if the very force of his longing to see her one more time would be enough to make the edges suddenly part.

"Pres?" nudged Beth, her hand falling lightly over his and squeezing. "Ready to go?"

"Uh . . . yeah," he murmured, finally pulling his gaze away from the stage and looking at his date. "Why didn't they bow?"

"Huh?"

"Don't actors and actresses usually take a bow after the play's over?" he asked, gesturing at the stage with annoyance.

Beth raised an eyebrow, then made a big show of looking around the almost-empty off-off-Broadway theater before catching Preston's eyes again. "Umm . . . not if there's no one to applaud."

Giving one last troubled glance to the curtain, Preston stood up, pursing his lips. "Well, it doesn't feel like the show's over without that part."

"I doubt it'll be around for much longer anyway," she said dismissively, taking her bag from the floor by her seat and rising to her feet. "Really awful stuff."

"Not *really* awful," said Preston thoughtfully.

The material was admittedly bad, but Elise Klassan had done her best and given a performance that was sticking with him, almost like it had hitched a ride on his back and was following him up the aisle and out of the theater. There was something about her. Something . . . well, he didn't know. He couldn't put his finger on it, but suddenly he couldn't stop thinking about her.

As they neared the exit, Preston was surprised to find one last audience member still sitting in his seat, his expression a mirror of the way Preston felt, staring at the stage thoughtfully as though waiting for more, and Preston paused beside him in the aisle.

"I'm going to freshen up. Meet you in the lobby?" asked Beth. She kissed his cheek and made her way out the theater door.

The man in the last row looked up at Preston. "Is she dead?"

"Excuse me?"

"Matilda. Is she dead?"

Preston chuckled, but the man didn't.

"I don't know," he replied softly, feeling his smile fade.

"What did you think?" asked the man.

"Not good."

"Hmm. And yet you were the last to leave," observed the man.

"Actually," said Preston, looking down at him, "you're the only one still sitting."

"What was 'not good'? The play itself?"

Preston nodded.

"What about the actors?" The man opened his program. "Mark, uh, Smithson. He played Cyril."

Preston shrugged. He didn't have a good opinion about Mark Smithson's performance, and he wasn't going to make one up for the sake of conversation.

"Paige Rafferty?" He glanced down at the program again. "She played Constance."

Preston looked out the small window in the door to the lobby, but Beth hadn't come out of the bathroom yet. Again, he really didn't have an opinion of Paige Rafferty's performance other than that was sure he wouldn't remember it by tomorrow. "She was fine, I guess."

"But unremarkable."

Exactly. Preston nodded.

Up until now, the man's tone had been convivial, almost playful. But now, he fixed his dark eyes on Preston's, hawklike and narrowed, and Preston wondered for the first time who he was. A reviewer? The director? Someone else associated with the play?

"And what about . . . Elise Klassan?"

Preston flinched. He didn't feel it coming, but he felt it happen. Then he licked his lips, which made his cheeks flush with heat, and he dropped the man's eyes in embarrassment.

"Mm-hm," rumbled the man, his voice smooth as warm honey. "Me too."

"She was good. She was . . ." Preston's voice trailed off, and he looked back at the stage for a moment, disappointed that the curtain was still closed and no longer rippled. The theater was so quiet and empty, it almost felt surreal, like there hadn't been a play at all.

What was it about it her that was affecting him so deeply?

He suspected that she was pretty under all that stage makeup, bouffant 1890s hairdo, and neck-to-ankle dress, and, as duly noted, her high, pert chest was undoubtedly a thing of beauty. But his feelings really weren't about beauty or attraction. They were about something else far less quantifiable or easily explained. The only words that came to mind? *Under his skin.* Her performance had gotten under his skin. The way her face had crumpled, the way her voice had broken when she whispered "Cyril," the profound sorrow on her face, and how terribly discomfited he felt at not seeing her alive and smiling one last time.

There was something about Elise Klassan that was special. Compelling. And she shone more brightly than hammy lines and mediocre costars. He was affected. He was moved. He was touched. And though he knew this was the point of theater, he found he didn't like it.

When Preston turned around, the man stood, his lips spreading into a wide, satisfied smile. "You've helped immensely."

"Have I? With what?"

The man nodded, reaching down for his umbrella and chuckling softly to himself before looking back up at Preston. "I wasn't sure if I was right. But now . . . seeing you. . . . well, I know I am."

He nodded once more, as if in thanks, then he sidestepped out of his row, winked at Preston, and exited the theater.

Look for *Proposing to Preston* at your local bookstore or buy online!

Other Books by Katy Regnery

A MODERN FAIRYTALE
(Stand-alone, full-length, unconnected romances inspired by classic fairy tales.)

The Vixen and the Vet
(inspired by "Beauty and the Beast")
2014

Never Let You Go
(inspired by "Hansel and Gretel")
2015

Ginger's Heart
(inspired by "Little Red Riding Hood")
2016

Dark Sexy Knight
(inspired by "The Legend of Camelot")
2016

Don't Speak
(inspired by "The Little Mermaid")
2017

Swan Song
(inspired by "The Ugly Duckling")
2018

ENCHANTED PLACES
(Stand-alone, full-length stories that are set in beautiful places.)

Playing for Love at Deep Haven
2015

Restoring Love at Bolton Castle
2016

Risking Love at Moonstone Manor
2017

A Season of Love at Summerhaven
2018

ABOUT THE AUTHOR

USA Today **bestselling author Katy Regnery** started her writing career by enrolling in a short story class in January 2012. One year later, she signed her first contract for a winter romance entitled *By Proxy*.

Katy claims authorship of the multi-titled Blueberry Lane Series which follows the English, Winslow, Rousseau, Story and Ambler families of Philadelphia, the five-book, best-selling A Modern Fairytale series, the Enchanted Places series, and a standalone novella, *Frosted*.

Katy's first Modern Fairytale romance, *The Vixen and the Vet*, was nominated for a RITA® in 2015 and won the 2015 Kindle Book Award for romance. Four of her books: *The Vixen and the Vet* (A Modern Fairytale), *Never Let You Go* (A Modern Fairytale), *Falling for Fitz* (The English Brothers #2) and *By Proxy* (Heart of Montana #1) have been #1 genre bestsellers on Amazon. Katy's boxed set, The English Brothers Boxed Set, Books #1–4, hit the *USA Today* bestseller list in 2015 and her Christmas story, *Marrying Mr. English*, appeared on the same list a week later.

Katy lives in the relative wilds of northern Fairfield County, Connecticut, where her writing room looks out at the woods, and her husband, two young children, and two dogs create just enough cheerful chaos to remind her that the very best love stories begin at home.

Sign up for Katy's newsletter today: http://www.katyregnery.com!

Connect with Katy

Katy LOVES connecting with her readers and answers every e-mail, message, tweet, and post personally! Connect with Katy!

Katy's Website: http://katyregnery.com
Katy's E-mail: katy@katyregnery.com
Katy's Facebook Page: https://www.facebook.com/KatyRegnery
Katy's Pinterest Page: https://www.pinterest.com/
 katharineregner
Katy's Amazon Profile: http://www.amazon.com/
 Katy-Regnery/e/B00FDZKXYU
Katy's Goodreads Profile: https://www.goodreads.com/author/
 show/7211470.Katy_Regnery